Praise for

Tempest in a Teapot

"An intriguing debut, brewed with a rich blend of tea and empathy."

—Virginia Lowell, national bestselling author of
Dead Men Don't Eat Cookies

"A well-written, charming novel with endless possibilities. Sophie is a smart, young protagonist . . . Cooper does a nice job of corralling the suspects and forcing a killer's confession at the end." —*RT Book Reviews*

"This mystery had me completely stumped until the end . . . Delightful." —Melissa's Mochas, Mysteries & Meows

"The mystery was complex and well-plotted, and I enjoyed trying to fit the clues together." —Book of Secrets

"In *Tempest in a Teapot* we are introduced to a charming and quirky cast of characters. This includes our feisty protagonist, Sophie Taylor . . . This lighthearted mystery becomes a page-turner of a read that I could not put down. It is well-plotted and kept me wanting to find out whodunit." —MyShelf.com

"Amanda Cooper writes an engaging mystery in her first book in this new series. With intriguing characters and a delightful setting, I can already tell this series is going to be a firm favorite. For tea drinkers all across the world I highly recommend this series." —Cozy Mystery Book Review

Berkley Prime Crime titles by Amanda Cooper

TEMPEST IN A TEAPOT
SHADOW OF A SPOUT
THE GRIM STEEPER

The Grim Steeper

Amanda Cooper

BERKLEY PRIME CRIME, NEW YORK

**BERKLEY
PRIME
CRIME**

**An imprint of Penguin Random House LLC
375 Hudson Street, New York, New York 10014**

THE GRIM STEEPER

A Berkley Prime Crime Book / published by arrangement with the author

ISBN: 978-0-425-26525-3

PUBLISHING HISTORY
Berkley Prime Crime mass-market paperback edition / February 2016

PRINTED IN THE UNITED STATES OF AMERICA

10 9 8 7 6 5 4 3 2 1

Cover illustration by Griesbach Martucci.
Cover design by George Long.
Interior text design by Kelly Lipovich.

Penguin
Random
House

Thank you to Samantha Hunter, who helped me understand the tangled and complex world of American higher education. You gave me invaluable information on college and university culture and politics. Also, thank you to author Susan Holmes. You graciously answered my *many* questions about being a college professor, and gave me fabulous insight into the technicalities of grading at the college level and the software used.

Any mistakes made are my own misunderstandings!

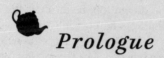

Prologue

Sophie Taylor stomped down the beautiful, moonlit Hamptons beach, her sensible shoes scuffing up little spurts of sand with every step. Once in a while every person has a miserable day to end all miserable days, and she had just suffered through a wicked awful one. It was a long walk back to the Hamptons home owned by her parents, neither of whom was in residence, but she needed every inch of it to cool down.

Her father was in Shanghai working on a business deal (as usual), and her mother had taken off for a vacation-slash-shopping excursion to Italy, or France, or Tahiti, or *somewhere more fun*, in her own words, than the Hamptons after the summer season had ended. Most other Hamptonites in their circle of friends had gone back to the city or elsewhere to work, like her father, or jetted off to foreign locales, like her mother, to shop or go on holiday.

But Sophie was trying to make a go of the job at Bartleby's

on Shinnecock, the seafood restaurant at which she had been
offered a sous chef de cuisine position by none other than the
new owner, Hendriques Van Sant, a lovely Dutch gentleman.
Her mother had gone to great lengths to set it all up, and Sophie
didn't want to ruin their tentative truce by letting her down. It
should have been a dream job, better than she had ever
expected after the disaster of her own failed restaurant in Manhattan, In Fashion, which ultimately led her to retreat to her
grandmother's tearoom in Gracious Grove, New York.

Except . . . She stopped, took a deep breath and tried to
focus on her lovely surroundings. This was the Hamptons
seashore in October, even more beautiful (to her, anyway) than
the Hamptons in summer! The tide was out, long stretches of
wet sand gleaming in the moonlight, rocky outcroppings dark
and mysterious, throwing shadows cast by the silvery light.

She growled at the moon, whirled and stomped on, unable
to enjoy so much natural beauty when the brutal day she had
suffered kept trudging through her memory, like an earworm
song one couldn't shake, the day's lowlights streaming on a
never-ending loop. Bartleby's was a great restaurant with a
lengthy, stellar history and reputation. Hendriques was a sweet,
wonderful man, a rare entrepreneur and restaurant magnate
who had not lost his human touch. He would be a dream to
work for, except . . . except the *actual* restaurant owner was
not Hendriques, who bought it, but his shiftless, difficult, and
spoiled-rotten son Adrian, to whom he gave it as a gift. The
chef de cuisine she had dreamed of working under and learning from had quit because he could no longer endure Adrian.
The new chef, Monty, was a talentless egoist who thought
being chef de cuisine entitled him to daily temper tantrums
that featured thrown food, broken crockery and foul language.
He was like Gordon Ramsay but without the talent.

The Taylor home loomed huge and dark against the night

sky, the glass facade reflecting back to the sea endless churning waves on the distant horizon overhung by the silvery gleaming moon. She scaled a sand hill, swishing through long dry beach grass, and circled to the side of the house where the door to the mudroom—or as they called it, the sand room—was located. She entered, shed her sturdy footwear and shook the sand out of her clothes. The housekeeper was on vacation, so she tried to be as tidy as possible in the woman's absence.

She strode from the sand room though the pantry and to the kitchen, which was lit only by under-cupboard lighting. She didn't bother with any other light, preferring it dim and quiet after the bright lights and constant din of the kitchen at Bartleby's. She opened the almost empty fridge, an enormous double French door stainless steel beauty, and snagged a bottle of Perrier, then found a lime in the crisper, quartered it and popped a wedge into the bottle mouth. She took a long drink, and sighed, trying to erase the awfulness of the day. Perching on a stool by the marble countertop, she flipped through the mail she had set there before she left in the morning.

Invitations, ads, catalogs and not much else. She had been hoping for a card or letter from Nana back in Gracious Grove, but she and her friend Laverne, the onetime employee and now partner at Auntie Rose's Victorian Tea House in upstate New York, were likely too busy, with Sophie gone. The yearning for her grandmother's soothing presence was an ache in her heart. Or was that heartburn brought on by too much tension, no time to eat, and the frenetic pace, all with a heaping helping of one horrible day on top? Thirty was too young for heartburn.

The wall phone rang and when she looked up, she noticed that the message light was blinking, too. She crossed the room and grabbed the cordless receiver, returning to perch on the stool again. "Hello?"

"Sophie, I'm so glad I caught you! You're not answering your cell."

"Oh, hey, Dana," Sophie said, leafing through the stack of mail and catalogs. It was Dana Saunders, a friend from Gracious Grove. "It's so nice to hear a friendly voice!"

"Oh, Soph, I'm *so sorry!*"

Sophie smiled. Trust word to spread about her awful day. "It's okay, I'll get over it. It's just one day, after all."

"What?"

"It's just one day. It has got to get better. Jason must have texted you, right? He's the only one I've told how rotten it's been lately."

"The only one you've told? Sophie, I don't think . . . haven't you heard about your grandmother yet?"

Sophie's heart thudded and she slipped from the stool, dropping the catalog she had been holding. "What about Nana?"

"Oh, lord, Soph, I thought you'd heard. Laverne called Bartleby's and some guy said he'd get a message to you. Your grandmother is in the hospital. She's had a heart attack!"

Two minutes later Sophie was punching numbers into the phone. "Chef Monty? I'm sorry to call you at home," she said, her voice shaking, tears welling in her eyes. Nana was ill, Nana . . . *Nana!* She hopped from foot to foot.

"What do you want?"

"Chef, my grandmother is ill. She lives upstate, so I'll have to take a couple of days off. Since you hired another sous chef, he can cover everything and I'll be able to leave tonight."

"Leave? I don't understand."

She explained, more slowly than she wanted, and repeated her request for a few days off.

"No. Absolutely not. You have to be here and show Craig the ropes."

"Show Craig the ropes? You hired him to be sous chef

over me three days ago; if he doesn't know the ropes by now, he never will. Chef, you made me do gueridon!" Gueridon was a way of cooking at the table in front of the diner. Traditionally performed by wait staff, it was technical, requiring deft handling of the food and dishes, combined with an actor's flair. Sophie could do it, but she was a little rusty, and tableside performance was not her forte. However, Monty had demanded she do bananas flambé that very night with no time to prepare, and it had gone terribly wrong.

Really wrong; splattering flaming sugar and rum on the guest was not a great performance.

He wasn't answering. "Monty, come *on*! Craig should be able to step in and work right away. If he's half the sous chef you claim he is—better than me, apparently—then he should be fine. I have to go."

That was when the chef started screaming unintelligible phrases that were jabbered so high, Sophie held the phone away from her ear. When he paused, she asked, "So, can I have time off?"

"No! I expect you in the kitchen tomorrow morning at eight for staff meeting and prep."

He hung up. She paused and got out her cell phone. Well, no wonder no one had been able to get a hold of her; she had it on mute and hadn't even put vibrate on. She scanned through her numbers and called Adrian. She explained what had happened at the restaurant, and then said, "But it's okay. If Monty wants Craig as sous chef, then so be it. There's no arguing with chef." She then explained about her Nana's illness, and that she had to take off for a few days.

"But it's just your grandmother!" Adrian said. "I didn't even go to my grandmother's funeral."

She held her breath for one long minute so she didn't shriek at him, then said, "Adrian, I'm not playing. I *am* going."

"Not if you want a job to come back to you aren't."

"I'm leaving tonight."

"Figures. You only got the job because your mother bribed Papa anyway."

"What?"

"Oh, you didn't know? Here I thought you knew all along. It surprised me how you worked like a busy little beaver when Papa wouldn't let me get rid of you. Said he'd promised your mom. She wanted you back here to snag some rich husband or another, so she *bribed* my dad to take you on as sous chef. That's how we got the catering contract for your mother's annual Hamptons June gala, you know."

She was stunned into silence by an overwhelming sense of bitter betrayal.

"I'll bet you don't even know the full extent of her interference in your life. You really ought to talk to your mother more."

"What do you mean?" she asked, finding her voice.

"Never mind. You can find out on your own. I told my father you'd prove to be unreliable. I knew I was right."

"Adrian, you're a pill, and Monty is a no-talent jerk. Good luck with him and with Craig, who doesn't know broccoli from broccolini, because I quit."

She was on the road in her mother's cast-off Jetta in fifteen minutes. She drove all night, nonstop. As she entered downtown Gracious Grove, she was exhausted, but relieved.

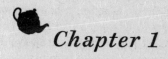

Chapter 1

"**N**ana, stop! You're not supposed to be down here yet!" Sophie jumped up from her chair in the kitchen of Auntie Rose's, and made her grandmother take her seat.

What they all had thought two weeks ago was a heart attack had turned out to be a severe and sudden angina attack for octogenarian Rose Freemont. It was a fortunate turn of events, but still, a warning, her doctor said; she needed to take it easier.

"I'm not dead yet!" Rose Freemont said, her tone on the edge of cranky. "I want to come downstairs and have a cup of tea with my best friend and my granddaughter. Isn't that okay?"

As Sophie cleared her teacup away and helped her grandmother sit, she stifled a chuckle and shared a glance with Laverne, now her grandmother's partner in the business. Sophie had been pleased to learn Laverne's long service at

Auntie Rose's Victorian Tea House had been rewarded by a share of the business. No one worked harder than her godmother, seventy-something Laverne, and partnership in the business would be some small recompense for years of devotion. "We want you to be careful. Once you're down here, we can't be sure you won't get in a tizzy at all the changes we've made while you've been laid up."

"Changes? What changes?" Nana had almost started up out of her chair, but then eyed Sophie and relaxed. "You're teasing me. I guess I earned that."

Sophie chuckled. Her grandmother's recovery was a huge relief, and in the past two weeks she realized how much she had missed seeing her every day since returning to the Hamptons and working at Bartleby's. Her mood darkened briefly when she thought of her mother; Rosalind Freemont Taylor was still traveling. She had offered to fly home when she heard of her mother's illness, but once it was diagnosed as something less serious that required rest and medication, she had decided against it. She was planning to meet up with dear, dear friends, and they would be *so* disappointed if she bailed out on them.

Nothing, not even a global catastrophe, would have kept Sophie away from her grandmother's bedside, but she and her mother were fundamentally different. She had refused point-blank to speak to her mother on the phone, not sure she could keep from blowing her top over what she had learned from Adrian before quitting Bartleby's.

Laverne and Nana chatted, while Sophie prepared her *mise en place* for the day's dishes. It was fall, so she was doing butternut squash for the cream soup of the day, and for the clear, a vegetarian confetti soup with red and white quinoa. She had already peeled and cubed the squash, so she piled that into plastic bags and stuck it back in the fridge. She then filled the stockpot with an assortment of vegetable stalks, stems and leaves, a can of tomatoes, some seasoning and a couple of gallons of water, set it on the burner to bring it to a boil, then returned to the little table that sat in a sunny nook by the window.

"What are you two cooking up?" she asked.

Laverne and Nana exchanged looks. "We were chatting about the Fall Fling Townwide Tea Party."

"The what?"

"We lost track of it while I wasn't well," Nana said. "It's something the town started a couple of years ago; you've never been here in autumn, but I thought I'd told you about it before. Cruickshank College has taken over management this time, coordinating with the Gracious Grove town council. I'm surprised Jason hasn't mentioned it to you. Every year the town has a Fall Fling Townwide Tea Party. This year the college is putting on some of the displays and holding a kind of tea market there."

Nana and Laverne explained that the tea party had been expanded this year and would include a tea convention at Barchester Hall, one of Cruickshank's most stately buildings. Vendors, including Galway Fine Teas from Butterhill, run by Sophie's friend and Auntie Rose's chief supplier of tea, Rhiannon Galway, would have booths, hand out samples and sell tea.

Sophie sipped her tea, smiled and said, "Maybe I'll actually be able to see Jason. We've only gotten together once since I've been back, and he seemed distracted."

"Is something wrong?" Nana asked.

Sophie played with the smooth handle of her large cup. "I wish I knew. He said it was nothing, but I felt like he didn't want to worry me because I was . . . well, because I was worried about you, and he knew it."

Laverne covered Sophie's free hand with hers, the strong

dark fingers curling protectively around her goddaughter's. "Ask him; I'm sure if there's anything wrong he'll be happy to talk to you about it, now that Rose is better."

"You're right," Sophie said, squeezing her godmother's hand with appreciation.

The phone rang and Sophie jumped up, answered it, but didn't hear anything except some heavy breathing. "Mrs. Earnshaw, you've called out again," she said, deducing that it was the next-door neighbor and owner of Belle Époque, still playing with her new cell phone. "Mrs. Earnshaw, this is Sophie, next door!" she said, more loudly. "You have to swipe the little phone receiver icon sideways with your finger. Or . . ." The line went dead and she hung up.

"That Thelma again?" Nana asked.

"I think so. Either her or a dirty caller breathing in my ear."

The two older ladies laughed.

"Now you scoot on back upstairs," Laverne said to her partner. "Sophie and I will take care of everything. You get some rest."

She looked stubborn for a minute, but Sophie came around the table and enveloped her in a warm hug, then ducked to look directly into her grandmother's eyes, pushing the fluffy white curls off her forehead. "Please, Nana?" she said, kissing her soft cheek. "You have a follow-up with the doctor tomorrow. If he clears you, you can start working again for an hour or so at a time."

She nodded. "All right, then, just to keep you two happy. I'll go up and read some more Agatha Christie while you two work too hard, as usual. But after tomorrow . . ." She gave them a look, her round face screwed up in a determined frown. "After tomorrow, nothing will keep me out of the tearoom."

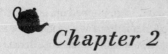

Chapter 2

It had been a busy day. After they closed up the tearoom and tidied, Sophie gave Laverne a strong hug at the back door. "I'm so happy to be back!"

"Good to hear it, honey. I think your grandmother is worried about you giving up that wonderful job you had."

"Wonderful job? Ha." Sophie snorted and released her godmother, staring into her warm, loving, dark eyes. Laverne was considerably taller than Nana, who was a short, round little lady, so she and Sophie were eye to eye. "I only stayed because I was afraid of letting Mom down. Now I know she lied to me and bribed the owner to get me away from Gracious Grove. I'm glad I left Bartleby's the way I did or I never would have known about that."

"Don't be too mad at your mother," Laverne said, cupping Sophie's cheek. "She did what she thought was right."

"As always. Too bad it's what's right for her, not me. Good night, Laverne."

"Good night, honey," she said, and gave Sophie a hug and kiss on the cheek. She picked up a cotton tote bag full of containers of leftover soup and goodies. "Time to go home and see what trouble my father has gotten into today."

"Mr. Hodge is my inspiration. I want to be exactly like him when I'm his age."

Laverne chuckled. Her father was well into his nineties, still had an active social life and an occasional girlfriend. "Horace and him are double-dating two sisters in their eighties," she said, mentioning Horace Brubaker, another nonagenarian member of Rose Freemont's Silver Spouts teapot collecting group. "I tell them to be careful around those younger women."

After Laverne left, Sophie hopped upstairs to her grandmother's apartment on the second floor and found that Nana was napping on the sofa, her book on the floor, with Pearl, her chocolate-point Birman cat, curled up in the crook of her knees. She stood watching her for a long moment, tenderness washing through her, gratitude for her grandmother's recovery swelling in her heart. Pearl looked up at her and blinked. Sophie put her finger to her lips and shushed the cat, who blinked and curled back up, tail over her eyes. Sophie picked up the book and set it on the coffee table, pulled a crocheted afghan over Nana's shoulders, then climbed the stairs to her own attic suite on the third floor.

She checked her phone. Several texts, and one message; Jason asking her to call when she had a moment free. "Hey, what's up?" She threw herself down on the soft sofa in her living room, eying her shelves of teapots that took up the entire wall, the only one that wasn't abbreviated by a slanted ceiling.

"I wondered if you were up for a basketball game at Cruickshank tonight?"

"Since when are you into basketball?"

"Since the dean has said that he wants all staff, teaching and otherwise, to support the Cruisers. He's spent a lot of money on the coach, and he's trying to soothe the alumni association and Board of Governors. Cruickshank used to have top-notch athletic teams back in the day, and he's being blamed for letting it slide. I need Dean Asquith on my side."

"Jason, I *know* something's wrong," she said, sitting up, reacting to the tension she heard in his voice. "If you were holding back because you knew how worried I was over Nana, she's fine now. She's going to the doctor tomorrow and expects to be cleared to start back working. So tell me if something is bugging you."

"Yeah. We do need to talk, because it's all going to blow up in my face and I don't want you to be shocked."

But despite those cryptic words, he wouldn't tell her more, saying they'd talk that evening, if she'd come out for the basketball game. They arranged where to meet and hung up. Through her open door she heard Nana stirring downstairs, so she descended.

"Hey, honey," Nana said as she put the kettle on to boil in her bright galley kitchen. "I'm making tea and a poached egg for dinner."

"How about I make breakfast for dinner, some Eggs Bennie, instead?"

"Would you? Oh, honey, you know how I love your Eggs Benedict."

"Well, I'm trying something a little different this time, cutting out some of the butter, so I hope you still like them when I'm done."

As Nana drank a cup of tea and read the newspaper, Sophie set to work in the narrow but well-appointed galley kitchen, first making no-cook Hollandaise in a food processor. It turned out tasty and healthy, with avocado and Greek yogurt as the base. It was lemony, silky smooth and delicious. Her trained chef's spirit recoiled from calling it Hollandaise, but it was lovely and would be a healthy substitute.

Coming home to her grandmother's place had made her realize many things, so perhaps the couple of months working at Bartleby's had been good for her. First, she had missed her grandmother fiercely. Almost as much she had missed Jason, Laverne, her friends and Gracious Grove. And then, with all the butter-drenched food she had been preparing at the restaurant, it was nice to come back to Auntie Rose's and have some control over what she put into each dish instead of going by Chef's recipe. Her first target had been the mayonnaise-rich salads, which she had lightened up using Greek yogurt and lower-fat alternatives.

She had also started producing vegetarian fare, at least one offering per day of soup, sandwich and salad. Nana had stiff competition out there now, though that still wasn't Belle Époque next door, which got by with frozen and bought goodies more often than not. Down the street a new tearoom had opened, owned by Julia Dandridge, Jason's literature department head at Cruickshank. SereniTea was a combination yoga studio and tearoom, so it didn't appeal to exactly the same demographic, but Sophie was determined to not let them take a bite out of Auntie Rose's profits. Healthier, lighter fare at Nana's tearoom would help compete.

They ate their Eggs Benedict on trays in Nana's cozy living room with the news on TV. Sophie fretted about what was bothering Jason.

"There's no point in fussing about it when you'll soon know," Nana offered. "At least he's willing to talk about whatever it is."

"But why didn't he tell me sooner? He knows he can talk to me, right? I feel like leaving when I did messed things up between us again." The Bartleby's restaurant offer had come in August just as she and Jason were beginning to get closer. It was a jarring reminder of the first time when they were teens; her mother had talked her into breaking up with Jason before taking her back for her last year of high school. Their breakup had been teary, painful and the effects long lasting.

"This time you had a talk with him, though, and didn't break up." She handed her plate and teacup to her granddaughter and folded the TV table.

"You can't break up when you're not really going together," Sophie said gloomily, stacking the dirty dishes, carrying them into the kitchen, putting them in Nana's sink and squirting liquid detergent over them. She washed, and her grandmother dried.

"But you're both adults now, and he understands that your career is important to you." Nana, her face lined with worry, eyed Sophie. "Which I am concerned about, too. I don't want you to stay here to look after me. You don't have to work at Bartleby's, you know; you could get a job at any restaurant in New York City. You *should* be doing what you love."

This was the moment Sophie had been hoping for. She turned and hugged her grandmother, keeping her soapy hands away from Nana's soft chenille robe. "I *am* doing what I love. Auntie Rose's gives me everything I need. And I get to do it with you, and my friends, and Jason nearby. I don't need to prove anything anymore. It's not that my drive is gone, it's just . . . shifted gears."

"Okay, I guess I have to accept that," Nana said. "But honey, I don't want you to be mad at your mother. She was doing what she thought right."

"You and Laverne sound like you're reading from the same playbook," Sophie said lightly, kissing the top of her grandmother's fluffy head. "Trouble is, Adrian implied there were more instances of Mom messing in my life, stuff I don't know about. I hope it isn't anything to do with In Fashion failing. I'd never forgive her."

"She would never do anything to hurt you."

"I know she wouldn't do it *purposely* to hurt me, but she and I have such different ideas of what would make me happy . . . I just don't know. Anyway, I'm so glad to be back here. And tonight, I've got a date for a basketball game!"

Nana was quite ready for bed. Sophie had found a complete set of *Murder, She Wrote* on DVD for her grandmother's birthday, and Rose was budgeting out one episode per night. Sophie left her happily curled up in bed with Pearl on her lap and Jessica Fletcher on her TV.

A frosty chill was creeping through the Finger Lakes region now that October was half-gone. Gracious Grove was set on a hillside that eventually descended to Seneca Lake. Wind swept down through the village, scattering colored leaves. Sophie dressed in skinny jeans tucked into tan Uggs, a jean jacket over a long-sleeved T-shirt with a brightly colored crocheted scarf—made with love by Laverne—wound around her neck. She was happy to have the Jetta, and took off as dusk crept over the town, heading to Cruickshank College, an old and venerable institution of higher learning about ten miles out of Gracious Grove. It still surprised her that Jason Murphy, teen love of her life and sporty boat-piloting boyfriend of fourteen summers ago, had become a college professor, spouting Blake and Milton and working on his PhD in literature with some incomprehensible (to Sophie) dissertation topic.

By the time she got to Cruickshank College, the sky was indigo, with just the last pinky golden rays illuminating the horizon beyond the lovely old towered main building. There were other buildings scattered around the hundred or so acres of the campus, like the red and gold autumn leaves that now littered the grassy commons. Apart from the main building, which was the administrative heart of the institution, there were dorms, two modern facilities, one for the arts and one for the sciences, as well as a lab, parking structure, convention facility called Barchester Hall and a couple of other buildings. She pulled around back and into the parking lot of the largest of the other buildings, a long low redbrick structure with an arched roof, named the Saul Spenser Arena after the college's most famous alumnus and supporter, an industrialist in the old-fashioned sense of the word. Jason had told her to meet him in the lobby.

She joined the few early-bird attendees, devoted fans who entered through the glass double doors. Many wore the school's colors, royal blue and silver. The entry lobby was a hardwood-floored cavernous section with huge glass arched windows over the doors, letting in some of the golden sunset light. She found Jason standing with several of her friends. "What a great surprise!" she said, as she hugged Jason hello and turned to face Cissy Peterson; Cissy's boyfriend, Wally Bowman, a deputy on the local police force; as well as Dana Saunders and *her* boyfriend, Detective Eli Hodge (Laverne's nephew) from the Butterhill PD. Everyone was better dressed than she was, especially for a basketball game. "What gives? I feel underdressed."

Dana gave Jason a look. "You didn't tell her, did you?"

He shrugged. "I forgot."

"Tell me what?" Sophie had an ominous sense she wasn't going to like what followed.

"We're attending a reception before the game for the new coach and his wife and some of the other staff, as well as our star point guard, Mac MacAlister," he said, his face blank of expression. Jason was thirty-one, lean, with longish straight brown hair. He had grown up, of course, in the years since he and Sophie went together, and was more serious, with long-term ambitions Sophie only barely grasped.

"A reception. And I'm in jeans and Uggs." She sighed and rolled her eyes. "Oh well, what can I do now?"

"Wow, you are *way* more chill than I would be," Dana said. She, of course, was flawless, in caramel-colored dress slacks, a burnt orange leather jacket and high-heeled leather boots. "Especially considering."

"Considering what?" Sophie asked.

"Considering Jason's in serious trouble," Wally said.

Cissy, dressed in a conservative wool skirt, boots and a sweater, nodded. "*Serious* trouble."

"What kind of serious trouble?" She glanced around the group and over at Jason, who shook his head, looking irritated at his friends.

"Don't look at me," Eli said. He put his arm around Dana and hugged her close. "This is the first I'm hearing about it."

"I told you everything; you don't listen," she teased, smacking his bicep.

"How can I listen when I look into those eyes?"

Argh, they are just too cute, Sophie thought.

"I'll tell you, Soph, but right now, I have to go over and meet Dean Asquith," Jason said. His expression was tense, and he visibly squared his shoulders before heading over to a group including a tall regal-looking man and woman, as well as Julia Dandridge, the head of the English literature department, and her husband, Nuñez Ortega, a local property developer.

She watched him walk over to the group, then turned back to her friends. "Great. I didn't want to make a big deal about it with Jason, but how crappy is this? I get to meet the dean looking like I'm schlepping to Wegmans on a Saturday morning, and there's not a thing I can do about it."

Dana eyed her critically. "Yes, there is."

Eli, a tall, dark and handsome fellow, looked on with a bemused smile as Dana proceeded to order Sophie around, swapping her fashionable boots for Sophie's Uggs, and her leather coat for Sophie's jean jacket. She took the string of pearls from Cissy's neck and hung it around Sophie's, then stood back and looked her up and down. "Better. We can't do anything about your jeans, but you at least look moderately chic and put together."

"Those are my grandmother's pearls!" Cissy complained, clutching at her naked neck.

"Then we know they came from the dollar store. Thelma Mae Earnshaw never spent more than a buck for anything in her life," Dana said. "Stop whining; you'll get them back."

Eli chuckled and hugged Dana to his side. She gazed up at him with adoration.

Jason returned to the group of friends. "They're opening up the reception room. We'd better go."

Wally took Cissy's arm. "Jase, maybe it would be better if we skipped the reception, and just you and Sophie go. Unless you really want us there we'll just be a distraction; you'll be busy with the others anyway."

Jason nodded. "You have a point." He included the others in a glance. "Thanks, guys, I really appreciate you showing up early like this, but Wally's right. You may as well just enjoy the game."

"And besides," Dana said with a sniff, "Now *I'm* the one who's underdressed!"

"You coming, Soph?" Jason asked, pointing toward the reception room off the lobby, where some of the college staff was already headed.

"I'll follow you in a sec," she said, and he smiled, then turned and headed across the lobby.

"We'd better go and get our seats," Wally said.

"But you . . . *you* go and mingle with Jason and the other professor types," Dana said, giving Sophie a little shove. "Make a good impression."

"Thanks Dana, Cissy, for the loan," Sophie said, touching the pearls and tugging at the jacket, which was a little loose, since Dana was more voluptuous than she. "Do you know anything about this trouble?"

Wally nodded, but Dana gave him a look and shook her head. "Keep your mouth shut, Wally. Jason will tell Sophie."

Sophie watched them walk away and head toward the sports floor of the arena, deserting her in her hour of need. She joined Jason and the other college professors and spouses who were now lingering near the reception room door. Jason introduced her as she waited to discover what her purpose was for being there with him. She met Dean Asquith, the tall, handsome, silver-haired gentleman in a well-cut blue suit, and his wife, Jeanette Asquith, also tall, silver-haired and handsome; she wore a cocktail-length dress in some shiny blue fabric, with chunky silver jewelry. A sullen-visaged, dark and swarthy fellow wearing a tweed jacket over a Cruisers team shirt was introduced to her as Heck Donovan, the new basketball coach. His wife, whose name Sophie didn't catch, appeared fortyish and wore glasses. She had a ravaged complexion, mousy hair done up in a messy bun, and she dressed dowdily in a blue jean skirt and oversized sweater. Sophie said hello to Julia Dandridge, the English department head—smartly dressed as always—and her husband, Nuñez Ortega.

"A few more of the teaching staff will be joining us, but shall we move in to the reception now?" Dean Asquith said. "I'd like Coach Donovan to speak briefly."

As the group followed the dean, Sophie took Jason's arm.

"What is going on?" she asked. "You *have* to tell me what trouble you're in. No one would say!"

"I'll tell you in a minute," he muttered as they entered a long meeting room, lined on one side by buffet tables laden with treats and urns of coffee and tea. "Let's say that tonight I need to make good with the dean. He is *furious* with me right now. Julia invited me tonight because she's doing her darndest to help me out, but she can't do it all alone. Soph, I'm sorry, but I have to go toady up to the dean and his wife. He quite literally holds my fate in his hands." He squeezed her hand and followed Dean Asquith to the mahogany bar at one end of the room.

That was all she was going to get out of him it seemed, so, always interested in food, she drifted over and scanned the offerings. There were the usual squares, tarts and cookies on a scarred foldout table—awfully tacky for a private college reception—and unfortunately they all looked like they came out of a food factory.

"They'll be from some commercial bakery in Buffalo or Rochester," Julia Dandridge, who had also drifted to the food table, said.

"Don't they believe in supporting local business?" Sophie said, with a slight smile to acknowledge the other woman.

"Officially they say they don't want to appear to be play-ing favorites, but I think the convention organizer who works for Cruickshank is getting kickbacks from a food factory."

"Kickbacks? Like, bribes?" Sophie asked, wide-eyed. "You can't be serious. At a college?"

"Hey, if Jason is being accused of taking bribes, I guess it could be happening in food services, right?"

Chapter 3

She grabbed Julia's sleeve. "What do you *mean* bribes? Julia, nobody is talking to me. You have to tell me, why is Jason in trouble?"

The professor, an undecided expression in her eyes, hesitated, staring down at Sophie's fist bunching her suit jacket. "If he hasn't told you . . ." She shook her head.

More people were entering the meeting room, some talking in clusters, others touring the mounted jerseys from bygone sports heroes that lined the wood-paneled wall, illuminated with small spotlights. Sophie took a deep breath and explained to Julia about her grandmother's illness, and why she thought Jason had refrained from telling her what was going on in his life. When she finished, she could see the sympathy in the older woman's blue eyes.

"I'm so sorry. I had no idea! I knew you had gone to the Hamptons to work, of course, but I didn't know why you came back to Gracious Grove. I had heard Rose was ill, but I didn't know how serious it may have been. I'm happy she's better."

The hum of conversation in the room was amping up. Sophie glanced toward the bar area at the end of the room, where Jason lingered on the fringe of a group of professorial types. "He said he'd tell me, but he needed to go over and talk to the dean first. I know that Jason would never do anything dishonorable, and he wouldn't do anything that would shame the college. He loves his job, and he loves Cruickshank." She met Julia's gaze. "Please tell me what's going on so I'm not lost when I talk to these people. I don't want to say the wrong thing."

Julia took Sophie's arm and drew her away to a quiet corner of the room, since people were now starting to inspect the snacks and drinks table, munching on tarts and canapés. "And to think I was sidling up to you to pick *your* brains. I'm worried about this upcoming Fall Fling tea party, whatever it's supposed to be. I'm out of my depth with running our tearoom," Julia said ruefully.

"We can talk about that, too," Sophie said. "But first I need to know what's going on."

Julia glanced over at the group. Her husband, Nuñez, a dark-haired, dark-eyed property developer, was talking to the coach, but he glanced over and smiled at Julia. She smiled back and touched her stomach. "Okay, here it is," she said, turning back to Sophie. "Cruickshank was a big deal in college athletics back in the fifties and sixties. I understand that in the last few decades the school had drifted away from athletic focus. The chess team was doing better at national tournaments than the basketball team. But college-level sports bring prestige and big bucks, both in donations and, for successful teams, merchandising. The Board of Governors and alumni association have been pressuring Dean Asquith to improve athletics at Cruickshank—"

"So they hired this new basketball coach, Heck Donovan," Sophie interjected, to speed the story.

"Right. They decided to start with the basketball program. Heck has been here for almost a year." Julia's attention was caught by someone who strode through the door, a tall, lanky, redheaded fellow, probably not more than twenty, wearing a Cruickshank College team tank shirt and baggy shorts.

"Who is that?" Sophie asked, as he looked around the room and caught sight of the coach. The younger man beckoned and the coach hustled over. They bent their heads together—or rather the basketball player bent from his lofty height and the coach looked up at him—and talked about something intensely, moving away from the crowd.

"The Cruisers' star player, Mac MacAlister. He's at the center of Jason's problem."

"Which is?" Sophie asked, beginning to get impatient. There was a stir in the room, and the chatter was louder. Some folks drifted out, and it was clear that the reception would soon end, as people found their way to their seats to watch the basketball game.

"After some poor showings academically, the dean was pressured by the state education department to more rigorously enforce their academic standards to maintain eligibility for scholarships."

"What is the standard?"

"C or better; let their grade slip below that, and they're supposed to be benched. Heck Donovan was none too pleased when the board decided that in future, his bonuses will be tied to his student athletes' academic standings rather than their performance on the court. I hear he was considering suing Cruickshank, because he says that's rewriting his contract."

"Does he have a point?"

"I don't know. I haven't paid much attention to any of this until Jason's name was brought up. Miraculously, MacAlister squeaked by with a C plus in the spring semester. But a writer for the student newspaper, the *Cruickshank Clarion*, accused the college of fluffing up MacAlister's grade to keep him eligible to play. He got an A in one of Jason's courses. If he hadn't gotten that A, his average grade would have fallen below the C, and he wouldn't have been allowed to start on the team this fall."

"So they think that Jason gave him an inflated grade?"

Julia nodded.

"He wouldn't do that. He cares about teaching."

"I know, but there's no disputing that MacAlister's grade was somehow inflated. Jason says he gave Mac a D, but that's not reflected in the official transcript recorded at the registrar's office. There's the registrar there," she said, pointing toward a man who was watching Mac and the coach talk, his expression betraying agitation. "That's Vince Nomuro."

Sophie eyed the Asian-American gentleman, a fellow of mid height, salt-and-pepper hair and thick dark glasses. He wore a GO CRUISERS! T-shirt over a dress shirt, and under a tweed sport jacket. As she watched, a younger woman with curly dark hair and metallic-framed glasses stormed into the room and approached the registrar, tugging at his sleeve and talking in an urgent fashion. He shook his head, said something sharp and pulled away from her. She stomped back out.

"And that excitable young woman was the assistant registrar, Brenda Fletcher," Julia said in an amused tone. "She works up a head of steam on a weekly basis."

"Couldn't the mark be a simple mistake?" Sophie asked. "Like, a typo?"

"Unlikely. As department head I have to approve the mark, but routinely don't question them. I rely on the professors and academic advisers to get things right. My records show that Jason gave Mac an A while he swears it was a D." She sighed. "I blame myself for this mess."

"Why?"

"If I'd been paying attention, I would have questioned the grade, given Mac's past failures in English literature courses. I've been spreading myself too thin for quite a while now. That was right when I was in the midst of buying the building and converting it to become SereniTea. I had some medical things I was dealing with . . . and now . . . well, Nuñez and I . . ." She blushed and smiled, putting one hand on her slightly rounded belly. "We're expecting."

Sophie gasped, then said, "Congratulations! I can't believe Jason didn't tell me!"

"He doesn't know," Julia said. "It took us eleven years. This was my third—and last—round of IVF. It's expensive, and hard on the marriage. I feel like I wasn't there for the rest of my life, the academic side, and I relied on my instructors and professors though it, even though they didn't all know what I was going through. It finally took, but I'm just barely at the second trimester. I haven't told anyone but family, so far."

Sophie was taken aback. Why had she then told her, a virtual stranger?

"I know we're not exactly friends, Sophie," she said, turning to her and clutching her forearms. "But I feel like we *could* be. I see you out with your girlfriends shopping and at the bakery, and I wish I could join you."

Her tone was wistful. Sophie realized in that moment

that the professor was actually lonely. "Julia, please *do* join us anytime you see us! The girls would love you." Sophie said, not sure if that was true. Dana might, but Cissy would likely feel intimidated and unsure of herself. As always. However, months ago she had decided she couldn't cater to Cissy's insecurities and self-doubt. "You don't have family in Gracious Grove, do you?"

She shook her head. "I moved here for Nuñez several years ago. It took me two years to get a job, and then I wasn't sure that Cruickshank was where I wanted to be."

"What's wrong with Cruickshank?"

"Nothing, really. But Dean Asquith and I—he's the dean of faculty, so I have to deal with him all the time—don't see eye to eye. Dr. Bolgan, the dean of arts and humanities, agrees with me. We'd like to see more rigorous class requirements in our department and some new, more-challenging courses." She sighed. "Even at Cruickshank, we have some undergrads who are reading at a high school level, and that's being generous. It's gotten worse since this push for athletic scholarships has gotten stronger."

"So, does that mean that other athletes are getting grades they didn't earn?"

Julia shrugged. "I'd love to see Cruickshank make a name for itself academically so it can attract more-dedicated students and become a prestigious school. But the dean sees the English literature department as padding, preferring our business and economics school. *He'd* like Cruickshank to become a mini Wharton, but he feels he needs to play ball with the alumni association and the Board of Governors if he's ever going to expand the business program." She rolled her eyes. "Like that is going to happen. He has ambition, I'll say that for him. He'd like to replace President Schroeder when he retires in three years."

"Is that likely to happen?"

Julia shook her head. "I don't see it. He lacks gravitas."

Sophie eyed the dean. "He sure seems dignified to me."

"He's aping President Schroeder. If you'd met the college president, you'd see that Asquith is performing a poor copy."

Sophie pondered Jason's problem as she watched him from across the room. He caught her watching him and shrugged. *Sorry*, he mouthed, no doubt realizing the discordant reception was not her idea of an entertaining evening. She smiled and fluttered her hand at him in reassurance. "Is this serious, Jason's problem?" she asked, turning back to Julia.

"People keep saying no one ever gets fired for this kind of thing, but I don't know if that's true, especially given that he's had a few run-ins with Dean Asquith before."

"Run-ins?"

"Jason has been extremely vocal in his support of Dr. Bolgan's and my attempts to beef up the literature curriculum, though he doesn't have our standing and isn't even on tenure track at this point, and won't be until he gets his doctorate. The dean is *not* pleased with him. He'd love to weaken our support and may see this as a handy excuse to point a finger, give Dr. Bolgan and me a stern warning, *and* take Jason down before he completes his PhD and gains professorship. And if he gets fired, he may not be able to find another job in the US, or at least, not one that pays decently. Adjunct positions are notoriously poorly paid. Others have had to go abroad to universities in Europe, the Middle East or Asia, to make a decent living."

"I need to help him, if I can."

"I don't see how anyone can, at this point. We'll have to sit tight while the grading thing is investigated. I don't believe for a moment he altered the grade. A rigorous investigation will point that out."

If it was an honest investigation. Sophie didn't like to think that Julia was naive, but who was to say the dean wouldn't imply that he investigated and found out Jason was the culprit? "I wish Jason had told me before." She realized that she didn't know a lot about his work; she had been intimidated by the whole atmosphere of the college, and so had avoided it.

But this was his life, and she cared. Witnessing Julia's close friendship with Jason, she had regarded her almost as a competitor for his affection, but she was wrong. This woman was a friend, and maybe she would become Sophie's friend, too. "Julia, we won't have time now to talk about the Fall Fling tea party, so why don't you come by Auntie Rose's sometime this week and we'll talk then? You can pick Nana's brain. She's been in the business for forty years, and there is nothing she doesn't know about running a tearoom. Maybe we can coordinate our block for the townwide tea party?"

"I'd like that. Now go and join Jason."

"But what should I say to people? What can I do?"

Julia smiled and said, "Just be yourself. I've watched you, Sophie; you're a people person, a natural charmer. Professors are just people, you know."

"I know, but when Jason gets going, I'm not even sure what he's talking about after a while. He's so different than he was when we were teenagers. I was the one who read poetry back then, but it was usually some summer reading list assignment from my boarding school, though I guess I never told him that." Her insecurity about that and where she stood with Jason came out in her words, voicing thoughts she hadn't expressed to anyone. She felt it was safe to say these things to Julia.

"First, there are all kinds of intelligence, Sophie. And second . . . professors need to be brought down to earth every once in a while. That's what Nuñez does for me. As a property developer and construction guy, he sees things in concrete terms. The college community is insular. There are friendships, but there are more enemies, gossip, rumors, backbiting and competition. Just because they're academics doesn't mean they aren't human."

"Thank you," Sophie said, meeting the other woman's gaze. "I appreciate the pep talk."

"Now scoot," she said, giving Sophie a push. "Help Jason out. He looks uncomfortable."

She tottered across the room, trying to maneuver in the unfamiliar high-heeled boots. Jason took her arm as she joined the group.

There was a momentary lull, and he spoke up. "Everybody, I didn't have a chance to say earlier that Sophie's grandmother is the owner of Auntie Rose's Victorian Tea House in Gracious Grove. They'll be taking part in the Fall Fling Townwide Tea Party this year."

The coach's wife pushed up her glasses and snorted with derision. "As if anyone cares about a freaking tea party!"

Nuñez Ortega, his expression neutral, said, "Mrs. Donovan, you haven't been here long enough to know, perhaps, but Gracious Grove takes its reputation as a tea town very seriously. The result, I suppose, of being dry for so long."

The woman jammed her hands into her sweater pockets and looked away. Sophie felt sorry for her and, as the conversation switched to some other topic important to the staff, sidled over. "It's an odd place, isn't it? Whenever I describe Gracious Grove to my New York friends, they're appalled that there are still dry towns in this country. I'm Sophie Taylor, by the way. I didn't catch your name earlier."

"Penny Donovan. This place sucks," she said. She squinted and wriggled her nose, then pushed her glasses up. "Heck worked at a high school before this. At least the teachers' wives and husbands weren't a bunch of snobs like this crowd."

"You've been here a year, right?"

"Heck has, but I just came this fall."

Penny had a grating nasal tone to her voice, a Long Island twang more exaggerated than any Sophie had heard from native Long Islanders.

"I had a contract position at a not-for-profit in the city," the woman continued, "so I didn't move here until the contract was up."

When anyone said *the city* in that tone, Sophie knew they meant New York City. "You must miss it. I lived in the city for a few years, and after that the slower pace in Gracious Grove is hard to get used to." She exaggerated a little to commiserate with Penny; one thing she *didn't* miss was the pace of life in NYC.

"I miss it like crazy. I had something to do there, something important! What I did mattered, and now . . . now I don't do anything but support Heck's job. It *sucks*." Her tone was fierce, and she shoved her glasses up on her nose with a brisk gesture. "I'm at the end of my rope."

"I'm sorry," Sophie said, not sure how to respond to the woman's vehement dislike of Gracious Grove and Cruickshank College.

Penny shrugged. "Whatever. So I hear your boyfriend is in hot water, right?" she asked, eyeing Jason, standing nearby. "Because of that goon, Mac MacAlister?"

Sophie, taken aback at the abrupt mention of a problem she had just learned about, stayed silent.

"Oh, okay, I get it. No talking to the staff's wife about it, right?"

"That's not it. But I don't know a lot about it, and I'm not sure what to say."

"What I would want to know is, who turned your fellow in? Who told a stupid school newspaper reporter? I mean, it has to be someone who has a grudge against Jason."

Sophie thought about that for a moment. "Not necessarily. It could be someone who doesn't like Mac, right? Or even someone who doesn't like your husband. From what little I understand, Mac is the star on the team. If he's benched, it would hurt their chances at making it into the play-offs, or whatever it is that college basketball teams do." When the other woman just stared at her, she added, "Or it could be someone with a grudge against Cruikshank, or the dean, or someone who feels strongly about athletes in general."

"Boy, you're full of answers, aren't you?" Penny turned and walked away.

Jason caught Sophie's eye and tilted his head toward the coach's wife, who stomped to the perimeter of the room and began browsing the food tables. Sophie shrugged.

Dean Asquith's elegant wife, Jeanette, detached herself from her husband's coterie of admirers and drifted to Sophie's side. "I understand you're Rosalind Taylor's daughter."

"Do you know my mother?"

"I do. My people have a home in the Hamptons near yours. I understood that you were working at Bartleby's. Such a lovely restaurant. What happened?"

"My grandmother got sick. I couldn't get time off, so I quit." That was the short answer, and one she was going to stick with. It was easier than explaining the circumstances. Out of the corner of her eye, Sophie noticed a girl who looked like a student edge into the room; she sidled over to the buffet table, filled a plate with goodies, then moved to a corner, eating, and watching everyone with a sharp gaze.

"Well, tell your mother hello from Jeanette Asquith, next time you see her."

"That's not likely to be for a while," Sophie said frankly, still watching the girl.

Julia Dandridge marched over to her and said something sharp. The girl seemed upset and put the plate down. Julia pointed to the door. It appeared that she was ordering the girl to leave. Maybe she was gatecrasher, not supposed to be at what was clearly a staff event.

As the dean's wife launched into some story about the family home in the Hamptons, Sophie watched the girl motion toward Jason and say something, but Julia shook her head and pointed to the door again. The girl sighed and moved toward the exit, as Julia rejoined her husband. "Excuse me, Mrs. Asquith," Sophie said, cutting the dean's wife off in mid-reminiscence, and heading toward the student, curious about what she had been saying about Jason.

The dean was now making some kind of speech. She should be over there, though she didn't really want to be, she thought, eying the group, who were all being polite—even Penny Donovan—though many looked bored or uncomfortable. And now the coach was saying something. Julia clutched her husband's arm and leaned her head on his shoulder.

It would have been nice if Jason had prepared her before throwing her into the lion's den of college politicking. She'd much rather talk to people who weren't professors or professors' spouses. Sophie turned to the girl; she was curvy and pretty, with blond hair in a smooth cap to her shoulders. Her skin was very pale, and it looked like she had used foundation to try to block out a smattering of freckles over her nose. She wore a short plaid kilt that showed plump knees above argyle socks and loafers, all very collegiate in an old-fashioned sense.

"Hi there," Sophie said as she approached. The girl had slowed as soon as Julia had joined Nuñez, and now lingered near the entrance. "Can I have a word with you?"

"Who are *you*?" the girl asked.

"My name is Sophie Taylor. I saw you gesturing toward Jason Murphy a moment ago. Were you here to talk to him?"

"Yeah. I'm in his Literary Migrations course." Sophie must have looked blank, because the girl explained, "We're examining the movement of literature in the English language to the Americas and other English-speaking nations."

"Ah. Okay. What did you want to talk to him about?"

"Nothing important," she said evasively.

Sophie wondered if she was personally interested in Jason. There must be dozens of college girls taken with him. He was good-looking, smart and charismatic. She'd have fallen for him hard at eighteen if he was *her* professor. "It looked like Julia wanted you to leave."

"Yeah, she's *way* protective of him, like it's her job to screen all his students or something. She's just jealous."

Julia caught sight of them talking, and signaled Sophie to break away.

"What's your name?" Sophie asked, turning instead toward the girl, her back to Julia.

"Tara Mitchells."

"Tara, you can level with me. What *did* you want to talk to Jason about?"

She hesitated, her eyes narrowed, but then said, "I heard he might, like, lose his job over the grading thing. Some of us who take his classes wondered if we should start a petition to keep him. None of us want to see him go because of a stupid thing like Mac getting a better grade than he should have. I mean, so what if Jason—I mean Professor Murphy— gave him a better grade than he deserved?"

"But he wouldn't do that," Sophie insisted. "I've known Jason most of my life, and he would never do anything unethical. He's gotten really proper since he was a teenager."

"What do you mean, '*since he was a teenager*'? Did he do bad stuff back then?"

The girl had a doubting expression, and Sophie well remembered being that age. You never thought your teachers or elders did anything like what you did. "Nothing *too* bad," she said, glancing over at him. "He drove too fast, drank a bit, and probably tried smoking cigarettes a couple times. Didn't everyone?" She looked back to Tara. "Once he took a boat out when he wasn't supposed to and it was reported stolen, but that was all cleared up."

"Really?" she replied.

"He loves Cruickshank, and he loves teaching. He'd never do anything to jeopardize that."

"Unless he didn't know his actions would jeopardize anything, right?"

"I guess." Sophie watched her. "So you're in one of his classes? What is he like as an instructor?"

She shrugged. "He's . . . uh . . . he's okay, I guess."

"Is he a good teacher?"

"Look, most professors are crap at teaching." Her attention was taken by something across the room; the speeches were over and the group had broken up. "Oh, look, *Kimmy* is here."

"Who is that?" Sophie asked, turning and following the other girl's gaze.

"That's Kimmy Gabrielson, Mac MacAlister's biggest fangirl. And I do mean biggest in every sense."

Sophie spotted a young African-American woman, heavyset and big bosomed, very pretty, with an angelic face: Cupid's bow lips, twisted ombré curls drooping over creamy dark skin. Tara's meangirl slight against Kimmy's weight registered, and Sophie eyed Tara with distaste, then looked back at Kimmy. The young woman was watching Mac and Heck, who were talking in the corner of the room. She approached them and held up a camera. Mac nodded and posed with the coach for a photo by a team sweater. "What's that all about?"

"Kimmy keeps taking pictures and trying to get the school newspaper to print them, like Mac is the only athlete on the team, or something. He's been suspended while the investigation is going on, and can't even play! And, like, she's his academic adviser! Can you believe it?" Tara glanced around the room, spotted Julia looking toward them, about to break away from her husband, and suddenly said, "I gotta go." She sped through the doors and was gone.

The party broke up as the game was about to start. Mac and Heck left the room together, followed by Kimmy, and Penny trailed the other faculty and spouses, her shapeless jean skirt concealing any hint of her figure. Sophie joined Jason and Julia and her husband.

"I was *trying* to get rid of that girl," Julia whispered. "I wish you hadn't talked to her."

"Tara Mitchells?"

"She's a tricky specimen."

"What do you mean?"

"She didn't tell you? She considers herself the star reporter for the *Cruickshank Clarion*. *She's* the one who broke the story about Jason and the grading scandal."

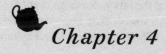

Chapter 4

Sophie spent the rest of the evening trying to decide if anything she had said was damaging to Jason, but all she had told the girl was that Jason would never do anything unethical and that he was a good man who loved Cruickshank. Nothing wrong in that.

The basketball game was a blowout, but unfortunately it favored the visitors, who whooped and hollered as they left the floor. Jason grumbled that it was because Mac wasn't allowed to play. He was the star point guard, the one they relied on. Cruickshank Cruiser fans were in a subdued mood as they filed out of the brightly lit auditorium into the spacious lobby. Sophie still could not stop worrying and wondering if she should be confessing about her conversation with Tara. Cissy, Wally, Eli and Dana had been sitting further up in the stands than Jason, as a staff member, and Sophie as his date, so they all met up in the lobby.

"Girlfriend, I want my boots back," Dana said, shuffling over to her. "How can you wear these Uggs? Ugh!"

Sophie laughed and tried to get the high-heeled boots off, but after hopping around on the hardwood floor for a few minutes, she said over the loud chatter of the visiting team's fans who now filled the lobby, "Let's go over to the chairs." Sophie pointed to a row of blue fiberglass molded chairs bolted to the wall. "These things feel like they're welded to my feet."

"Great, your foot sweat in my boots."

"I didn't *ask* to borrow them," Sophie said.

"They made you look more professional. Don't be ungracious."

Sophie tottered over to the chairs, followed by Dana.

"Oh, hey . . . I see someone I have to talk to," she said. "I'll be right back." She headed off, still wearing the Uggs.

Sophie sat down, slung her purse onto the chair next to her and unbuckled one long boot as she tuned in to a conversation between a man and a woman, around the corner.

"Vince, they're pressuring me for a statement and I don't know what to say."

Vince . . . why does the name ring a bell, Sophie wondered as she worked on getting the boots off her swollen feet. *Oh, right! Vince Nomuro, the registrar.*

"Who are *they*?"

"The school paper, who else? It hasn't hit the national news. Yet."

"Say nothing; that's the best strategy."

His voice was calm, precise. Was he discussing the grading scandal, or was that too big a stretch?

"I *have* to say something! They keep implying it had to happen in our office," the woman said. "I told that girl there are a dozen people who could have tampered with the grades, but I don't think she believed me. I know *I* didn't do it. Did you?"

"What an awful thing to suggest!"

"Murphy says it wasn't him, that he never gave Mac an A. I'm just sayin' . . . if it wasn't him, it wasn't me, and it wasn't you, who the hell *was* it?"

"Good God, Brenda, it could have been any one of a number of people: Paul, Julia, Heck . . . even the dean himself! Until an official body gets involved and investigates, keep your mouth shut."

Brenda . . . that was the assistant registrar I had seen approach him earlier, Sophie thought, pausing and listening rather than tugging on the boot.

"Well, jeez, Vince, I hate to keep you from something important, but I kind of thought the cheating thing that could taint our whole department was important enough to talk about. You've been avoiding me lately. When *are* we going to talk about it?"

"I'm trying to keep my eye on the dean," Vince said, his voice holding tension. "I don't trust him, not while he's anywhere near the Board of Governors or alumni. He's desperate for this thing to go away and not hurt fund-raising or his job."

"He's such a jerk," she replied, her tone full of contempt. "He comes after me, and I'll be telling the alumni association and anyone else who will listen about him and his girlfriend Sherri Shaw at the Marriott in Rochester last month."

Sophie's eyes widened; the dean had a girlfriend?

"If he comes after *me*, I'll threaten to tell the association about Jeanette and her boy toy Paul," Vince replied. "I think *that* would be more embarrassing to Asquith than his fling with Sherri."

Brenda chuckled. And her voice got louder as she said, "What a pair!"

Vince Nomuro and the short, curly-haired young woman came around the corner, but Sophie had turned away, working on her boot as they passed. She looked up and watched them, pondering what she had overheard. What a hotbed of gossip this place turned out to be! She tried—and failed—to imagine either the dean or his elegant wife with randy younger bed partners. She was giggling to herself when Dana returned, tugging Kimmy Gabrielson by the sleeve.

"What are you laughing about?" Dana asked. "And really, do you need a helper to get those boots off?"

"Yes, please! I don't know how you manage to get these off alone."

"Who said I managed alone?" Dana said with an arched eyebrow. She glanced over her shoulder at Eli, who was watching her with a smile.

"You got them off all right earlier."

"Yes, well, my feet are daintier than yours. Sophie, this is Kimmy Gabrielson, who works here at Cruickshank. She comes into the bookstore all the time. We're in a book group together."

"Hi," Sophie said and held out her hand.

The other woman took her hand and shook, her palm slightly damp. "I saw you in the reception room. Dana says you're with Jason Murphy, right?"

Kimmy's voice was low and husky, not at all what Sophie had expected from someone with such a sweet youthful face and beautiful bow lips. "We're old friends," Sophie said, still not sure what their real relationship was. "You're an academic adviser, right?"

She looked startled for one brief moment, her dark eyes wide, but then she nodded. "I am, to several students here. I saw you talking to Tara Mitchells; she's the one who told you that. I'll bet she also told you I have the hots for Mac MacAlister, right? That girl . . . watch out for her."

A second warning about Tara. Sophie's stomach twisted as Dana pulled one boot off her foot and began working on the other one. "What should I be looking out for?"

"She'd make a great writer . . . for the *scandal* sheets. Tara is the worst kind of gossip, the kind who makes it into a job, not just a hobby."

"Oh." *Fudge.*

Kimmy regarded her, a thoughtful look in her dark eyes. "I'll bet she was there to pick up the dope on the grading scandal. That's why Julia tried to get rid of her." Kimmy held the long boots while Dana slipped off the Uggs and handed them to Sophie. Dana plunked down on a seat and began the process of wriggling her feet into the fashionable boots.

All she did was stand up for Jason, so she had nothing to worry about, Sophie told herself again. She pulled the Uggs on and gave a groan of contentment. "That feels so much better. How can you wear those torture devices, Dana?" Sophie asked.

"Beauty is pain, darling," she said. "Now give me back my jacket."

The exchanges made, they started across the cavernous lobby to rejoin their group, which was gathered by the doors ready to leave. As Dana sprinted ahead and threw herself into Eli's arms, Sophie lingered behind and walked with Kimmy. "So you'd know better than anyone; is Mac smart enough to have gotten that A on his own?"

Kimmy cast her a sideways look. "I like the guy, but no way. He's not that bright. I've spent a lot of time with him, and I know people are talking, but it's because he is a sweet fellow. I've been trying to get him to change majors from business admin to something less challenging."

"Like?"

"Sportscasting, something like that, at a college more suited to his abilities. He's kinda dumb, but likable."

Sophie was sure sports journalism students wouldn't appreciate Kimmy's assessment of their brains. "I'm naturally concerned for Jason. I don't get the whole grading thing. Jason says he didn't give Mac an A, but who else could have changed his grade in the computer?"

"Me, for one," she said.

Sophie laughed out loud, more because she was startled by the other woman's candor, than that she thought it was funny.

Kimmy halted her with a hand on her arm before they joined the others, and drew her away to a shadowy area between sconce lights along the curved brick internal wall. "You're worried for Jason. I know him, but not well. He doesn't seem the type who would cave to pressure. But if you're interested, I'll tell you; there is a finite number of people who could have done this."

"Like who?"

Kimmy cocked her head to one side. "You're not going to let it go, are you?" She shook her head, her spiral curls trembling. "Jason *is* the most likely, but Julia also could have done it. I could as well, because I have access to official grading programs. Vince, the registrar, and even Brenda the assistant registrar, I imagine. We all can access the CMS."

"CMS?

"Content management system. I don't know what internal safeguards Vince has in place, all I know is it's password protected, but passwords are easy to figure out. There's even software you can use."

"Anyone else?"

She shrugged. "The dean?"

"Could Mac or the coach have done it?"

"Mac, no way. Students can't get into the program." Her expression turned doubtful. "I don't *think* Heck could have done it. He wouldn't know how and wouldn't have access to the software. If both Julia and Jason are telling the truth, then the grade was changed after Jason entered it, but before Julia reviewed it."

That was a telling point, one that she was sure had already occurred to both Julia and Jason. "I've heard of this stuff happening at a few other schools. How was it managed there?"

"Grade fixing? You're probably thinking of the big scandal at UNC a few years back. That was different. There had been years—decades, even—of what are called paper courses, set up with few requirements and little oversight. Students barely had to hand in course work, and there were no actual classes. They got automatic As or Bs, or the coach told the instructor or professor what mark was needed to boost the student athlete's overall average."

"That didn't happen here."

"No." Kimmy hesitated, but then said, "Okay, I can tell you're worried about this, but Jason will weather the storm. If he didn't do it, then the investigation will uncover who did, or at least a likely culprit. Don't worry about your man; he's going to be fine."

Sophie smiled. "Thanks. You're good at cheering a person up." She could see why Kimmy would make a good adviser; she was intuitive and empathetic, not minimizing the source of worry, but not overstating the case, either. However, Julia had expressed concern, and she was closer to the problem. As they started back across the lobby toward the group, she asked, "Are you joining in on the Fall Fling Townwide Tea Party?"

"I am," she said. "My book group is doing the tour. We just read the English translation of *The Tea Lords*, by Hella S. Haasse, about the Dutch tea trade. Do you read?"

"Not much. I'm more of an action person, you know? I like cookbooks, and I do read magazines."

"That's okay," Kimmy said, patting her shoulder. "Not everyone likes the same things, right?"

Sophie was sure she didn't mean it, but she could hear the pity in the other woman's voice, much as there would be in her own toward someone who didn't like to cook. They reached the group and joined up. Jason smiled down at her. "Now you look more like yourself," he said, putting one arm around her shoulders. "Come on; let's go have a coffee and I'll fill you in on all the drama."

T he next morning, bright and early, Sophie was in the tearoom kitchen finishing up some dough, one for scones, another for cheese biscuits to go with the soup, and yet another cookie dough, which she was rolling into logs to be refrigerated and sliced as needed for fresh-baked cookies. On the big six-burner professional stove were two pots of stock, one for the cream soup of the day, a vegetable chowder, and another for the clear soup, her own take on a minestrone.

Laverne let herself in the back door and set her tote bag down on one of the chairs by the small table close to the window. As she unwound a hand-knit variegated scarf from around her neck, she said, "You've been busy. Everything smells so good!"

Sophie hugged her carefully, keeping her wet hands away from her godmother's tidy outfit, a dark skirt and maroon blouse. "I'm enjoying this so much. It's like I have time to think and innovate while I cook. I didn't have that luxury at either In Fashion or Bartleby's."

As Laverne got a cup of tea and sat down for a morning tea biscuit, Sophie told her about what was going on at the university, and how it impacted Jason. She and Jason went to a café and had a long talk after the game. He admitted he hadn't told her what was going on because he knew how upset she was about her grandmother's health scare. "He's been dealing with it all on his own; he hasn't even told his folks yet!"

"That poor boy," Laverne said. "You know, Eli's younger sister works at Cruikshank in the admissions office."

That wasn't a huge surprise. Laverne had so many nieces and nephews, she always said it was a good thing she didn't have children herself, what with so many other children who needed a maiden auntie to knit and crochet for them. "Admissions," Sophie mused. "Would she know about this grading thing?"

"She might. Why? Are you snooping again?"

Sophie shrugged and wiped her hands on a towel, then flung it over her shoulder as she sat down opposite Laverne. "I'm worried for Jason. Julia Dandridge said the dean and him have clashed before, and that's why Dean Asquith might not protect him and could try to pin the blame on him, to get the scandal over with and move on. But if Jason gets fired, he could damage his reputation and have a hard time getting another job at a university in the US."

Laverne patted her hand across the table, "Now, honey, don't go borrowing trouble."

"Borrowing *what* trouble?"

Nana was at the bottom of the stairs, dressed in one of her favorite jewel-toned velour tracksuits, this time in a sapphire that made her blue eyes twinkle. Sophie jumped up and went to hug her. "Doctor's visit this morning, right? Laverne's going to drive you?"

Nana eyed her. "Don't think I don't know what you're doing, deflecting attention. Yes, Laverne is going to take me to see my handsome young doctor, then I am going to come back, have lunch, and work for a sensibly short period in the tearoom, which means I'm going to sit by the cash desk for most of the day like Thelma and watch you both work your tailbones off. But before then, you are going to tell me what it is you're not supposed to borrow trouble over."

Sophie stifled a chuckle. Nana was back in rare form. She sat her grandmother down, brought her a cup of tea and a biscuit with homemade seedless raspberry jam, and talked as she worked on the soup, telling her grandmother what she had told Laverne. After discussing it at length, she said, "Oh, and Nana, Julia Dandridge is going to come around to pick our brains about SereniTea and the Fall Fling. I said you might be able to give her some info."

Laverne and her exchanged a look. "So when did you decide Julia wasn't a devil woman set to steal young Jason away from you?" Laverne asked.

Sophie shrugged. "I know, I'm an idiot. They're just friends." She hesitated, then added, "She and her husband are having a baby, but don't tell anyone."

"Who would I tell?" Nana asked. "The doctor?"

The phone shrilled in the peaceful kitchen, and Sophie hopped over to get it. "Hello?" Nothing but heavy breathing. "Mrs. Earnshaw, you've dialed out again!"

No answer, then a click.

Thelma Mae Earnshaw sat and stared down at the screen of the tiny thing in her hand, not much bigger than a credit card. Just then Gilda, her only steady employee at Belle Époque, came back from doing the shopping, laden with about ten plastic bags from the bargain store and the dollar store.

"This thing is broken!" Thelma groused, banging it on the table surface.

Gilda struggled through the door, lugged the bags through to the kitchen and plopped them down on the floor near the fridge, panting and moaning about her sore shoulders and aching feet.

"Get me a cup of tea while you're there," Thelma hollered, staring down at the screen and poking at it halfheartedly. How could a million kids get this so easily and not her? It had to be defective, that's all there was to it. "Cissy got me a lemon," she said about her granddaughter, Cissy Peterson, who ran Peterson Books 'n Stuff, the "stuff" being note pads and stationery, candles and crystals, and all manner of New Agey crap, as Thelma thought of it. Still not as bad as that new tearoom down the street in the old Sinclair house. What the heck did they call it? Sireny Tea? Sore End It Tea? Something like that. Yogurt and tea; whoever heard of such a foolish notion?

"Gilda, you coming with that tea? I asked a half hour ago."

Gilda thumped a mug down in front of her. "I haven't been home ten minutes, and you didn't ask, you demanded!"

Thelma glared up at her frizzy-haired factotum, then chuckled. "You look like one of them fuzzy-headed chickens that squawk around the barnyard in a fluster. Don't go getting your knickers in a knot," she said affably. "Sit down and have a cup with me, and thaw a couple of those pumpkin spice muffins Sophie sent over while you're at it."

Minutes later, soothed by the buttered muffins and tea, Gilda said, "You'll never *guess* what I heard at the market."

"No, I couldn't guess," Thelma said, still glaring at the cell phone on the table. "Why don't you just tell me without a whole bunch of roundaboutation?"

She couldn't avoid the hesitations and meandering, but Gilda eventually told Thelma a tale about Cruickshank College, which Thelma didn't care about one way or the other, and some kind of scandal attached to Sophie's young fellow, Jason Murphy. But then it appeared that that wasn't at all what she meant when she had challenged Thelma to guess what she overheard.

"And you know that professor woman who owns the new tearoom? Girl at the bargain store, her sister cleans at that new tea shop, and says the professor told her this morning that she's going to be ganging up with Rose next door to take over the Fall Fling tea walk thing and leave you out of it. We'll be left in the dust!" Gilda said, her eyes bugging from her head. "Going to squeeze us right out!"

Thelma straightened to attention. "What did you say?" she said.

Gilda repeated herself.

"And she told her cleaning lady all this?"

"Well, not exactly," Gilda said, and goggled slightly, her protuberant eyes wide. "I think . . . I suppose the cleaning lady overheard it when the professor woman was telling it to that scrawny manager girl I've seen jogging around the neighborhood."

Didn't matter who she said it to, she supposed; Thelma saw red. No one was going to sideline her, not a soul. She'd do whatever it took, and if that meant dirty tricks even though she and Rose Freemont had made a kind of truce, then so be it.

"Fall Fling, my great aunt's patootie," she muttered, as she heaved herself to her feet. "I'll fall fling 'em right to kingdom come."

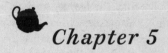

Chapter 5

A clean bill of health and the okay to work a few hours every day had put a spring in Nana's step and a twinkle in her eyes. She behaved herself, and only spent a few hours working in the tearoom each afternoon. But Friday had been especially busy, so Sophie sent her grandmother upstairs to rest and Laverne home to look after her nonagenarian father. She shared leftover soup with her grandmother for dinner, then nipped back downstairs to set up the tearoom for the last Silver Spouts meeting—the Spouts was Nana's teapot collecting group—before the Fall Fling tea stroll on Sunday.

The tearoom was kept mostly spotless by Laverne and Sophie, with a little heavy-duty cleaning help once every couple of weeks from a local woman, for a reasonable fee. But to Sophie, the tearoom was showing its age. The carpeting was worn in spots, and even the rose toile wallpaper, above white wainscoting, looked tired. The tiny shop off the tearoom proper was still fine; it held all the wares that Auntie Rose's sold, from Fitz and Floyd teapots to Grace's Teaware's pretty teacups and saucers, as well as books on tea, tea-scented candles, children's tea sets, "tea" shirts with tea-themed sayings, and last but not least, Auntie Rose's Tea-riffic Tea, blended for them by Galway Fine Teas in Butterhill. Rhiannon, her friend and the proprietor, was going to have a booth in Barchester Hall at Cruickshank for the first night of the Fall Fling. Sophie had already texted her to bring a box of their tea with her.

Sophie moved tables aside and made a ring of ten or so chairs facing the tea-servery area that looked out onto the kitchen. Once she had arranged the seating, she looked around at the room again. One thing that was very right about Auntie Rose's was Nana's amazing collection of tea-pots. Antique sideboards and buffet hutches filled with tea-pots of all kinds lined the walls. An ornate Eastlake buffet held floral teapots, while a heavy Victorian held chintz designs. On floating shelves in between there were animal shapes, people, royal family tributes, red hat society teapots and too many more to name.

But on a separate shelf, right near the door where every-one would see it, was her Nana's favorite . . . a shelf entirely devoted to Old Country Roses teapots and teaware. Sophie crossed the dimly lit tearoom and examined the shelf of teapots. OCR, as it was known by enthusiasts, was a classic Royal Albert design featuring red and gold roses with gold trim on a white background. It continued to be so popular the company was always coming up with lovely new designs, so Nana was still collecting. There were OCR teapots in different shapes, as well as the novelty teapots: a set featuring bunny teapots with the OCR pattern on them, another one with a raised pierced rim that was highly sought after, and a whole array of figural ones shaped like a table with OCR teapots and teacups atop them!

"You're so quick, my Sophie!" Nana said.

Sophie whirled and eyed her grandmother. Nana stood in the doorway to the tearoom and appeared rested and fresh in a pale blue tunic over rose-colored pants. "It would have taken Laverne and me a while to do all of this."

"It's nothing, Nana. I told you I was good to do it on my own."

"You always were the little girl who said that," Nana said with a fond smile. "*I can do it on my own!*"

"Are you expecting the whole group tonight?"

"I think so. We may need more chairs, if everyone makes it." She gazed at the semicircle of chairs and counted, then said, "Yes, another five, if all show up. Gilda has taken to coming over with Thelma, now that she lives upstairs at Belle Époque. And Laverne is bringing her niece Cindy; you remember Cindy."

"I do." Cindy, the youngest of Laverne's many nieces and nephews, was tall for her age, an exceptionally pretty girl with a demure demeanor and green lovely eyes. "Does that mean Josh will be here, too? I hope so; I haven't seen him since I got back."

Josh Sinclair was the youngest official member of the Silver Spouts, having just turned seventeen. He had a crush on Cindy, but Cindy's parents thought she was too young to date, so the two teens had merely been friends.

"Oh, I do think he'll be here," Nana said with a slight smile. "Cindy turned fifteen a few weeks ago. I have a feeling Josh is going to ask if she can go out with him now."

They worked in silence for a few minutes, with Nana

mostly focused on the teapots she intended to talk about, and some notes on the Fall Fling Townwide Tea Party, or "tea stroll," as she called it, since folks would be walking from tearoom to tearoom. Sophie pulled up more chairs, spaced them and made sure everyone would be comfortable.

"I like that Julia," Nana said, finally sitting down in one of the chairs.

The new tearoom owner had indeed dropped in and picked Nana's brain about running SereniTea, three doors up the street from Auntie Rose's. The house had been Josh's grandmother's home before Julia and her husband bought it. They had done a quick makeover in a modified Japanese style, with shoji doors and screens, a space for meditation, a Zen garden in back and a large room for yoga classes. It was so completely different from Auntie Rose's and Belle Époque that it didn't count as competition. Nana was able to advise her on some of the nuts and bolts of running a tearoom. Julia had a manager, a young woman who was also the yoga instructor, but neither had retail experience, and both were struggling.

"I do, too," Sophie said. "She's trying to help Jason get past this grading thing. I hope they figure out what happened."

Nana reached out and took her granddaughter's hand. "It'll all work out, sweetheart. I believe in Jason."

"I do, too, but that isn't always enough."

Rose watched as her granddaughter leaped up to work some more, dashing into the kitchen to prepare snacks and set up trays for the Silver Spouts. Sophie had been hurt deeply by the death of her restaurant, but had been recovering nicely over the spring and summer in Gracious Grove. Then Rose's daughter Rosalind showed up, tempting her daughter with the offer to go back to her career as a chef in a fashionable restaurant in the Hamptons. The mother and daughter's relationship had never been smooth, since their ideas of what would make Sophie happy were many miles apart. Sophie had hoped that going to the Hamptons to work and be near her mother would help their fragile relationship, but what she saw as her mother's betrayal had hurt her deeply.

Rosalind had called and offered to come when Rose was sick, but she hadn't a lick of good bedside manner; they both knew that. And with Sophie and Laverne to help, she wasn't necessary. Maybe that was the problem; Rosalind was *never* necessary. Being needed was one of the great gifts of life, and Rose's daughter had been denied that for most of her life. Or had she managed her life so she would never be counted on? It was an interesting thought.

Regardless, that had to change. Whether either of them knew it or not, Sophie needed her mother, and Rosalind needed her only daughter. Rose would give anything to see the two mend their rift.

The Silver Spouts arrived, and the volume of chatter in the room rose. They had their talk and discussed the Fall Fling Townwide Tea Party. Snacks were served, and the most enjoyable part of the evening for many commenced, with several of them breaking off into smaller groups to chat. Horace Brubaker and Laverne's father, Malcolm Hodge, both nonagenarian but active and busy, sat apart at a table with two of Rose's friends, Annabelle and Helen. Thelma and Gilda sat at the table right next to them and shamelessly eavesdropped on the foursome.

Rose and Laverne were enjoying a cup of tea with Cindy and Sophie when Josh, who had had his reddish-brown hair closer cropped so he looked older and more mature, approached. He said hello to each, then turned to Laverne.

"Miss Hodge, I was wondering, now that Cindy is, uh . . . has turned fifteen, if it would be okay if she accompanied me to a natural sciences exhibit at the college."

Seventeen going on forty, Rose thought, smiling at the boy. He had an old-fashioned air about him, as would any teenage boy who collected teapots. Cindy blushed and looked down at her cute shoes, a pair of Mary Janes in light blue.

Laverne regarded him sternly, her handsome face set to avoid smiling too broadly. "Well, Mr. Sinclair, I've discussed this with her parents and we've decided that since she is now fifteen, it's up to Cindy, so you will have to ask her yourself."

He looked a little shocked, and his freckled cheeks flushed pink, just as hers were. But he turned to her and said, "Cindy, would you like to go to the traveling exhibit at Cruikshank next week?"

With an unexpectedly shrewd look, she cocked her head to one side and said, "What kind of exhibit?"

"It's uh, it's amphibians and reptiles of the rain forest."

Rose stifled a sigh. He was inviting her to go see lizards and frogs? Did he not know girls at all? She waited for the sniff of disgust.

Cindy hopped in her chair and said, "I'd *love* to go, Josh! I like snakes best. Will they have snakes? Pythons? Anacondas?" She paused and clapped her hands together. "*Boa constrictors?*" Her dark eyes were wide and sparkling.

Josh smiled broadly. "I hope so. I like lizards better than snakes. Do you mind frogs? Some girls don't like frogs."

Rose burst out laughing. "Well now, in my day if any boy had asked me to go see snakes and frogs with him, I would have bopped him on the nose."

Josh and Cindy broke away and sat together discussing the exhibit, words like *herpetology, semiaquatic, neurotoxins* and *tetrapod* floating toward the adults.

"She's interested in many kinds of animals," Laverne explained. "Cindy wants to be a zoologist and travel to Africa someday. She may be the last kid to benefit from the Laverne Hodge college fund." Laverne had always set aside some money for her nieces and nephews; those who needed it could apply to her for a school loan, which was eventually repaid, no interest needed, to benefit the younger nieces and nephews.

They chatted with some of the others about the Fall Fling tea stroll.

"I think we're ready for it, aren't we, Sophie?" Rose asked.

"We're better than ready," she said, with her special brand of brisk confidence, revitalized by being in charge of the menu at Auntie Rose's once again. "We're setting up a table outside for the strollers, with tea and snacks; I'll be manning that. But the tearoom itself will be open, too, with you two inside for those who want to sit for a moment, or warm up."

"This tea walk . . . yet another attempt by Cruickshank to improve relations between town and gown," Horace, who had been listening in from the next table, croaked, his voice hoarse from a cold he was finally defeating. He cleared his throat. "I know Dale Asquith; his family had a home by the lake, and he spent summers at it. Even then, his parents insisted he keep up with his schooling. He was one of my troublesome piano students back when I taught. He always was a pain in the tush, and from what I hear, he still is."

"Horace, people do change with time," Rose said.

The elderly man tapped his cane on the floor and chuckled a rusty sound. "Now, Rose, you are too sweet and gentle a lady. Take everything I say about him and multiply it to the power of ten. One of his greatest faults is a tendency to not take responsibility for those faults. It was always someone else who kept him from practicing: his brother, the maid, a door-to-door salesman." He glanced over at Sophie and his smile disappeared. "You make sure he doesn't try to do that to your young man with this grading problem, because he will, if it will save his butt."

The meeting broke up. Sophie sent her grandmother straight up to bed, and Laverne home, since she had to drop off Cindy first. She rearranged the tearoom for the next day's business, but it was only nine when she was done and trotted upstairs. There was a text on her phone from Dana to call her, so she did.

It was odd, Sophie thought as she listened to it ring; Cissy Peterson was the one who had wanted to be friends when they were teens, and they were, but now that they were all adults it was Dana who Sophie gravitated toward. Dana Saunders had once been jealous of her, she had admitted, because of Sophie's wealthy family, but recently they discovered that they clicked.

"Hey, Dana, what's up?" she asked when the phone clicked.

"I'm so sorry, Soph. You must be worried sick!"

"Worried? What are you talking about? What's wrong?"

"Oh, for heaven's sake; hasn't anyone told you yet? It's the article in the *Clarion*. I'll send you the link."

A few seconds later, Sophie looked at her phone screen and clicked on the link from the Cruikshank College newspaper, the *Clarion*.

PROF'S FRIEND ADMITS
POSSIBLE GRADE HIKE FOR MAC
By Tara Mitchells

*Sophie Taylor, instructor Jason Murphy's "friend,"
insists that while he would never knowingly do
anything to jeopardize his position at the college,
he could easily have hiked Mac MacAlister's grade
if he wasn't aware how it would impact him. She
further stated that the fun-loving prof, who as a
wild youth was known to drink, smoke and steal on
occasion, has cleaned up his act and is desperately
trying to stay on the straight and narrow . . .*

"Oh, *no!*" Sophie wailed, not able to read further.

"Damn straight, *oh no*," Dana said. "You'd better call
Jason. I'm hanging up right now. *Call* him!"

Jason answered immediately.

"I saw the article. Jason, I'm so sorry! It sounded . . . I
didn't mean . . ." What could she say?

"One question: Did you really say I could easily have
hiked Mac's grade?" His voice was filled with tension, and
harder edged than normal.

"I said nothing of the kind."

He sighed. "Okay. I didn't think you would. Tara needs
to be told she's wrong."

"More than that! They should print a retraction, Jason."

"What I want to know is, where did they get the stuff
about drinking and stealing? I don't get it." When she didn't
respond, Jason said, "Sophie? What's up?"

"Okay, the night of the basketball game I didn't know who
she was. I may have said something . . . I mean, you remember

that incident with your cousins' boat? You took off for a joyride and got in trouble?"

He was silent.

"And I mentioned . . . remember the summer you and Phil Peterson hung out together?" Phil Peterson was Cissy's older brother, a lifelong troubled soul who was now apparently living out of state trying to get his act together. But when they were teenagers and even beyond he was always trying to smuggle booze into school events, and had been known to sell an ounce of weed occasionally. He had dragged Jason into his mess once or twice, though Jason wised up to the danger of inappropriate friends pretty quickly.

"Why did you get into that with a student?" he said.

"I don't even know," she said, feeling about two inches tall. She put her head in one hand. "I don't normally babble; you know that. But I was uncomfortable, and she looked so harmless. I'm sorry. I need to learn to keep my mouth shut."

He sighed heavily. "It's okay. You couldn't have known the girl was a writer for the newspaper."

"She said she was there in support of you! That she wanted to start a petition to *help* you."

"She's a muckraker. She ought to do well in media."

"I'm sorry."

"Okay. It's all right."

"Jason, who do *you* think did it?"

He was silent for a moment. "I wouldn't want to accuse someone unjustly."

"I promise I won't say a word to anyone. I've learned my lesson."

"It has to be someone who either loves the basketball team or cares about Mac personally. I'm thinking either Heck Donovan or Mac's academic adviser."

"Kimmy Gabrielson. She told me herself that she was

one of the few people who could have done it and had access to the content management computer program. Would she tell me that if she had done it? If you know what I mean?"

"Would she have said that to you if she was the one who changed the grade? She's smart. It would be a great bluff."

"True. She didn't think Heck Donovan *could* have done it. She said she's not sure he would even have had access to the software."

"You've discussed this in depth, haven't you?"

"Jason, you never told me a thing. I was blindsided and shell-shocked," she said, stung by his acerbity. She flung herself down in a chair in her living room and tossed a pillow at the wall. If he wanted to get into it, then she'd tell him the truth. "I think that's why I talked about it; I was so taken aback."

There was silence from his end, and she worried she'd offended him. But then he said, "You're right. I'm sorry, I'm just . . . this is a mess. Anyway, as you know, Mac was benched pending the investigation, and Heck is furious. He and the dean had a battle royal, I guess. Dean Asquith's secretary spread the tale across the campus. Heck came storming into my office this afternoon and gave me what for."

They talked a few minutes more, then said good night. Unsettled by the whole thing, Sophie was tired but edgy. She watched some TV, her favorite true crime stories, and then went to bed to toss and turn with wild dreams of running through the halls of her old boarding school, plaid kilt flapping around her knees, escaping from some maniacal killer who specialized in schoolgirls. After that disquieting night she was happy to awaken in the pretty bedroom and descend to the sunny kitchen to bake scones and cookies and make soup and stew.

Before the tearoom opened she called Dana. She wanted to tell her friend what Jason had said about who he thought was responsible, but Dana didn't even let her finish her first sentence.

"Soph, I hate to say it, but I just heard from Kimmy. The dean made a public statement to the students and press this morning. He said in light of the grading scandal, that the one responsible has been discovered and will be dealt with summarily."

"But that's good, right? If they've found out who did it?"

"I'm not so sure of that. Kimmy thinks they're going to scapegoat Jason."

Chapter 6

Sophie hung up quickly, told Nana she'd be down to open with her, then ran upstairs and texted Jason to call her. She didn't want to bug him, knowing that weekends were filled with course work, grading tests and essays, and work on his doctorate, but she needed to know what was happening. She paced and fretted, biting her nails, an old habit she thought she had grown out of. He called back ten minutes later.

She breathlessly asked him about the dean's address to students and the media, and he said she had heard correctly. He sounded tired and worried; she wished he was beside her so she could give him a hug.

"I haven't been suspended from teaching yet, but it's not looking good. I don't think he's brought in outside help, but the dean has one of the college staff sniffing around asking questions. One of my buddies in the science department said someone told him that he was asking if I've been behaving any differently lately, or if I bought anything unusual."

"What does that mean?"

"I guess they think there may be bribery involved. I don't know! It's making me crazy. I can't even defend myself because no one is saying it outwardly, they're whispering behind my back!"

"Oh, Jason, this is awful. As if you'd ever do anything like that!"

"Anyway, even if they don't suspend me, I feel like everyone is watching me now, judging me, thinking I cheated. I don't understand what's going on. I didn't *do* anything, so I know there's no evidence against me. Unless the dean's got someone else in mind and he's just not saying, I don't know what to think. He and I have never gotten along, but I don't think he would take it out on me to cover up the problem."

She didn't say what she was thinking, which was, what if it was the dean himself who did the grade altering, not expecting it to come out? "What will you do if the worst happens?"

"The worst? You mean, what if I'm fired? I don't even know if he *can* do that to me, but I know he'd love to. We don't get along, and everyone knows it."

"When do you find out?"

"He's going to make the official announcement after the weekend. He doesn't want anything taking attention away from Fall Fling, he said."

"What are you going to do in the meantime?"

"I'm going to go ahead as if all is okay. I didn't do anything. If he tries to pin it on me, I'll fight it, but who knows what'll happen from there?"

"I know it'll be okay, Jase, really. You didn't do it, and they can't prove you did."

"I guess you have more faith in the system than I do. Oh well, there's always Paris."

"What do you mean?"

"I've always wanted to go to France. Maybe I'll go there to work."

Thelma Mae Earnshaw prodded Gilda with one boney finger. "Now get on over there to Rose's joint, cozy up to Laverne and find out what they're doing for that dumb tea fling. I know what we're doing, but I couldn't overhear a thing at the Spouts meeting about what they've got planned."

"What am I supposed to find out?" Gilda wobbled over to peer into the oven, then tugged at her frizzy hair and sighed. "I don't know what you want, Thelma." She grabbed two mitts and opened the oven door, giving the scones a poke.

Thelma ducked her head and eyed the side entrance to Auntie Rose's through the smeared window. "I need to know what they're serving to folks, and when they're making it. And how are they going to keep tea hot all evening for the strollers. Hmph. Sounds like they're going to be carrying babies; *strollers*!" She picked up her cell phone. Cissy had programmed in some numbers and said all she had to do was find someone's name and she could call them. She had also explained a few other nifty features, like the camera.

A camera on a phone! She was like a modern-day spy, and could take photos while pretending to call or text, whatever that was, but Cissy said it all the time. Thelma found the little gadget on the screen that looked like a camera, aimed the phone at Gilda's butt as her employee pulled the tray of scones out of the oven, and hit the little button, but the darn thing jiggled and all she got was a blur. Dang!

Gilda plunked the tray of scones on the counter and pulled off the oven mitts, grumbling under her breath. Then she cast Thelma a sly look. "I guess I *could* go over and have a cup of tea with Laverne. Maybe pick her brain?"

"And find out what they're doing. Now, scoot! Just don't be too long. We got a tearoom to run."

When Gilda had tripped out the wide door in an all-fired hurry, Thelma pulled some sugar packets out of her pocket. Maybe she could pull a few harmless pranks on Rose, just so she'd stay on her toes.

I t was the end of a long day that had started badly, with the news about the dean's press conference and Jason's worries, and continued weirdly, with Gilda, from Belle Époque, coming over and quizzing them all on their Fall Fling plans. Sophie and her grandmother had eaten dinner together, but tomorrow was a big day. Nana was going to bed early to get a good sleep.

Sophie pulled on her skinniest skinny jeans and her beloved pair of Uggs, wound a scarf around her neck and slipped on her blue jean jacket, then paused. October in upstate New York; it could get kind of cold in the evening, but still . . . she was driving the Jetta, it had an excellent heater, and she'd be going directly into Barchester Hall to meet up with Rhiannon Galway and help at the Galway Fine Teas booth. She'd be fine, she decided. She closed her apartment door, raced down one set of steps and nipped through Nana's apartment to her bedroom, where her grandmother was tucked in bed with Pearl on her lap, a cup of tea at her side and Jessica Fletcher on the DVD player.

She stuck her head in the door. "I don't know what time I'll be home. You have my cell number if you need me, right?"

"I do," Nana said with a sleepy smile. She stroked Pearl's head gently.

"You haven't been overdoing it have you?" she asked, watching her grandmother.

"No, Miss Bossy," Nana said with a chuckle. "I'm getting up there in years. Everything takes twice as long and is twice as hard. But it's so nice to be back in the tearoom again." She eyed her granddaughter. "I hope you know how much I appreciate you coming back here, but . . ."

"But what?"

"*But* I never want you to feel you have to stay here if you'd rather be elsewhere."

Sophie crossed the bedroom and bent over her grandmother, giving her a fierce hug. "I am *exactly* where I want to be. I think it took going back to the Hamptons to get that in my head. I have friends here, and you and Laverne; what else could I want?"

"And Jason?"

"And Jason," Sophie said, trying to keep her tone light. What would happen between them if he had to leave? She didn't even want to think about it.

"Are you going to see him tonight?"

"I don't think so."

"Say hello to Rhiannon for me."

"I will. I'm bringing back a fresh box of our tea. We'll need extra for tomorrow night."

"Good thinking. Night, honey."

"I'll be quiet when I come in. Good night, Nana. And Pearlie-Girlie," she said, dropping a kiss on the cat's fluffy head. The Birman stretched and yawned, then curled up in a goofy ball, feet pointing skyward.

Barchester Hall, one of the buildings from when Cruickshank was expanded to accommodate the influx of returning

GIs going to college on the GI bill, was a large building with cement columns separated by aqua, salmon and glass panels. It housed an auditorium theater for speakers, as well as a big room for conventions and displays. She parked and entered the retro lobby, which featured starburst and amoeba designs, veering off toward the convention hall.

The event was in full swing. A few hundred people strolled the long aisles, perusing tea-related displays of all kinds of vendors, from tea blenders, porcelain makers, teapot artisans, antiques merchants and many more. She rushed along the line of tables until she came to Rhiannon's and hopped into the booth, giving her friend a quick hug.

"I'm so glad you're here." Rhiannon, her auburn hair pulled back and woven into a braid, pulled off her emerald-green apron and flung it down on the table. "I need to go to the bathroom!"

"Drink too much tea?" Sophie asked with a grin.

"Funny. Look, can you hold down the fort for a minute? Tell anyone who asks I'll be back in a sec." She grabbed her purse and rushed off.

Sophie looked around, familiarizing herself with the booth. It was roughly a ten-by-twelve space, with square shelving units holding a variety of Galway's special blends in both loose-leaf and tea bag types, as well as imported teapots, infusers, strainers and Irish linens. Rhi had some thermal jugs set up that dispensed hot tea in five different blends.

Folks drifted past and some paused; she served them tea blends, telling them the difference between the two black blends, and the green, Earl Grey and chai teas offered. She pointed out the excellent quality but plain teapots, various steepers, strainers and infusers, and packaged loose-leaf teas.

Rhiannon came back, shoved her purse under the counter and picked up her apron. "I'm lucky you came along when you did. That time of the month, you know?" She grabbed an extra apron and thrust it into Sophie's hands.

"Happy to be of assistance," Sophie said, donning the apron, which had *Galway Fine Teas* in white script across the chest.

They worked together, with Sophie directing folks who had more complex questions or orders to Rhiannon. In between they talked about the problems that Jason was having at the college. Rhiannon said that Cruickshank had always had a lousy athletic program, and she knew because she had gone there on a women's volleyball scholarship.

"We did our best, but college leadership wasn't very encouraging," Rhiannon said, flinging her auburn braid back over her shoulders. She perched on the edge of the green-tablecloth-covered table. "We were ranked first in our division and *still* couldn't get any money or gym time. Don't laugh, but back then, besides us, they had great bowling, fencing and archery teams. Totally random, right? Nowadays they don't have *any* good teams."

"All I know is, Jason didn't do what he's being accused of."

A passel of locals came by. Sophie recognized some of them from the businesswomen's association in Gracious Grove. She hailed Elizabeth Lemmon, owner of Libby Lemon's, a kitchenware store in downtown Gracious Grove.

"Hey, Sophie, Rhiannon," the woman said, pushing back her dark fluffy curls.

"You two know each other?" Sophie asked.

"Sure. We talked about carrying Rhiannon's tea in our store. We still may do that!"

They chatted business, in between Rhiannon helping customers and talking about tea. As Rhiannon moved into the concourse to talk to some folks who were interested in having her do a talk on tea for their church group, Elizabeth leaned in to Sophie. "I've been hearing about what's going on with your fellow, Jason. You know the dean's wife, Jeanette Asquith? She's a gossipy soul, and has been spreading the word through every group in town she belongs to."

Dismayed, Sophie said, "Why would she do that?"

"Jeanette seems frosty, but once you get to know her, you find out she will talk your ear off about anything. She's a bit of a self-important pain, if you ask me, but she's such a good customer I can't shut her up."

"What did she say? What is she telling people?"

The woman took Sophie's arm and drew her out of the booth toward a private curtained area behind, which was storage for the vendors. It was dimly lit and lined with boxes. "In the last couple of days she's been telling anyone who will listen that one of the instructors has been caught red-handed upping one of the athlete's grades. It doesn't take a rocket scientist to guess she means Jason Murphy. It was being talked about even before that story in the *Clarion*."

"Do people in Gracious Grove actually read the *Clarion*?"

"Off-campus students live in town, so a lot of places carry it and many local business advertise in it. I don't; no student is in the market for high-end kitchen gadgetry. But Peterson Books 'n Stuff carries it and advertises in it, especially since they supply school texts to a lot of Cruickshank students."

That was how Dana knew about the newspaper article before anyone else. "I don't get why Dean Asquith's wife would be spreading around the rumor."

Elizabeth touched her arm. "Look, you didn't hear it from me, but she's got a friend on the side."

"I've already heard that. What has he got to do with it?"

"Paul Wechsler is systems engineer at Cruickshank."

Sophie, mystified, shook her head.

"*Think* about it! Who could change those grades easier at any point than the fellow who has access to every area of the computer system?"

"But why would he?" Was she being dense? She didn't get the connection.

"Okay, let me spell it out. You're not the gossipy type, right?"

Sophie shook her head.

"Okay, well, the scuttlebutt is that Paul is so in love with Jeanette that he'd do anything for her. He wants her to leave Dale Asquith, but knows she won't do it as long as Paul just works for the college. I could be wrong, but I think he may have done it for a bribe from Mac MacAlister's parents, who are already wealthy, but hoping he gets an offer from the NBA. His dad played here back in the seventies. Their dream is for him to play for the Knicks. If the bribe was big enough, Paul thinks he could start the IT company he's been talking about for a year, make it big and tempt Jeanette away from Dale."

That seemed like a particularly tortured theory to Sophie, but she took it in and thought about it. "So you're saying Jeanette, knowing what Paul did, is trying to throw shade on Jason, hoping her boyfriend won't get caught?"

"Exactly!" Elizabeth said. "You go to the head of the class."

Sophie peeked around the drapes; Rhiannon was swamped, so she excused herself from Elizabeth and returned to the booth.

"You're Sophie Taylor, right?" said a young woman who stood with a friend looking over the teapots.

"I am! How'd you know?"

"My aunt described you. I'm Vienna Hodge."

"Laverne's niece? Eli's little sister?"

"One of the many . . . nieces, I mean," the young woman said with a laugh. Midtwenties and slim, wearing a peacoat over leggings, she had the most gorgeous long-lashed hazel eyes. Her dark hair was shiny and short, sleeked forward and dyed mahogany on the ends. "Eli's my half brother; I'm from Daddy's third marriage. Anyway, Auntie Lala called me and said you would be here, and asked if I could stop in and talk to you. She wouldn't say what about."

Well, this was awkward. Vienna's similarly slim but blond and blue-eyed friend was talking to a fellow in the aisle. "I don't want to take your time. You work in admissions here, right?"

The young woman nodded.

"I really just . . . it's about Jason Murphy. He's my friend, and is in trouble, as you likely know."

"That's all anyone is talking about. None of us want to see him fired," she said, motioning to her friend. "He's the hot prof, you know? The one all the girls have a crush on. *And* he's nice, not a jerk like some of them. Whenever he comes in to the office, he always stops to chat. But what can I tell you? I'm just an assistant in admissions."

"I guess I'm grasping at straws. You know these people, though; have any of them been acting odd? Or has anyone said anything about who the dean is leaning toward blaming?"

"My boss is friends with the registrar, Vince Nomuro. Do you know him?"

"Just enough to recognize him." Sophie explained about the basketball game she had attended.

"Yeah, no doubt. Vince is such a big basketball fan that he's at *every* game. I overheard them talking this morning, the registrar and my boss. Vince is worried. I don't know if he did it, or if he just worries in general, but I *did* hear him say that he won't go down without a fight."

Vienna and her friend were meeting people at the Crook's Lair, the on-campus pub, so they bustled away. Sophie pondered what she had just heard; surely it would be an even more serious thing for someone like Vince Nomuro, whose whole career was based on trust with data on students. He had certainly seemed nervous at the basketball game, and was keeping his eye on Dean Asquith.

The evening was winding to a close and the hall was emptying, with the last few customers chatting to vendors and finalizing orders. Sophie helped Rhiannon tear down the booth. They loaded the shelves and product on a dolly cart and wheeled it through the convention center, with Rhi pausing to talk to people along the way. At one of their stops, Sophie noticed Dean Asquith speaking to a thirtyish woman with auburn wavy hair and a curvaceous form, hugged by an expensive dress. Asquith looked around with a nervous twitch, then grabbed her by the elbow and hauled her away. Interesting.

But irrelevant.

They circled the active area of the convention floor, beyond the long curtains, and threaded through pallets of boxed products to a garage-style door. "Wait here, and I'll go get my van and back it up to the door," Rhiannon said.

Sophie sat on the edge of the dolly cart and considered what she had learned so far. Paul Wechsler, Jeanette Asquith's boyfriend, had the motive and could easily have changed Mac MacAlister's grade in exchange for a bribe from some source, possibly the guy's parents. When one considered the size of the paychecks NBA players received, a bribe could well be worth it, but would it matter if he got good grades or completed his schooling? Couldn't he go directly to the NBA if he was so talented? She didn't understand all the ins and outs of the athletic and academic worlds. Maybe there was some scouting opportunity Mac needed to be a part of, or maybe getting into the college basketball finals would bring him to the attention of NBA scouts more surely than anything else.

Vince Nomuro, according to Vienna Hodge, was worried about his own job, though. He was certainly in the best position to change the grade, but why would he do it, unless bribery was also his motivation? Or was he so much of a basketball fan that he would have done it out of love for his college team's prospects? That was a big jump to imagine him risking his good job to keep Mac on the team.

Another merchant wheeled a dolly cart into the area, raised the steel door with a loud rattle and pushed the laden cart out to a waiting cube van, where the driver helped him load up. They left the door open and drove away, with a roar of the engine and smell of exhaust fumes. A cold wind swept in, along with some dried leaves. What was taking Rhiannon so long?

Sophie got up and paced away from the big open door. It was getting colder. There was a protected spot beyond the open door where she could still keep the loaded dolly cart in sight. She squeezed herself into it, and warmed her hands under her armpits. Another set of people left, loading their few boxes in a car trunk and taking off. Where was Rhiannon?

She heard voices again, but this time they were just beyond the long heavy curtains that separated the storage and loading dock area from the convention center floor. ". . . you can't keep me hanging on. I won't have it!" a female's shrill voice complained.

A male voice with a condescending tone responded, "You'll have to put up with it, Sherri. I'm not getting a divorce, and neither is my wife. I like things the way they are."

"To hell with that, Dale."

"Hey, you're seeing other men; don't try to tell me you aren't. I have spies everywhere, Sherri."

"That was just . . . I *wanted* you to know, Dale. I wanted you to know I can have anyone I want."

"Look, let's end this as friends. No hard feelings, okay?"

"No! I'm *not* going to put up with this anymore. You made promises, Dale. I'll talk; I swear I'll talk, and you won't like what I have to say. I know that some of your precious student athletes aren't doing all their own work, are they? What about that? A nice, fat, juicy cheating scandal."

"You will not say a word to anyone!" There was a bit of a scuffle, and the curtain wavered, then there was silence, and the sound of a woman weeping, and more words, soothing in tone, as they both appeared to move away.

Dale? That was Dean Asquith's first name, if she was right. Sophie nipped across the open space and peeked out of the curtains just in time to see the tall figure of the dean with his arms around the flame-haired woman Sophie had seen him with earlier. Well, that was interesting; so that was his mistress. If Sophie was a gossip, she would spread that little scene around, but she couldn't care less. More important was the news that cheating at the college may not be confined to grade hiking. How bad a scandal would that be, if students weren't doing their own course work?

At that moment Rhiannon backed the van up to the door and got out, apologizing. "Darn thing wouldn't start! I had to get some guy to give me a jump. I can't shut it down in case it won't start again, so help me load up and I'll get out of here."

Sophie grabbed the box of Auntie Rose's tea out of the back, got a lift across the parking lot to her Jetta and drove home.

Chapter 7

Auntie Rose's was closed, as it was a Sunday. Most Sundays were quiet, calm, peaceful days. Nana would spend it reading or talking on the phone to friends; sometimes she accompanied Laverne to church. Sophie would piddle around in the kitchen, inventing new recipes, getting ahead on prep and enjoying the sunshine that streamed through the window.

But this Sunday was crazy busy, as they were getting ready for the Fall Fling Townwide Tea Party. Laverne had helped with organizing, her strong suit, but then headed home to have a nap. Sophie made her grandmother go upstairs to lie down, telling Nana she would not let them open otherwise. Sophie tiptoed around for a couple of hours, preparing everything she could, then had a sandwich for dinner while reading restaurant reviews in an old *New York Times*.

And then it was showtime. Sophie was actually nervous, more so because the tea walk would mean the dean and many others from the college would be stopping by, and she wasn't sure how to talk to them, especially with all she was thinking and feeling about how they were treating Jason. But she needed to set that aside for one night. She would be herself. At In Fashion she had hosted senators and movie stars, authors and fashionistas, among other luminaries, so a college dean and his entourage should be small potatoes, as Nana said.

There was still that niggling doubt in the back of her mind, though. Academics seemed a whole different breed to her, and academic culture was strange, insular, snobbish, almost inbred.

Cissy Peterson was helping her grandmother and Gilda at Belle Époque, and Dana had offered to help Sophie at Auntie Rose's, but both were late. Sophie lugged a sturdy folding table out to the front of Auntie Rose's. The structure itself was a big white clapboard house, the entire main floor converted many years before into a tearoom. Nana had explained to Sophie when she was a child that when she lost her husband, she needed to find a way to make a living, and she had always loved tea and enjoyed baking, so opening a tearoom was her answer.

Sophie understood more now about how much Nana had suffered many years ago, losing her husband and a son—her oldest child had died in Vietnam—and having the other son disappear. No one had heard from Jack for forty years, though Nana had hired a private detective at one point to try to find him. He had drifted into the drug scene in California in the nineteen seventies, the detective was able to discover, but then he disappeared. The tearoom and Laverne's friendship were her saving graces.

The garden in the front of Auntie Rose's was kept simple so that maintenance would be easy. It was contained by low box hedges, and much of the area was graveled with white marble, though there was a section of lush green lawn, too, with a flowering crabapple tree. In one corner by the front window there was a pretty Japanese maple. Sophie hung a teacup mobile in the tree, tied a light to the branch and ran an extension cord thorough the front window. She set the tea table up under the light and spread a plastic cover over it, clipping it with clothes pegs in case a breeze came up.

Dana pulled up with Cissy in the passenger's seat of her car. Cissy jumped out, waved to Sophie, shouted "We're late!" then trotted into Belle Époque as Dana pulled around back and parked. Thelma's establishment was almost identical to Auntie Rose's in front. Not surprising, Nana said, since Thelma had her grandson, Phil, copy her ten years before when she had the front redone. It, too, had a hedge, though it was scrubby and undergrown, and unlike the flowering crabapple tree in front of Auntie Rose's, Belle Époque featured a small ornamental tree. Sophie snorted back a laugh. She'd name Nana's crabapple tree Thelma.

Dana approached from behind the tearoom. There was something different about the always-gorgeous woman, Sophie thought, examining her. She was wearing cinnamon-colored jeans and a heavy cable-knit sweater with a fleece vest over it. Somehow she managed to make even that warm outfit chic. Then Sophie looked down at her footwear. "You're wearing Uggs! I thought you said they were ugly. I thought—"

"That was before Eli said I made them look hot."

Sophie chuckled and asked her friend to retrieve the box of tea stuff from the tearoom. In between dashing in and out of Auntie Rose's to fetch things, Dana chattered nonstop about Eli. They had met in the summer in Butterhill, an hour's drive away, while Sophie and the others were up there at a teapot collectors' convention where a murder had happened, a murder that her nana was a suspect in! Eli had gotten himself assigned to the case, concerned about his aunt and grandfather, and intent on apprehending the killer. Dana had spotted him immediately and fell for his good looks, intelligence, but most of all his care for his family. The couple's relationship had moved swiftly, but Sophie was still surprised at one of Dana's confessions.

The setting sun lit the golden streaks in her gorgeous mane of hair, which she tossed back over her shoulder. She turned toward Sophie. Her voice trembling with excitement, she said, "Soph, I think Eli is going to ask me to marry him."

"Really?" Sophie paused as she reclipped the tablecloth for the outdoor table and stared at her friend. "But you've only known each other . . . what, three months? Not even?"

Dana shrugged. "When you know, you know. And I *know*. I knew right away, and I think he did, too. I love him and I want to marry him."

It seemed awfully quick to Sophie, but who was she to judge? "He seems like a great guy."

"He is a wonderful man, kind, thoughtful, sweet. He loves his family, and he's good to his nieces and nephews. He'll make a great father." She grinned and dropped a saucy wink. "And it doesn't hurt that he is smoking hot."

Next door, Cissy hauled a table out front as Gilda gabbled at her, flapping her hands. Poor Cissy, having to deal with cranky Thelma and flighty Gilda. "Dana, I've got this under control. Do you want to go help Cissy?"

"No. But I will anyway."

Sophie laughed. The Earnshaw-Peterson family was sometimes a trial to get along with. As much as she had tried to get Thelma involved with her and Julia's plans for their street's part in the Fall Fling, Mrs. Earnshaw seemed to have a chip on her shoulder and had refused or, rather, ignored her offer. At least Cissy was there to help, but her old friend, usually a pleasant companion, could be petulant and moody if she felt she wasn't the center of attention. Dana crossed the drive and helped Cissy, who brightened up and sent Gilda back in to work with Thelma on the inside preparations.

Laverne pulled in, driving the stately old car she had owned since it was new, in the seventies. She parked in back, where Auntie Rose's and Belle Époque had a modest joint parking lot, room enough for a dozen or so cars. Laverne stuck her head around the corner. "You need any help out here?"

"No, I'm good. Just go in and make sure Nana doesn't try to do too much."

"Honey, I'll try, but she's a grown woman. You can't stop her from doing what she wants."

"I don't know what I'd do if I lost her."

Laverne's dark eyes were warm with love. "I know, Sophie. She's the big sister I never had. You know I'll take care of her."

"I don't know when I became such a worrier."

Nana had a vintage electric samovar stored in the attic. Sophie had retrieved it, cleaned it up and now had it full of water, from which she would make fresh pots of Auntie Rose's tea as the evening progressed. Nana had insisted on using some of her jumble of assorted teacups and saucers for the full Auntie Rose experience. Sophie stacked them up, plugged in the samovar and got the plastic tubs of treats, setting them on a stool beside the table. She set up a couple of the domed treat plates and filled them, stacking more on a triple cake stand.

She checked her watch. It was seven, and their section of the tea party stroll was just starting. In fact, as she looked down the street, she could see some folks parking cars and gathering, starting at SereniTea, as she and Julia had suggested. Gracious

Grove, as a dry town, had an inordinate number of tearooms and cafés. The committee had decided that groups would be directed to the three "districts" in the town where tearooms were clustered. The first had been visited at five, the second at six, and their string, SereniTea, Belle Époque and Auntie Rose's, was last.

Sophie and Dana at Auntie Rose's, and Cissy and Gilda at Belle Époque were to stand outside, pour tea, talk about the blends and hand out treats. Sophie was going to guide inside those who wished to warm up or have a tour of Nana's teapot collection. Poor Cissy was wrapped in a winter coat and still hopped from foot to foot, her fragile frame not affording her enough internal heat to ward off the October evening chill.

A few strollers started with Auntie Rose's. Some folks said the tea tasted off but when Sophie took a cup herself, it tasted fine, and most found it perfectly delicious. Maybe some weren't used to the blend, or the strength. Kimmy Gabrielson and her book club arrived and took their time, enjoying the tea and treats. Kimmy and Dana chatted, then the group wandered on to Belle Époque and from there to SereniTea.

The treats were a big hit with everyone. Nana had made lemon bars and Hello Dolly squares, while Sophie had made macarons—delicate egg white, powdered sugar and almond flour cookies—in the college's royal blue, as well as cupcakes with blue icing, dusted with silver. Dana, who skipped back and forth between the two side-by-side establishments, reported that Thelma was offering platters of store-bought cookies, which was probably a safer bet than her usual homemade fare.

It seemed a thin crowd to Sophie, but at about a quarter to eight she found out why. A large group moved down the street toward them, many more than were supposed to come to each establishment together. She noticed the tall figures of Dean

Asquith and his wife, Jeanette, in the center of a group o
older, well-dressed individuals. With them was Mac MacAli
ster; what was the basketball player doing on the tea stroll'
He was accompanied by an older couple, the woman tiny an
birdlike, but the gentleman almost as tall as Mac, his larg
head covered in a spray of sparse hair with faint tinges of a
ginger hue among the gray hairs; the pair had to be his par
ents, or even grandparents.

The big group also comprised duos and singles: Vinc
Nomuro with a natty tweed duffer cap pulled low, and Brend.
Fletcher wearing a black-and-white peacoat with a fluffy
white scarf; Heck Donovan, looking as hangdog as usual in
a rumpled trench coat, and Penny with an odd assortment o
colorful scarves wrapped around her; Julia and Jason strolling
together, looking uneasy; Sherri Shaw, of all people, whose
exotic style had been toned down. She wore a tan shawl
collared wool coat over camel dress slacks.

The crowd broke up into smaller clusters. The dean an
his wife stuck close to the well-dressed men and women who
Dana explained to her were Cruickshank College's Board o
Governors, mostly responsible for fund-raising, cultivating
alumni to encourage gifts and bequests, and scholarship pro
grams. Dean Asquith appeared grim, as he tried to herd them
together and keep them close while avoiding his mistress
who lingered nearby, though she never spoke to him.

It was an oddly assorted group. It appeared to Sophie tha
the MacAlister clan refused to break away, grimly shadowing
the dean like jaguars following a wildebeest. Jason waved t
Sophie, and she waved back, but he stuck by Julia close to th
dean's group, as did the coach and his morose wife. Vince
eyeing them all with trepidation, sipped tea and kept his ey
on Asquith, though his assistant drifted away and texted or
her phone in a pool of light from the streetlamps.

Lurking beyond the college crowd were a few strays. Tara Mitchells hung back in the shadows snapping photos, her flash illuminating startled expressions. Maybe she was shooting the tea party for the *Clarion*. Sophie hoped that was it, and that she wasn't there to stir up trouble. There was a nice-looking dark-haired fellow who appeared to observe; he never got a cup of tea, nor did he eat anything, he just watched. Kimmy Gabrielson had evidently parted from her book group and joined with the college crowd. She trotted up to Mac, taking him by the arm and pulling her aside. They spoke for a moment, with vehemence on her part, but he shook his head and pried her grasping hand off his arm. She appeared miffed and stood with her arms crossed over her bosom, looking like she was trying not to cry.

Tara Mitchells was taking notes, Sophie noticed; it would do the academic adviser well to not wear her heart on her sleeve, because no matter what she said, it appeared she had deeper feelings for the basketball player than just a professional relationship, on her part at least. Dana approached her and they chatted for a moment, then Kimmy walked away, back toward downtown Gracious Grove, where she had probably parked. Even as Sophie kept an eye on them all, she served and chatted with the three older gentleman and two ladies, the Cruickshank College Board of Governors members.

"These are lovely macarons," one tall older lady said, giving the cookies the correct French pronunciation, rolling the *r*. She was neatly dressed in a gray wool skirt suit with a dark blue caped jacket, her iron-gray hair stiffly waved under a sophisticated little hat. A Cruickshank College crest adorned the jacket. "I haven't had such lovely ones in ages, certainly not here in America."

"Thank you!" Sophie said.

"Did you make them?"

"I did. I make them regularly for the tearoom, usually in pink and green, Auntie Rose's colors." She told them about her education in New York, and her restaurant, In Fashion.

"And you run this establishment?" the woman asked, looking up at the Auntie Rose sign.

"No, this is my grandmother's place. My name is Sophie Taylor."

The woman stopped and eyed her. "Ah, the instructor's friend."

Sophie noted the frostiness in her tone. "Ma'am, I don't know what you've heard, but Jason is *not* involved in that grading problem. I've known him a long time, and he'd never do anything underhanded."

"Young lady, when you have lived as long as I, you will know that even people you think you know can surprise you, and not in a good way. He and Dean Asquith do not get along; Dale has told us all about it. It sounds like spite or revenge to me. I'd be more careful who you back."

Sophie stifled the urge to snarl, and simply said, "He didn't *do* anything, and if Dean Asquith says differently, then he's the one who will look like a fool." She took a deep breath; there she went running her mouth again. Judging by the woman's angry stare, it hadn't gone over well. Stiffly she added, "If you'd like to go in, my grandmother, Rose Freemont, and her business partner, Laverne Hodge, are inside giving tours and talking about her teapot collection."

"That would be lovely," the woman replied, her tone frosty. "I may want to hold a tea here one day for my sorority sisters. I went to Cruickshank, you know, in the sixties, and now I am *chairwoman* of the Board of Governors." Sophie opened the door and held it for the group. Vince and Brenda surged in after the board members. The dean's gaggle had lingered at Belle Époque. Cissy was doing her best to help them, but it didn't look like it was going well, and it didn't help that Gilda appeared to be berating the dean. *What on earth?*

Dana slunk across the lane to listen in, then scooted back, her eyes gleaming with malicious amusement. "Gilda is telling them what horrible people they are for sidelining Thelma and ignoring her. She told the dean's wife that Thelma Mae Earnshaw was twice as good as Rose Freemont, but that Rose was always stealing her thunder and copying her ideas."

"Oh, lord, Dana, we have to *do* something!"

The dean waved Gilda off and led the way to Auntie Rose's. He cast a long, steady look back, and Gilda, eyes wide, shot into the tearoom.

"That is one exceptionally strange woman," he was saying to his wife, as they strolled up to Sophie's tea table. He eyed Sophie. "I know you. You're Jason's young friend."

Jason moved forward. "Sophie Taylor, sir. You met the other night at the basketball game reception."

Sophie glanced at him; his voice was tight with tension. What was up?

The dean leveled a long, steady look at Jason, his heavy-lidded eyes expressionless and his mouth turned down. "Yes. Just so. Why was that . . . that *woman* saying you steal all their ideas?" he asked, turning to Sophie.

How to explain? She took a deep breath. "That's Gilda Bachman, sir. She works for Thelma Mae Earnshaw, the owner of Belle Époque. She's, uh . . . overly loyal and imagines schemes where there are none. Julia Dandridge and my grandmother, Rose Freemont, got together to plan our Fall Fling offerings. We tried to include Mrs. Earnshaw but . . ." Sophie shrugged. "She wasn't interested."

"Dale, enough chitchat," his wife said. "We came to sample the tea."

Sophie served tea and told the dean that the Board of Governors members had gone inside. He and his wife entered Auntie Rose's to look around; Sophie was relieved, knowing that Nana and Laverne would soothe the gentleman and make a good impression. But the couple was only in there a few minutes when he came out and shoved his cup at her, splashing tea over her clean white chef's coat. "Is this your idea of a joke?" he bellowed, his words echoing in the crisp evening air.

"I beg your pardon?"

"My tea is *salty*. Is this because of Jason and his troubles at Cruickshank? If that's the case, you have chosen poor timing for a joke or some . . . some petty revenge." His voice was carrying. They were joined by the board members and the others, who drifted out the door and toward the dean. "This is outrageous!" he declared, as his audience grew.

The chairwoman sniffed, clutched her purse to her chest and said, "I'm not surprised."

"I'm so sorry," Sophie said, mortified. She took a sip of what tea was left in is cup; it *was* salty. What was going on? "I'll make you a fresh cup, sir."

"Never mind. I don't want any now. Who knows what would be in it next?"

"But I assure you, sir—" Sophie glanced over at Belle Époque and saw Thelma Mae Earnshaw's pouchy face in the wide window of the tearoom. There was a grin on the woman's face. Somehow, some way, that woman had something to do with the salty tea. Sophie had thought Mrs. Earnshaw's long history of dirty tricks was over, but apparently not.

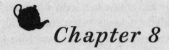

Chapter 8

The college group stalked away in the wake of the dean's departure. Vince and Brenda trailed them, and they were shadowed by Sherri Shaw, Tara Mitchells and the unknown dark-haired fellow, who caught up with the dean and drew him aside.

"*She* did it! I don't know how, but she did it," Sophie muttered to Dana.

"Did what?"

"Tampered with our sugar." Sophie grabbed a fistful of the sugar packets and held them up to the light. Sure enough, a couple looked like they had been slit open. She tore into one of the tampered-with packets, licked her finger and tested the contents. "I don't believe it! This is the absolute worst. She actually filled these with salt and put them in with our others."

"*Who* did?"

Sophie cast a look across the lane. "Somehow, some way, Thelma Mae Earnshaw did it."

The strolling tea party ended in a jumble of good-byes, voices calling out through the dark, people hugging and saying adieu. Some folks lingered, chatting. Others headed for cars, parked along the street or downtown. Sophie watched, pondering the evening, wondering what would become of Jason now that she had single-handedly torpedoed his shot at making nice with the dean. It was depressing. She felt like marching right over and telling off Thelma Mae Earnshaw and her frizzy-haired henchwoman Gilda, but she knew she would never do it. It had been hammered into her early (by Nana) to be respectful of her elders, even if those elders were frustratingly juvenile and impossible to deal with.

And besides, she had done much worse by railing at the chairwoman of the Board of Governors, who was likely at that very minute poisoning Jason's chances by spewing lies into the dean's ear.

Jason loped toward her. "Soph, how are you doing?"

"I'm so sorry, Jason!" she wailed, as he hugged her tight. She explained about the salted tea and the dean's accusations, and her own attempt at intervention in his plight.

"Not your fault," he said, stroking her hair and hugging her tight. "Not your fault at all. It's not over 'til it's over. That's what they say in sports, and I believe it."

"So it's okay? Do you know who he's going to announce as the guilty party?"

His expression in the dim light from the lamp over the table looked evasive, to Sophie. "We had a talk earlier, that didn't . . . well, it didn't go quite as I'd planned. But I'm going to talk to him again right now, corner him and *make* him listen. I won't be blamed for something I didn't do," he said, his voice hard with anger. "I'm going to point out to him that if he pins it on me and an investigation finds the real culprit it won't look good for the college." He hugged her tightly, then released. "I have to go if I'm going to catch him. I saw him talking to that woman, his, uh . . ."

"His girlfriend? I know about her, Jason. I saw her here."

"Oh, okay. Yeah. I saw him talking to her a few minutes ago. I'm going to catch up with him."

"I also saw him talking to another person, a guy, dark haired, average height."

"Crap." He scanned the street, but the dean had disappeared. "I'll have to find him. I *need* to speak with him. Talk to you later!"

Rose sipped a cup of tea at the table in the tearoom kitchen as Sophie, downhearted, cleared the last of the clutter, in and out from the front of the tearoom. It had not gone as her granddaughter had hoped and worked toward, which was unfortunate, since it was one more "failure"—not really, but that was how she would see it—that she had caused. Rose wished she could impart the wisdom of over eighty years, that few things were as important as they seemed at the time, that failure was never final, that success in life was often not felt until the twilight years. Sophie was young but, burdened with a mother who seemed to deliberately misunderstand the stellar value of her daughter's work ethic and talent, she mistrusted herself, underestimating her own value.

Sophie toted in another box and set it down on the kitchen counter, unloading the empty treat plates and trays to wash by hand in the deep stainless steel sink.

"Honey, sit for a moment," Rose said, patting the table opposite her. The kitchen blinds were drawn and just the light over the sink was on; the kitchen felt cozy and intimate.

"I have some stuff to do, Nana," Sophie replied, taking off her stained chef's coat and draping it over the back of a chair. "I want to get it all done and go to bed."

"Sit! I need to talk to you."

Sophie obeyed, sitting down in the chair opposite her grandmother and slipping her phone out of her jeans pocket, glancing down at it. She was likely waiting for a text from Jason. She was worried, Rose knew, that the events of the evening had damaged whatever little reliance remained between the dean and Jason Murphy. She was blaming herself for not noticing Thelma's creative interference, which Rose would deal with on the morrow, and for speaking up in her friend's defense, ill timed as it was. "Honey, listen to me," Rose said.

Sophie looked up from her phone, then laid it screen down on the table, folding her hands and paying attention.

"You did everything you could to make it all work out. Jason's career does not hang by the slim strand of a tainted cup of tea. Jason is a good man; even if things go badly, he'd never blame you for something so silly. I know Thelma did this somehow, but in the end it won't be what hurts Jason's career, nor will it be your harangue at the chairwoman. It will be someone who sabotaged him at the college, or the dean, too lazy to find the real culprit behind the changed grade."

"That's what Jason said. He's not going down without a fight."

"He's a winner, honey, and he's like you; never count him out."

Sophie sighed. "I guess you're right. I feel like I let him down."

"You didn't. Put that thought right out of your head. I've learned the hard way that you can't single-handedly make or break someone's life. If I could, I'd have changed my relationship with your mother long ago, but it has to be a two-way street."

"What do you mean?"

"I handled Rosalind all wrong when she was a teenager, minimized her feelings. Didn't take her worries about her weight seriously. I feel like I created, in a way, her obsession with her looks, her aversion to fat. If I could go back, I'd change things. I have tried to talk to her in the years since, but I believe now that it has to come from her. She has to be prepared to talk and to listen. I'll keep telling her how much I love her. Someday I hope she'll come around."

"I don't understand what that has to do with this."

Rose thought for a second. She was tired, and had to take her time to sort her thoughts out. "I guess I've been thinking about your mother a lot lately. You're right; it doesn't have much to do with this. What I'm trying to say, honey, is that we're all doing the best we can in a difficult world. *You* did the best you could, and Jason knows that. If the dean is going after Jason, it won't be because of salt in his tea or a miffed board member."

"Okay, message received," Sophie said, springing up and kissing her grandmother's cheek.

Laverne and Sophie cleaned up the last of the debris, finding paper napkins in the Japanese maple's branches, cupcake liners in the hedge and even an upset teacup on the ground under the tree. Gilda and Cissy were tidying over at Belle Époque, but Sophie was in no mood to talk to anyone. She was tired and cross and resentful. Thelma Mae Earnshaw, despite what Nana said, had been a thorn in her side for years. Just when Sophie thought they had everything worked out, the woman got into a snit and went at it again.

Laverne drove home with some treats in a container for her elderly father. Cissy left, too, without a word to Sophie, whether out of embarrassment over her grandmother's trick, or upset about something. As usual. Nana was already in bed softly snoring, Pearl curled up with her, so Sophie tiptoed upstairs and sat cross-legged on her bed hoping for a text or call from Jason to tell her what happened with the dean.

It disturbed her deeply that Jason was being blamed for something he didn't do. The unfairness of it rankled, as unfairness always had. When she was a kid, her brothers could do no wrong. While at the Hamptons, if they tracked sand and seaweed all through the house, it was "boys will be boys." But her mother expected Sophie to be ladylike and demure, when all she wanted to do was follow her brothers and do what they did. So it was always, *Sophie, you're getting filthy*, or *Sophie, can't you stay out of the dirt for two minutes?*

There was a noise outside, the vroom of a car engine and the sound of a car door closing. She looked at the clock; 10:03. Could that be Jason? She jumped up, dashed to the window that overlooked the front of the tearoom and looked down. If it had been him, he would have parked at the curb and she would see the car, but she didn't. And yet . . . there was *someone* out there.

She squinted into the dark; there was a car parked across the street, but it wasn't in the pool of light from the streetlamp, so she couldn't tell much about it except that it was smallish. She then noticed movement near the maple tree in front of Auntie Rose's; it was like . . . like two people embracing? Or dancing? Weird. But she didn't care to accidentally spy on anyone's love life, so she turned away from the window and went back to her bed, checking her phone again, hoping for a text saying Jason had sorted everything out with the dean.

He texted her that he had tried to talk to Dean Asquith again, but the man avoided him. Instead Jason went to Julia's tearoom after the stroll to talk to his department head about what to do, though she didn't have any answers. The dean was apparently making his announcement the next morning, and Jason hadn't even had a chance to talk to him, present his case and hear what proof, if anything, the dean had on him. Asquith was now not answering his phone, so Jason was going to get up early and go directly to the dean's home and confront him.

She could feel the frustration and worry in his words, and sent back a note telling him it would all work out (even though she wasn't so sure it would) and that she'd call him in the morning to find out how it went. She hoped he was doing okay, not worrying too much. What she didn't say was that she'd worry enough for both of them.

She'd only been back in Gracious Grove for a few weeks, and here she was worried about losing Jason again. When this mess was over, she needed to have a real conversation with him about their relationship. How did you start, with the ominous phrase *we need to talk*? That always seemed to indicate the end of the party for one person or the other. But she needed to know, was this all one sided? She knew he cared for her, but did he really *care* for her. The difference was subtle but real. He could care for her as a friend, or he could care to take it one step further, back to real dating.

All she knew was how she felt every time she saw him, and whenever he took her hand. It was electric. He was special to her, even more so for all the time they had spent apart. But there was so much she didn't know about the years between them saying good-bye, and her coming back to Gracious Grove last spring. She knew one thing about his relationships in between those times; he had been engaged a couple of years before, but she didn't know to whom, or how it ended.

They *definitely* needed to talk.

She heard another noise and jumped out of bed, dashing to the window again. It was Gilda dragging a garbage can out to the street. Garbage collection must be the next day! She'd entirely forgotten and so had Nana, but with the stuff she had tossed from the tea, she couldn't afford to miss the week's trash removal.

She slipped on a hoodie, grabbed a flashlight and tiptoed down the stairs to the side door, then scooted out. In the time it had taken her to do that, Gilda had already gone back in, and Belle Époque was closed up tight, lights out. She had a strange sensation that there was someone else around, but shivered and shrugged it off.

She trotted around back to the darkest corner of the backyard, shone the flashlight on the little wooden cabinet in which the garbage can was locked, and worked the combination lock, snapping it open. The cabinet kept the garbage can safe from foraging raccoons; the lock was overkill, in her estimation. Though who knew? Raccoons, clever little thieves, might develop number recognition and opposable thumbs. Then Nana would have to use a padlock with a key. She snickered as she pictured a raccoon bandit spinning the tumblers while another shone a penlight on the lock.

She dragged the plastic can down the lane toward the street, the sound echoing in the still, cold night air. Slowly, carefully, she made herself move at a snail's pace, afraid that the sound would awaken Nana, who habitually left her bedroom window open two inches except in the dead of winter. Finally, she got it to the road. Their street had no real curbs, just a grassy boulevard and then the pavement. So she checked to be sure the lid was on tightly, and wiggled the can until it was secure on the dew-dampened grass. If you didn't do that, a random dog or raccoon could easily tip it over, and she didn't want food all over the place.

She turned away and saw something glinting in the corner of the graveled section of Auntie Rose's front yard near the Japanese maple. What had she and Laverne missed, another teacup? She shone the flashlight that way and saw a piece of fabric with what looked like a shiny button. *What the heck?*

She moved toward it, speeding in one second from unaware to horrified. By the brilliant beam of the flashlight she saw Dean Asquith's face, eyes wide, drool hanging out of his open mouth, his suit jacket ripped and blood seeping through his torn white shirt. He was twisted, contorted, his hands clutched into claws, and he was dead . . . very, *very* dead.

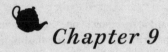

Chapter 9

She shrieked, the sound echoing in the still night air, then bolted back along the lane into the kitchen, not waiting to run upstairs. She called 911 from the kitchen phone, taking the cordless handset back outside with her as she gabbled the facts to the dispatch, answering questions she didn't remember later. Lights came on inside as the wail of sirens scythed through the cold clarity of the night. A dog howled in time with the keening sirens, a duet of mourning and horror.

Nana flicked on the light and opened the front door of the tearoom as she knotted the tie of her robe. Pearl sleepily stuck her nose out the door at her feet. "Sophie, what's—"

"Nana, go back inside!"

"Why? What's going on?"

"I f-found Dean Asquith."

"Is he okay?" Nana stepped outside anyway, pushing Pearl back in with her slippered foot as the police car creamed up to the curb. Gilda came running out of the front door of Belle Époque, shrieking unintelligible questions. "Oh, my dear lord, the poor man!" Nana said, staring down at him. She clasped her hands together, whispered something, then looked up at Sophie. "Are you okay, sweetie?"

"I am," Sophie said. She glanced to the police car. Thank goodness! It was Wally Bowman getting out. He was an old friend and now Cissy Peterson's boyfriend, someone she could trust and explain the situation to. "It's cold out here tonight, Nana; you should get back in where it's warm."

But as Wally approached, Nana was examining the scene with a surprisingly calm demeanor. Sophie looked down, forcing herself to face it, the overhead light illuminating the scene much more clearly than had her small flashlight. Hours ago Dean Asquith was alive, vital, the center of things in his academic world, and now he was dead.

She focused on individual features, trying not to let the fear overwhelm her. Drool: There was still a string of it dangling from his mouth. Surely that must mean he was killed recently? His body: Why was he contorted so? His fingers: She shuddered at the way they were cramped, like he suffered agony. And the blood seeping from his chest: Where did that come from? She didn't dare touch him. This was a murder scene, and she mustn't move an inch. "Wally! I'm so glad it's you," she said, looking up at the officer.

"Sophie," he said, with a curt nod. He muttered something into the radio that was clipped by a nylon thingie that looked like a carabiner to his epaulette, then studied her. "Are you okay? You look pale."

"I'm okay."

Wally knelt beside the dean and studied him, then stood back up. "Ma'am, if you could go back inside, I'll talk to you in a moment," he said to Nana. She stepped back in the tearoom without a murmur. Wally turned to Sophie. "You and I are going to move back to the street, and you can tell me what happened." He took her arm in his gloved hand and guided her to the street near his cruiser, as another cruiser pulled up, lights flickering. "Wait here a moment," he said, then approached the other car and spoke to the female officer who climbed out. She nodded curtly and radioed in.

Sophie explained everything that had happened from the moment she served the last customer to the second she first laid eyes on the fluttering piece of fabric that had drawn her to the dean's body. As she explained what went on, she kept thinking that it was going to be a long, awful night.

T helma was having a nightmare—or at least she hoped it was a nightmare—that she was being attacked by the clucking chickens from the farm she had been raised on. Gabble, cluck, peck! She felt like she was swimming, then someone was hauling her up out of the water and . . . she opened one eye. Gilda leaned over her, babbling about something, spit raining down from her dentureless mouth while she shook Thelma by the shoulder.

"What are you quacking about now?" Thelma asked, swinging her feet over the edge of the bed and squinting at the clock. "It's eleven at night, you stupid hen!" she growled.

"Thelma, oh, Thelma, we're in so much trouble!" Gilda's frizzy hair partially restrained by prickly curlers, waved her hands around and plucked at her fuzzy pink housecoat.

"What do you mean?"

"Over at Auntie Rose's! You remember you wished someone would die there sometime so *they'd* be known as the murder tearoom and not us? Well, you've wished it right into being!" Gilda's eyed widened as she stared down at her employer. "You wished for this to happen! And the salt . . . oh my! Those packets will have my fingerprints on 'em because I'm the one who snuck them into their stuff. And that awful, *awful* man, the college dean . . . I told him off. They'll be coming for me soon!"

Thelma, now fully awake, stared up at her employee. "I don't understand one word in twenty that you're cackling!"

Once Gilda calmed down and explained, Thelma tottered over to the window, joints popping and feet aching, and stared down over the street scene below, cruisers with top lights blinking cheerily, and lights ablaze over at Auntie Rose's. "What did you say? Who was it that was killed this time?"

"That college dean, the mean one who helped Rose exclude you."

Thelma felt a chill, like a goose had walked over her grave. "You talking about that dean feller that was running the whole shebang?" Reasoning it out, she decided that as usual, Gilda had gotten it all muddled around in her brain and the previous night's kerfuffle with the dean had added to Julia Dandridge and Sophie Taylor's shutting them out of the whole deal. "He's *dead*? Come on, you're imagining things. Had a nightmare. Go back to bed, you chicken-headed idiot."

And then there was a rapping at the door, *thud, thud, thud*, like in a horror movie when death comes knocking. Gilda squawked and flapped her hands, dashing around the room clucking in anxiety.

Thelma swallowed hard. What if Gilda wasn't imagining things? "We didn't do anything but put some salt in a couple o' sugar packets, that's all. Nothing else," she said. "A little salt never killed anyone."

Or could it? She wasn't sure. But she did remember when the dean drank the salty tea and made a fuss over at Auntie Rose's. Sophie Taylor had looked directly at her as she stood

in the window gloating over the fuss. That girl . . . she had
her grandmother's sharp eyes, for sure. Wouldn't take her
but two minutes to point the shameful finger of blame at
poor Thelma.

Thud, thud, thud again. "We'd better get going," Thelma
said. "You go down and hold 'em off."

"Me?" Gilda squawked again, jumping like she'd been
scalded. "Why me?"

"Because you're already decent. I've got to get my housecoat on and splash some water in my eyes. Make some tea,
while you're at it. My mouth feels like the bottom of a barnyard boot."

When Thelma finally got downstairs, Gilda, now with
her teeth in, was sitting quivering, with Wally Bowman
asking her about what she saw.

"N-nothing!" she stuttered.

"Look, Miss Bachman, Sophie Taylor says you hauled
the garbage out to the street just before she did; that's how
she was reminded it was garbage night. She heard you, then
looked out the window and saw you. Did you see anything?
Anyone?"

Gilda shook her head. Wally sighed and made a note in
a booklet, then looked up at Thelma. "What about you,
ma'am? Did you see or hear anything?"

How much to say? Thelma eyed Wally; he was Cissy's
beau, and she didn't exactly want to lie to him, but she sure
wasn't going to tell him the truth. She had to think that over,
first, for sure. Then she'd decide. "After I told Gilda to haul
her butt down and take out the garbage, I hopped into bed
and was dead asleep in two seconds flat. Gilda had to come
wake me up just now. I was in la-la land dreaming of Rock
Hudson and Cary Grant engaging in fisticuffs over me at

the Gracious Grove Methodist Church picnic. Is it true it's
that school dean that's dead?"

"I can't comment on that, ma'am."

"Oh, come on, Wally," she said, eyeing the boy slyly. She'd
known him forever, since he was a little boy, and then a boney
skinny teen kicking a Hacky Sack in her driveway, trying to
make up to her granddaughter. He flushed up to the roots of
his sandy hair and looked away. "Now, you're my Cissy's
steady fellow. Surely you can tell her poor old grandmother
who raised her something about it, so I don't worry? Is there
some mad killer on the loose? Should I be getting out my
daddy's shotgun?"

He swiveled and stared at her, wide-eyed, an uneasy look
on his face. "You don't really have a shotgun, do you, Mrs.
Earnshaw?"

She stayed quiet, puckering up her lips and squinting.

"Okay, okay! It is Dean Asquith; I guess there's no harm
in telling you that much. But I can't say anything more. We
won't know a lot until the autopsy is done. But you don't
need to worry. The police will be watching your houses,
and Detective Morris will be around to talk to you."

"That's that woman detective?" Thelma asked.

"Yes."

"Changed my mind about that one. Maybe *more* women
ought to be detectives, since we're a whole lot smarter than
most men."

S ophie felt like she was going to jump out of her skin, she
was so agitated. Wally had sent her back to the tearoom
kitchen to sit with Nana as the night commenced. More police
had arrived, the whole street lit up like the Vegas strip.

"What do you think they're doing?" Sophie asked her grandmother.

Her lined face weary, she cradled Pearl on her lap, slowly petting the chocolate-point Birman as the cat purred her pleasure. "I don't know, and I don't think you should dwell on it, honey."

"I can't help it. I keep seeing the dean's face." It was the contrast between the last time she saw him, disapproval etched on his aristocratic face, distaste twisting his mouth, and then in death . . . the string of drool, the contorted hands, the slack mouth, the eyes, wide and startled. She saw again the blossom of blood on the white shirt under the wool blazer. And a bloody wound on his neck; what was that, a knife cut? It all kept coming, unbidden, into her mind. She needed a distraction. "Nana, do you think the dean was killed by someone in his group tonight?"

"We won't know what happened until we know what actually killed him."

"His skin looked bluish, to me, and so did his lips," Sophie mused. "He had a cut on his neck, but then he had some kind of wound on his chest, too. His white shirt was saturated in blood, and the cloth was kind of in tatters. I didn't hear a gunshot; I think I would have, right?"

Nana nodded. "You were in your room right at the front of the house. I'm sure you would have heard a gunshot." Her grandmother eyed her but remained silent.

"Is something wrong?" Sophie asked. "I mean, other than the obvious? You seem concerned."

"I was wondering if it had occurred to you that this might change how things go for Jason."

"I'm glad *you* said it. I felt like a monster for even thinking it, but I don't know. Whatever Dean Asquith was going to say will be said anyway, right? He must have written down his conclusions, and put into effect his intent."

Nana nodded and stroked the cat. "I hope . . . I don't mean to alarm you, honey, but I do hope . . . I mean, I know he didn't *do* anything . . ."

Sophie got the gist of what her grandmother was not saying. Her stomach twisted. "You're hoping they don't blame Jason for this. He lives alone, and that's not much of an alibi. We were texting back and forth though, so that ought to help. I hope." She sighed and rubbed her eyes, glancing up at the clock. It was now well after midnight. She wondered how Jason would find out about the dean's death. They likely would have gone to the dean's wife first, to inform her of her husband's death, the wife who had a lover on the side, just as he did.

She frowned down at her hands; Dean Asquith had a lover he was trying to dump, and who was angry at him. His wife had a boyfriend. People other than Jason were upset about the grading scandal. And then there was whoever really *did* alter Mac MacAlister's grade. Did someone fear they were going to be exposed as the culprit, not Jason? "It seems to me that there were a dozen people angry at the dean, and any one of them could have killed him."

"You're so right, honey. I have a feeling this isn't going to be an easy case to investigate unless someone confesses."

Finally, at about one in the morning, Sophie and her grandmother were briefly interviewed by Detective Morris, who then strolled across to Belle Époque to interview Gilda and Thelma. Sophie wished her well of it. It had come out, during the interview, about Thelma and/or Gilda's tampering with the Auntie Rose sugar packets.

Sophie felt bad exposing Thelma and Gilda to the detective's questions, but she was not going to hide anything, and at some point the dean's reaction to his salted tea, when he implied that Sophie was targeting him for his behavior toward Jason, would come up. It was better coming from her. The detective heard her out, nodding, but there was a definite twinkle in her eye. She was familiar with Thelma Mae Earnshaw from the past, but it was difficult for Sophie to tell if Detective Morris most dreaded or looked forward to confronting her again.

Nana toddled over to the counter and peered through the dark across the lane at Belle Époque. Absently, she picked up a cloth, wet it and began wiping down surfaces that were already spotlessly clean.

"Remember what the doctor said?" Sophie asked her grandmother. "You're to get enough rest."

"My darling Sophie, I know that," she said, turning back to Sophie. "But a man has been murdered on our doorstep. It's terrible. I feel like I'll never sleep again. I know it doesn't seem so to you, but to me he was so young! So much life to live."

"My darling Nana," Sophie said, leaping up to her feet and hugging her grandmother, hovering over the tiny lady with a fierce desire to protect her. "That's true, I know. But I don't care about him, as hard as that sounds. I care about *you*. You can't help him now, but you *can* take care of yourself. Go upstairs and get some sleep."

"What about you?"

Sophie straightened. "Didn't you know I'm invulnerable? When I ran In Fashion, I made do on about three hours of sleep a night. My sous chef claimed he thought I was an alien who lived on the energy of other beings. One sleepless night isn't going to kill me." She made a face when she realized what she had said. "I mean, it won't hurt me."

"What are you going to do?"

"I'm going to do what I do best when I'm thinking; I'm going to cook." In her mind she added, *And I'm going to figure out who did this on our doorstep so that Auntie Rose's Victorian Tea House doesn't become synonymous with murder, and so that Jason Murphy isn't for one second suspected of the dean's murder.*

And that was that!

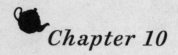

Chapter 10

Nana agreed and toddled up to bed, with Pearl softly thumping up the stairs after her.

Sophie got out some ingredients and began to cook. She went back to basics and made trays of cookies and muffins, mindless chores she had been doing since she was a child. While she worked, she reviewed what she knew about every person who had a reason to be angry with the dean. That she knew of, anyway; there could be a legion she didn't know about.

Vince Nomuro, the registrar, had been shadowing him at the basketball game, and openly told his assistant that he didn't trust the man. He had been named as one of the people who could have changed the grade. His assistant Brenda Fletcher was likely just as capable.

Sherri Shaw, his mistress, was angry at him, while he appeared to be trying to get rid of her. And yet here she was, hanging around, clinging to him. Didn't the woman have any dignity? That was a puzzle to Sophie. But was she angry or hurt enough to kill him? Sophie pulled another tray of muffins out of the oven and tested them for "bounce back." They seemed done, so she set them on a rack to cool.

The spouse was always a suspect, and in this case there were numerous reasons why Jeanette Asquith could want the dean dead. He had a girlfriend, she had a boyfriend and then there was money. There was *always* money. Did she want to get rid of him but didn't want to leave the marriage without financial security?

Sophie didn't know who, in that relationship, had the most money. He was the one working, but for all Sophie knew Jeanette had a job, too, though she doubted it. On the other hand, the dean's wife had spoken of her family's home in the Hamptons, and she knew Sophie's mother. Rosalind Taylor drifted in exclusive circles; Jeanette might be the one with wealth, and maybe she didn't want to share it in a divorce.

Sophie needed to know more about the woman, her past and her marriage, and she had a ready-made source. She would call her mother and ask about Jeanette Asquith. That meant speaking to her mother, and she wasn't sure she was ready for that yet, given how angry she still was about the bribery of the restaurant owner, but . . . she had to talk to her sometime.

The police would be looking at Jason; that was a given. She eyed her phone, sitting on the small table by the window, but wasn't sure if she should try calling or texting him just yet. Would it look like she thought he was guilty if she warned him about the dean's death?

And then there was the grading scandal, and the number of people who could be angry with or worried about the dean's involvement and impending announcement. Among those, there were several at the tea: Vince Nomuro and Brenda

Fletcher, who she had already considered. Kimmy Gabrielson. Tara Mitchells was there, too; Sophie wondered if it would be worth talking to her as a source of information. The girl had an agenda, true, but it didn't mean she wasn't a sharp-eyed reporter who noticed things. What had she seen last evening? Even though she was furious with the girl for tricking her into talking about Jason and then twisting her words for the newspaper, she could talk to her, if it came to that.

Of course the very best source of information at some point was going to be right down the street from Auntie Rose's: Julia Dandridge. The professor had been with those people all evening, and had further insight into their character and interactions that even Jason didn't have. Sophie's stomach rumbled. Were her nerves finally getting to her? Was it the fear of Jason being railroaded with accusations? He had a powerful motive to be angry with the dean, but she hoped his innocence would protect him.

Her stomach rumbled again. It was now three in the morning; she hadn't slept and hadn't eaten since her sandwich supper the evening before. She slunk through the dark tearoom and peeked out the front window. The body was hidden by a white canvas tent ablaze from within by brilliant lights, mysterious shadows moving inside as investigators did their job. She moved to look out the window on the other side of the door. Out by the road there were cruisers lining the street and uniformed officers clustered in groups, illuminated by the streetlights.

Every one of them must be hungry and tired, maybe more so than herself. One thing she could do was feed people. She slipped back into the kitchen and fortified herself with a muffin and glass of milk while she put on the big coffee urn. She pulled over a stepladder and got down paper cups from the highest cupboard, and set to baking more comfort food. Tea biscuits, mini-muffins and cookies. By four she had coffee made and another big batch of muffins baking in the double industrial oven. She grabbed her hoodie, pushed her feet into runners and snuck out the side door, down the alley and to the front.

There was Detective Morris alone, by the front bumper of a cruiser. Sophie strolled close, her ears perked, and heard the detective muttering into her phone, but the woman caught sight of Sophie and stared at her as she put her phone away in her suit jacket pocket. "Yes?"

Sophie folded her arms over her chest. "I thought you all might be tired and hungry and cold. I've put on a big pot of coffee and got out paper cups. I've made muffins, too."

"I appreciate the offer, Sophie, but we can't accept. I can't allow my guys to have anything from your kitchen. Not right now."

Her stomach clenched and her hands trembled. "Why?"

The woman shook her head and sighed. "I can't explain."

"Please, tell me. I don't under—" She broke off as it came to her. There *was* only one possible explanation; they suspected the dean may have been poisoned. Her mind raced and she turned away, examining the scene, remembering the man as she had last seen him, bluish and contorted, with the string of drool from his mouth.

The small front yard of Auntie Rose's was bordered by hedges. Why was the dean there? She recalled something she had told the detective already, about the sound of the car door, and looking out the front window to witness what had looked like two people embracing or dancing. A chill raced down her spine as she truly realized that she had quite likely witnessed the dean and his assailant. Perhaps he was being wrestled into the graveled area under the tree, dead or still alive. But why? Unless . . . did the killer want to pinpoint the blame? Did he or she want Sophie or Jason to be implicated? Or had they witnessed the dean's reaction earlier when he drank the salted tea and thought to use that to point blame at Auntie Rose's? If only she had run downstairs when she saw the two!

She turned back and noted the detective calmly watching her, sharp eyes focused. "You must think that I could be involved in the dean's murder, given the drama lately. But you'll discover that I wasn't, and Jason wasn't, either. If you wait until you figure that out, though, the killer might have already escaped."

The detective took a deep breath, clearly suppressing her first reaction.

"I'm sorry. That sounded snarky, didn't it? I didn't mean it that way," Sophie said. "I've thrust my foot in my mouth more than once lately."

"You were helpful last time, when the murder next door occurred," the detective said evenly. "But you can trust me to not jump to conclusions. Just because I say we can't have anything to eat or drink from your place, and you know we are investigating you and your friend as suspects, it doesn't mean we aren't casting a wider net. There are officers right this minute questioning many others, across our whole town. Some are knocking on doors in this very neighborhood. No stone will be left unturned."

Sophie nodded, tears welling in her eyes. "I'm sorry if it seemed like I was questioning your ability, or your methods, Detective. I have nothing but respect for you and your team. I hope . . ." Her voice caught and she cleared her throat. "I guess I'm scared. I'm so sorry this happened, and it's only complicated things for Jason and me, truly. This is the *last* thing either of us wanted to happen."

The detective nodded but said nothing more.

"Okay. I'll go now." She returned up the dim alleyway and slipped inside the warm kitchen as the timer went off. She took the muffins out of the oven, set them on a rack to cool and turned away from the dark window, tears clogging her throat, like a lump she couldn't swallow past. Pearl had descended and sat at the bottom of the stairs looking up at her. Sophie plunked down cross-legged on the floor and picked the soft fluffy cat up, cradling and stroking her. It was instantly calming as the Birman purred and snuggled down with a contented sigh.

Her phone chimed. She grabbed it off the edge of the table. There was a text from Jason; all it said was, Sophie, you up?

She tapped back Yes, and waited.

It chimed. "Jason?" she said.

"So it's true?" he said. "The dean was found dead outside Auntie Rose's?"

They talked over their shock about what happened, but he seemed distracted. "Are you okay?" she asked.

"Soph, I didn't want to upset you last night. You were so busy and stressed! But the dean and I had a run-in before the fling. I tried to talk to him but it got out of hand. I told him he needed to hold off if he was thinking of accusing me, because I wasn't guilty, and he'd look like an idiot—actually I said he'd look like a cloth-headed oaf of infinite absurdity—if it came out later who really changed Mac's grade."

"Cloth-headed oaf? That probably wasn't the smartest thing you've ever done."

"I know. I've been reading too much Shakespeare lately. But he had just told me that I should think about getting my resume in order. It was the way he said it, with a smirk, and in front of the Board of Governors! I'm sure every one of them will tell the cops how I reacted. I lost my cool, Soph. I yelled."

"But you're always so calm!" What a time for him to lose it.

"I love Cruickshank, and . . . you and I are just getting to a good place."

Sophie was silent for a moment, processing everything that he had said as she stroked Pearl's silky fur. It all tangled in her mind until she didn't know what to think, but it meant a lot that he included their relationship in his concerns. "If you end up leaving Cruickshank, will it affect your PhD, too?"

"I don't think so. Hold on a sec; I'm getting another call."

He was silent for a moment, then came back. "That was Julia. She heard about the murder and wants us to meet her at SereniTea. Are you up for that?"

"Sure. Right now?"

"In one hour."

She had a shower, dressed in yoga pants and a sweatshirt, pulled a hoodie on over top and left a note for Nana. It was still dark when she slipped out the side door once again, but a light gleamed through an upstairs window next door. Mrs. Earnshaw or Gilda must be awake. She could only imagine what the Belle Époque owner had told the detective about the previous evening. She and Nana had talked about Mrs. Earnshaw a lot over the years, but Sophie still didn't understand her. The woman was more impetuous than a teenager; you never knew how she was going to react. She saw any exclusion as a slight, and would not listen to reason. That behavior, along with impulsiveness and a tendency to fume, had been constants in her life, from what Nana said, since she and Thelma were teenagers and friends.

Hearing how Mrs. Earnshaw's lack of self-awareness had caused her to never grow beyond her flaws had taught Sophie that if she wanted to cure her own youthful faults, it would take work. Therefore, she decided that when she talked to her mother, she would do her best to have a rational adult discus-

ion. She emerged from the dark alley to the street. The detec-
ive was no longer there, but uniformed officers, including
Wally Bowman, were still in abundance. She gave a brief
wave, and he acknowledged her with a nod, then turned away.

Sophie dug her hands into her hoodie pockets and strode
up the dark street toward SereniTea, three houses up the
street. A car engine thrummed from the other direction,
coming closer. She paused at the street as Jason drove up in
his aging Chevy, killed the engine and got out, slamming
his car door shut, the sound echoing loudly in the quiet
neighborhood. Sophie felt eyes peering at them from behind
blinds and curtains. Residents on the street, awake since the
sirens wailed, were watchful, waiting until dawn so they
could scurry about and share notes on what had happened
at Auntie Rose's after the Fall Fling tea stroll.

Jason strode over to her and took her in his arms. She
leaned against his chest, then turned her face to look up at
him. He surprised her with a kiss: warm, lovely, unexpected.
Her heart was pounding and she melted. This was not how
she had planned her first kiss from him in years, but it was
so very lovely. Reassuring. He cared about her; she felt it
now and didn't need to ask.

But there was no time to react. He took her arm and
tugged her hurriedly toward SereniTea's new entrance,
through a redwood pergola. The door was unlocked and
the place was cool and dark. He led her through the teahouse,
actually several rooms constructed like individual Japanese
tearooms and then one large open area that was used for
yoga classes.

"Where are we going?"

"Back to Julia's office. She had a space created for book-
keeping and staff. Her manager lives in the apartment
upstairs."

"I heard about that," Sophie said. They emerged from the teak and tile world of the tearoom to a more humble and Western-looking kitchen, and through that to what had been a sunroom at one time, off the back of the house. It was a long and broad space, broken up with two L-shaped desks opposite each other and along the back wall of the house, with the other three walls taken up by windows covered in Roman shades.

Julia sat in an office chair staring at a computer screen. She looked up when they entered, and jumped to her feet. "You both came! I'm so glad." She came around the desk and hugged Jason, and then Sophie. "Sit, sit!"

Jason pulled two office chairs forward and offered one to Sophie, then took the other, sitting across the desk from Julia. "This is so awful," he said, leaning back and scrubbing his face with both hands, then running his fingers though his longish hair. "I don't know what to think. This is *so* not good for me. I don't want to be selfish, but self will intrude."

"As Jane Austen would say," Julia added with a fleeting smile. "I'm in shock," she admitted, her voice shaking. She shut down her computer and leaned back in her chair, her hand resting on her small belly. "Do we know what happened yet? Sophie, did I hear right that you found the body?"

She nodded, and told them what she saw. Both had already been questioned by the police, so she felt free to give them what she knew. She told them about the scrape on his neck, the bloody wound and copious blood on his white shirt, the bluish cast to his skin and even the drool and contorted hand. She finished with what the detective had said, about not being able to let her team eat or drink anything from the tearoom, and Sophie's assumption that there was a fear that he had been poisoned.

"Poison?" Julia said. "I never would have imagined that."

"But a bloody wound, too," Jason added. "It doesn't make any sense. Was there maybe more than one assailant?"

Sophie frowned down at her fingers, interlaced on her lap. "I can't see that. More than one attempt on his life in one night? That seems unlikely. You've known Dean Asquith longer than Jason," Sophie said to the professor and tearoom entrepreneur. "What did *you* think of him?"

"Me? I have thought for some time that if any man was asking to be murdered, it was Dale."

Chapter 11

"**W**hat do you mean?" Jason and Sophie chimed in at once.

At that moment a slim woman in a pink fluffy housecoat and bunny slippers, her springy hair up in a topknot, poked her head into the office. "Hey, Julia, tea?"

"Thanks, Kirsten. For all of us?" she asked, catching both of their gazes. "Jason, do you drink tea?"

"If I have to," he said, with a quick smile.

"Kirsten, this is Jason, a colleague, and Sophie, who helps her grandmother run Auntie Rose's, down the street. This is Kirsten Frawling, who manages SereniTea for me."

"I'm mostly a yoga instructor, part-time tearoom operator," she said and gave a self-deprecating shrug. "I've spoken to your godmother—I *think* she's your godmother, Laverne Hodge?— in the grocery store a few times," she said to Sophie. "I just had to talk to her; she has such an old soul. I felt her aura, and it was, like, kind of a deep blue, you know? Very warm and kind, compassionate. She's so proud of you."

"Laverne *is* my godmother. She's almost as much family to me as my grandmother."

Kirsten smiled and nodded. "I'll make some oolong, unless anyone wants something else? And for you, little mama, mint tea!" she said pointedly to Julia.

Jason frowned. "Little mama?"

Julia flushed and nodded, touching her stomach. "Nuñez and I are finally having a baby."

Jason jumped up, circled the desk and hugged Julia. "I'm happy for you both. I know you've been wanting this for a while."

He sat back down next to Sophie and took her hand in his. She felt absurdly happy, even given the gravity of what was going on; Jason's warmth toward Julia was friendship and nothing more.

"What did you mean by what you said about the dean?" Sophie asked the professor.

Julia glanced at the screen, clicked the mouse and turned off her monitor. She sat back and sighed wearily. "This is going to be such a mess," she commented. She met Sophie's open gaze, indecision in her eyes. "I guess I can't say something like that and leave it, right? I've been at Cruickshank awhile, and known Dale longer. He was on the committee at Salisbury College when I was doing my doctorate, and helped me a lot. But it took a while before he got the hint that I was not interested in anything but the work."

"He hit on you?" Sophie said, as Jason squeezed her hand.

"*Hit on* is too mild a phrase. He did everything he could, even bribed me to sleep with him."

"That's disgusting!" Sophie said. She flicked a glance over

at Jason; he was rigid, a shocked look on his lean face. "So the fact that he had a girlfriend on the side wasn't odd."

"No, oh, no, not odd. He was never *without* a girlfriend. Lately I think he had moved on from Sherri—I could see the signs—but to whom?"

Sophie nodded, thinking back to what she had observed and overheard at the tea convention. He had certainly seemed eager to get rid of Sherri, though she was sticking like glue. "But if he's been doing this for a long time, he wouldn't suddenly be murdered for it."

"His philandering wasn't the only thing about him that caused havoc. He was the most narcissistic man I've ever met. It was all about image with him. That's why he never would have divorced Jeanette. She is exquisitely the perfect example of a dean's wife and willing to overlook his . . . dalliances."

"I know what you mean, about his narcissism," Jason said. "He's famous among the profs and instructors for his three-hundred-dollar haircuts and overly expensive suits. *And* for bragging about them."

"It's more than his appearance, though," Julia said. "He truly did believe he was mesmerizing, like a fabulous speaker, personally riveting, magnetic, all that crap. At a faculty meeting I attended, he informed Dr. Bolgan, Jason's doctorate adviser, that she needed to feminize her appearance. He said that she looked like an old . . . well, it was an unpleasant word I won't repeat. He said her appearance didn't reflect well on the university."

Sophie was aghast. "That's beyond narcissistic; that's just *rude*!"

"It is."

"If you knew Dr. Bolgan," Jason said to Sophie, "you'd know how disgraceful that is, to listen to her speak, and then focus on her appearance. She's *amazing* both as a professor and as a writer, something that Dean Asquith would not be able to appreciate even given a hundred years. She's also kind. That's rare in our circles. But she's not so kind that she doesn't tell me when I'm full of it, or writing nonsense. She's the perfect doctoral adviser."

"What did she say back to the dean?"

Julia smiled. "For a while I treasured the memory and brought it out whenever I was angry with Dale. Alice told him that because his ideal woman required paint, powder and a good designer, he would be blind to the great women going about their business all around him. But they, she said, would always recognize him for the 'vast wasteland of intellect' he was. She said he was 'barren of emotion and understanding because he judged everyone by the standards of his own abject failure.'" She sighed. "I hate to go all fangirl, but it was awesome!"

"Brava, Dr. Bolgan!" Jason said.

Sophie shifted impatiently. "That's all very good, guys, but people don't get murdered because they're rude."

"Sophie's got a point," Jason said. "What do you know about his relationship with his wife?"

Sophie nodded eagerly. "Exactly. You know, on most of the true crime shows I watch, it's the significant other who either did the murder or planned it."

"You want me to believe that elegant, perfectly poised Jeanette Asquith bopped her husband on the head, or gave him a cup of hemlock?" Julia said, her light brows raised in amusement.

Sophie was stung by her derision and was silent.

Jason glanced over at her and then at Julia, and spoke up. "Jean Harris was an elegant and refined lady, too, before she went to prison for shooting Dr. Tarnower dead."

"You've got a point." Julia sat back in her chair as Kirsten brought in a tray with tea and some cookies.

"Hey, guys, here's the tea, and I made some quinoa honey cookies yesterday for the tea party. Try them!"

Sophie took one, bit into it and chewed. And chewed. She took a long swig of tea to wash it down. Kirsten anxiously waited, watching Sophie.

"I know you're a chef," the woman said finally. "Just tell me what you think."

"A little dry," Sophie said honestly. "But the taste is good. It needs some kind of fat. Did you use . . ." She thought for a moment, eyeing the reed-thin woman. "I'll bet you used applesauce instead of a fat component, right?"

The woman nodded.

"The trouble is, that doesn't give it the right texture; it will always be crumbly and dry. You need to add a healthy oil, to give it a moister crumb. Maybe try coconut oil?"

Kirsten nodded again. "They seemed too dry to me, too, but I didn't want to add butter. I'm learning to cook Asian foods, and I'm not bad at that, but baking has always been a mystery to me."

"I always say cooking is art and baking is science."

"Kirsten, you met Jeanette and Dale Asquith last night, right?" Julia said.

The woman nodded and rolled her eyes. "I don't like to, you know, speak ill of the dead, but he was over-the-top pompous." Her voice was light and high, with a burble of humor in it. "I had a prof like him at Smith. Thought he was God's gift to women the world over. Dean Asquith managed to hit on me, even though his wife and members of the Board of Governors were right there in the room. Asked me if he could come back for a 'private session,' wink wink." She shuddered.

"Maybe that was one flirtation too many for Mrs. Asquith,"

Sophie said, as Kirsten murmured something about having a shower and getting dressed, and drifted away.

Julia took a long drink of her tea and planted her hands on the desk surface. "Look, let's be blunt. The police are going to look at Jason as well as others."

"And our best bet is to be able to point them toward who might be guilty," Sophie said. "I'm so glad you're on board, Julia, because you know a lot about these folks."

"Who did you have in mind?" she asked, as Jason looked back and forth between the two women.

"Well, there are other possibilities, but what about some of these people from Cruickshank? Like the registrar, who everyone says is the most likely person to have changed the grade. Was Dean Asquith maybe going to announce that Vince Nomuro was the guilty one? Or his assistant, Brenda Fletcher? I think it would be an even more serious matter for one of them than for Jason, right?"

Julia nodded, her eyes thoughtful. "They would probably be fired. As a matter of fact . . . I don't know if I should say this." She paused, her brow wrinkled, and sipped her tea.

"Come on, Julia, spill." Jason was impatient and shifted in his seat, pushing aside his own tea.

"Okay, all right. But this goes nowhere," she said, glancing around. She leaned over the desk. "Dale pulled Vince aside here, in SereniTea. I had a moment of feeling nauseous, so I was behind a shoji screen catching my breath and overheard. Dale said he had been wondering about Vince's home renovations, and how he could afford to take all those trips. He said, was there a little extra money coming in from students anxious for good grades? He said he knew there were problems in the registrar's office, and he was going to dig into it until he had the truth."

"But he had already said that he was going to make an

announcement this morning about who was guilty!" Jason blurted out. "So . . . he didn't really know? What was he going to say?"

She shrugged. "Maybe he was just fishing, trying to see what Vince would say?"

"What *did* Vince say?" Jason asked.

Julia shrugged. "I'm sorry, but that's all I heard. They moved away, and Kirsten came looking for me."

Sophie thought for a moment. "Did the dean say he had the guilty party in his sights and was going to announce it Monday to satisfy the college president?"

Julia said, "That would be quite the risk to take unless he was sure."

"But that was so like Asquith, you know that, Julia," Jason said. "He had this overweening sense of invulnerability, that no one could touch him."

"True." But she still seemed doubtful.

"So maybe Vince is the one who changed the grade *and* killed Dean Asquith," Jason said.

Julia frowned and shook her head. "I *wish* this was over with. I wish Dale wasn't murdered. I wish . . ." Her eyes teared up.

It seemed an overly emotional response until Sophie considered that the woman was pregnant, at long last, and it was supposed to be the happiest time of her life. Instead, her tearoom wasn't doing so well and the college was wracked with problems, both internally and image-wise. "We'll get to the bottom of this all, Julia," Sophie said, including Jason in her glance. "We've done it before and we can do it again."

The professor nodded and drank some more of her mint tea, taking a deep cleansing breath and letting it slowly out. "I saw someone *else* around last evening that surprised me. Paul."

"Paul Wechsler? I did see him hanging around, but I couldn't figure out why," Jason said.

"You don't pay attention to gossip, do you?" Julia said. "Paul is Jeanette's boyfriend."

Jason looked stunned, and shook his head.

"Okay, I've heard of him," Sophie said, remembering Elizabeth Lemmon's information about Paul and Jeanette. "But I'm not sure I completely understand his job."

Julia turned to her. "He's the systems engineer responsible for all technical aspects at Cruickshank. There's supposed to be a systems security manager, but the position has been open for almost a year now, with no qualified candidates, from what I understand. So Paul takes care of everything. He's overburdened and underpaid, if you ask me. He takes care of pretty much the whole computer system except for an IT specialist, some data management clerks and a few other random employees."

"Is he dark haired? Medium height?" Sophie asked, and Julia nodded. "I saw him! He lingered on the periphery, but then he accosted the dean near the end. Why would he do that?"

"Mmm . . . sounds odd. Was there an argument?"

Sophie shook her head. "No, he kind of drew him aside and they walked off talking."

"Yes, well, before that they were talking outside Sereni-Tea when we were gathering to move on down the street, though I wasn't close enough to hear them. That exchange looked heated."

"Was that before or after the dean's conversation with the registrar?" Sophie asked.

"After, I think. I'm pretty sure." Julia chewed her lip, her gaze unfocused. "I've been wondering ever since the grading problem came out if Paul was a culprit. He'd know *exactly* how and when. And he'd even be able to make it look like someone else did it. The timing of the grade change was perfect to pin it on Jason. Knowing Paul was talking to Dale last night makes me worried. I've thought all along that Dale should bring in an independent forensic technician to go over the computer data, but no, he didn't want gossip to spread. Said we'd handle it 'the Cruickshank way,' whatever that is."

"Hushing things up and hoping for the best," Jason interjected.

"But why would Paul Wechsler do that, alter Mac's grade?" Sophie asked.

"Bribery? The gossip is that Paul wants Jeanette to leave Dale. He's intent on starting his own business, and for that he needs money. In fact, to do *anything* with Jeanette he needs money."

This echoed what Sophie had heard from Elizabeth Lemmon, and was a kind of independent verification of the theory. Elizabeth wasn't the only one pointing the finger at Paul Wechsler. "Okay. So he's a candidate, for sure. But we can't get stuck on the theory that whoever did the grade alteration also killed the dean. I mean, if we're going for affairs, then the dean's mistress was there; I saw her," Sophie said. "She seemed upset because the dean was ready to move on, or already had."

Julia bit her lip, then said, "You know, gossip is so the worst trait of the college community. However, it could help us figure this out right now. The scuttlebutt is that Dale was playing hardball with Sherri. She thought she could pressure him into making a commitment to her by openly dating other men."

"So him trying to dump her was a power play?"

Jason furrowed his brow and looked from one to the other of them. "What do you mean?"

"Don't you just love him?" Julia said, hitching her thumb in Jason's direction. "So clueless. Because he's a nice guy and would never manipulate someone or treat anyone like crap, he doesn't realize that other guys do it all the time."

"I know. It's adorable." Sophie ruffled his hair.

He jerked his head away. "Stop. I don't get it."

"The games people play, Jason," Julia said, folding her arms on the desk and leaning forward. She was fully back to professional, smart, even-tempered Professor Dandridge now. "Sherri Shaw wanted Dale to leave Jeanette and was trying to make him jealous by going out with other men. She thought he'd try to keep her. Instead, he decided to break it off, or maybe he said so to keep her in line, you know . . . make her aware of her place in his life."

"In the shadows," Jason said.

"Oh!" Sophie was reminded of the night before. "In the shadows!" She told them what she had seen, and both agreed that the dean was too big for someone to wrestle his body into the hedges. "So if that was him I saw with someone else, he was alive at that point."

"How much time was there between what you saw and you finding his body?"

Sophie thought back. "About half an hour, I'd say?"

"Okay, on to other people outside of the Asquiths' affairs. What about Heck Donovan?" Jason said.

"The coach?" Sophie said. "That's stretching things, isn't it?"

"You didn't see all the interactions I did, Soph. Dean Asquith and the coach had a heated argument that evening."

"I did notice them all there," she replied. "The coach, his wife, Mac and what looked to be Mac's parents?"

"That's what started it all," Jason said. "I was sticking to the dean's group, trying to get a chance to talk to him before today. I thought the tea stroll was my only shot. Once he made his announcement, I figured he'd be stuck with the story or risk embarrassment, and if you know—knew—Asquith, he doesn't—didn't—do embarrassment."

Julia nodded in agreement. "I thought it was your only hope, too, if Dale was actually going to announce he had proof you did it." She shook her head and added, "Even though we know he didn't, not what *we'd* call proof, anyway."

Sophie watched Julia, and a sudden thought assailed her. What if Julia was the one who changed the grade? SereniTea was not doing as well as she had hoped, and now she and Nuñez had a baby on the way; wasn't she the perfect candidate for bribery, over anyone? They only had her word for it that when she saw the grade it was already an A. She glanced at Jason. He'd never believe it about his friend and colleague, not in a million years, and it was nothing she could ask either of them about. It *was* something she had to think about. However . . . Julia would never have killed the dean. Sophie was not wedded to the theory that the grade changer and the killer were one and the same.

And on the subject of grades . . . "Were any other grades changed? It may not be just Mac MacAlister's A we're talking about, right?" Sophie suddenly asked.

Julia looked shocked. "No one has said. Maybe there *are* others, and they haven't come to light yet!"

"But that doesn't mean the dean didn't know about them."

"That's true," Jason said.

"Or maybe . . ." Sophie considered what she knew and didn't. "Could there be more that haven't been discovered yet, and the dean was close to finding out about them? That would be motive for killing him."

Julia put her head in her hands and moaned. "It's too much. There are too many possibilities here!"

"But we can narrow them down," Sophie insisted. "Some folks will have alibis. You two can talk to people that I can't. Most of them are from the college, and I'm sure you can find an excuse, especially given what happened and your connection to each other, right?"

Julia watched her speak, wide-eyed, then said to Jason, "I hope you know you've got a keeper here. This girl is smart, ten times more than half the grad students at Cruickshank."

That was a mixed compliment, Sophie thought, meaning that Julia hadn't expected her to be so smart because she didn't attend a traditional college. But she smiled, deciding to take the good, which was that Julia appeared to see them as a couple.

Jason reached around and put his arm over her shoulders. "I knew my two favorite ladies would hit it off!"

They parted ways, with Jason and Julia agreeing they would *try* to find out where some of the players were when the actual crime happened. Julia was also going to try to find out what the dean was actually going to say that day. Maybe he would have cleared Jason of suspicion and fingered someone else, though Jason seemed pretty sure he was being railroaded for the deed.

Sophie was going after whomever she could find to question. Tara Mitchells was first on her list; she was going to approach her, ostensibly to chew her out over her *Clarion* story. There was also Kimmy Gabrielson, who seemed so attached to Mac that she'd do anything for him, maybe even change his grade. If she got caught by the dean, what would the consequences be to her career? But she also decided not to rely on Jason and Julia for the others, and would take any chance she could to go after those at Cruickshank; as employees of the college, they might be wary of questioning people they knew, like the registrar and his assistant.

There were two questions they needed to answer: Who changed the basketball star's grade, and who killed Dean Asquith? Sophie was keeping an open mind, because those two questions may or may not have anything to do with one another.

Thelma sat at her window overlooking the lane between her and Rose's establishments and simmered; *stewing in her own juices*, her cranky grandma used to call it when little Thelma Mae Hendry would sulk and gripe. There came Sophie in the dark, back from who knew where, trudging up to the side door like the world was on her shoulders.

That girl wouldn't know about trouble until she lost her husband, her daughter, and had a sulky teen granddaughter and a troublesome grandson to worry about. Even years after her daughter's lingering illness and death, trouble hadn't stopped coming for Thelma; she still worried about her grandkids. Cissy was okay, she guessed, but Phil . . . he was *always* a concern. He was coming home soon from working in Ohio at some kinda trucking company. As much as she would be happy to see him, there also came the worries of what he would be up to next. Nearly got himself in jail so many times she'd lost count. Heck, he'd been in the pokey a time or two.

The light went on in Auntie Rose's kitchen as Sophie slunk in. That girl had been up all night, baking and fussing, talking to that detective woman. Her heart compressed a skosh. The trick she'd pulled on Sophie with the salt, that was nasty. Behindsight was twenty-twenty, folks said, and Thelma could see now that she'd just had her nose outta joint. Sophie had *tried* to include her even if that professor woman hadn't. Sophie was a nice girl, and she'd been kind to Cissy more than once. Why had Thelma gone and ruined it like she always did?

Maybe she could make it up to her. She picked up her cell phone and examined it, squinting at the tiny screen. Okay, so Cissy had put in the phone numbers she'd most likely need from a list Thelma had given her. There was a thingie that looked kinda like a telephone receiver; she poked at it, and the screen lit up and showed a list of people. She used her stubby finger to make the screen do what the kids called scrolling, though there was precious little scrollwork that she could see. She stabbed one number and watched out the window across the alley.

Sophie raced and picked up the phone after glancing at the call display. "Mrs. Earnshaw, you've dialed out again."

"Sophie? That you?"

"Yes, Mrs. Earnshaw. You've accidentally dialed out again. Over here. To Auntie Rose's."

"Not an accident. Why does everyone think it's always an accident?"

"Oh. What can I help you with, Mrs. Earnshaw?"

The girl was polite; she had to give her that. Sophie Taylor had been raised right, not like those hooligans nowadays who wouldn't move out of the way when she was trotting down the sidewalk. Maybe she'd get herself one of those scooter thingies and run 'em down. Like a cartoon, she could see little hooligan bodies flying to the right and left of her as her scooter, with flames painted along the body, plowed through 'em. Then who would have the last laugh?

"Mrs. Earnshaw?"

"Yeah," she said, coming back from a pleasant daydream. "Sophie. Right. I think we oughta get together. Counsel of war, you know, a powwow."

"I don't think that's what a powwow is—a counsel of war, you know—and I'm not sure you should say powwow nowadays anyway, ma'am."

Thelma squinted and looked at the phone. Almost sounded like that girl was laughing at her, but that couldn't be right, because she was dead serious. Dead, as in Dean Asquith dead. Asquith; if ever there was a name deserved to be laughed at, that was it. "I saw who did it, Sophie."

"Did what?"

"I know who killed that miserable man, that cheating dog of a dean, Asquith."

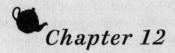 *Chapter 12*

S ophie was silent for a few seconds. What was Mrs. Earnshaw saying? "I don't understand. Who is it? How do you know?"

"I'll tell you all later. You bring Rose and Laverne over at ten and we'll talk. I got something else to do right now."

Sophie was about to demand more information, when the phone line went dead. She glanced through the kitchen window over to the main floor kitchen of Belle Époque and saw Mrs. Earnshaw get up from the table with difficulty and toddle out of the room. The police had probably told her what they had told Sophie and her grandmother, that both establishments would be closed for at least that day, so she couldn't be going to get ready to open up. Besides, she thought, glancing at the clock, it was only six in the morning.

Something else to do right now, she had said. It crossed Sophie's mind that that could be ominous, or it could mean she was going to get something to eat. She cleaned up the kitchen and packaged the extra food she had made, tucking it away in the freezer. Nana descended, and they had breakfast, of course talking about the crime, and she told her grandmother about the meeting at SereniTea.

"Then something weird happened," she said, glancing over at her grandmother. She told her about Thelma's phone call and ominous last words. "What do you think she meant?"

Pearl had ambled down the stairs and now stood on her hind legs, patting at Nana's blue housecoat. Nana picked up the cat and settled her on her lap. "Who knows with Thelma? Maybe it would be wise to give Cissy a call, just to be on the safe side."

"Good idea. I want to talk to Dana anyway. She's in a book club with Kimmy Gabrielson, and I need to talk to that girl about Mac MacAlister and her own whereabouts last night after the tea walk. Cissy may be at the bookstore, too." Peterson Books 'n Stuff, Cissy's business, employed Cissy's best friend, Dana, as sole employee, while Cissy drifted in and out, taking care of the business end of ordering. Dana did the actual work of deciding what books would be bought, since Cissy's favorite part was the "Stuff": pens, mugs, stuffed animals, crystals, jewelry, greeting cards and book-related paraphernalia, like bookmarks,.

She was actually very canny about all of that, and with Dana's exquisite design sensibility, the store was a cozy welcoming nook. But as in many college towns, one steady source of income was used textbooks. Even in a digital age, physical books were still needed; Cissy wisely capitalized on that, building a thriving buy-and-sell used textbook business. Her store was a haven for thrifty Cruickshank students.

It was nine; the bookstore would be open and hopefully Dana would answer first.

"Peterson Books 'n Stuff," Dana said on answering the phone.

"Hey, Dana."

"Oh, hey, Sophie. I was about to call you, but I wanted to get a coffee first. So, now you're knocking off college deans outside your tearoom?"

"Ha-ha, very funny," Sophie said. Her all-nighter was beginning to wear on her, she realized, and she threw herself down on the sofa in her living room. "I called for a few reasons."

"Wait a minute, girlfriend. Not so fast, You are going to tell me every second of what happened last night, as I listen breathlessly and inhale a cup of coffee—Eli stayed over last night and I did not get a lot of sleep, if you know what I mean—but I want to hear it all."

Sophie complied, knowing it would take longer to talk Dana around to what she wanted to know, than to explain what happened and move on from there.

"Wow," Dana said when Sophie finished her tale. "That's awful!" She sounded more serious, not as flippant. Death had a tendency to do that to a person.

"I know. The reason I'm calling you is—"

"Hold on a sec; Cissy just came in." Dana put the receiver down and Sophie could hear a muffled conversation in the background, with some exclamations, and a few *Wow*s and *Oh no*s

After a few minutes, Dana came back with a clatter of high heels and clanking jewelry. "Hey, Soph . . . sorry, but Cissy had news."

"Really?" She hoped it wasn't news of the sort of who kissed who, or which of their friends was getting married next, but more along the lines of the murder investigation. Given that Wally and Cissy were practically living together—though no one whispered a word of that to Thelma—it was possible.

"Really. I guess her grandmother called her last night about the dean being killed, and so when Wally came home, Cissy grilled him but good. He was tired and trying to shut her up—okay, so that's how I saw it, not what Cissy said—and ended up telling her stuff he probably shouldn't have."

"Like? Don't be a tease, Dana. I have to go over to Mrs. Earnshaw's; she's called some kind of meeting and told us all to come over."

"Nuh-uh . . . first, you have got to tell me . . . what did it look like the dean died of, to you?"

"Hard to tell. He looked contorted, and there was drool hanging from his mouth. He appeared bluish to me. I saw a wound on his neck, too, and a lot of blood soaking through his shirt at the chest." She paused and shuddered. "I wasn't exactly giving him a physical."

"That's enough. Okay, so from what Wally told Cissy, there are signs of poisoning so they're doing toxicology tests, and he did have a scrape on his neck. But he *likely* died from the stab wound in his chest."

Sophie stilled. Poisoning, a wound on his neck *and* stabbed? Someone had wanted him very dead. Like, dead enough for two people. Was it possible that there was more than one assailant? Or was it one very determined killer?

"Sophie?" Dana said.

"I'm here. Stabbed; crap, that's serious. Thanks for the info. Is Cissy still there?"

"Sure. She's checking our inventory of used textbooks. Thanks to her, we're making a killing—pardon the pun—from Cruickshank students."

"May I speak to her?"

"Okay, but first, who do you think did it?"

"I don't have a single idea. But I sure do know of a lot of people who may have wanted him dead."

"Besides Jason?"

"Dana!" She heard the stifled chuckle, but this was nothing to kid about. Sometimes Dana's sense of humor came out in odd ways. "Yes, besides, Jason. Like Kimmy Gabrielson. She says she doesn't have any feelings for Mac MacAlister, but that's not what I saw last night. I'd say she has it for him bad, and that's not appropriate given their professional relationship."

"Kimmy? No way would she kill anyone. I've known her two years, and that girl is a solid-gold sweetheart."

That had been said about murderous females before, Sophie thought. "There are the two love interests of the dean and his wife, then there is the registrar and his assistant, the basketball coach, and who knows who else."

"Sounds like a handful."

"Dana, can you get me in touch with Kimmy Gabrielson? I mean, I'll bet you're right, but I'm wondering what she may have noticed last night. She's smart, she's observant, she may know something or have seen something."

"Okay," Dana said. "Why don't I believe that's all you want to ask her? I'll give her a call this morning. Actually, she has some books that just came in from a special order for the book club, so I need her to come pick them up anyway."

"If I know when she's coming in, I can just *happen* to be at the store and I'll take it from there."

"I'll send you a text. Here's Cissy."

They greeted each other, and talked a bit about the shocking end of Sophie's evening, and what Cissy had pried out of Wally. "Cissy, I am a bit concerned. Your grandmother has told me, Laverne and Nana to come over to Belle Époque at ten, and said she has something to do. Have you talked to her yet today? Do you know what that's about?"

Cissy sighed. "No, I don't have a clue."

"Can you visit and be there when we come over?"

There was silence for a moment, then a long, drawn-out martyred sigh. "Okay, I guess I can. I was going to get a manicure but I'll put it off for now, even though it messes up my whole day."

"Good," Sophie said, refusing to be drawn in by her oh-woe-is-me attitude. "See you there."

Laverne was in Nana's second-floor tiny kitchen having a cup of tea with her friend and business partner when Sophie descended.

"Oh, honey, I'm so sorry you had to go through that," Laverne said, getting up and hugging her goddaughter. "Finding the dean."

"I'm okay," Sophie said, her voice muffled against Laverne's hand-knit sweater, inhaling her White Shoulders and baby powder scent. "Laverne, can we talk about last night?" she said, once her godmother released her and sat back down. Sophie sat on the third chair at the tiny table in her grandmother's small, pale-blue-painted dining area, drawing her knees up, heels on the edge of the seat.

"Sure, honey. I suppose you want to know if I saw or heard anything?"

"Well, from both of you," she said, gathering her grandmother into her gaze. "The dean and his wife and party were inside, too, and I wasn't. So were the Board of Governors members and some others. Did you notice anything odd, or any interaction? Before the dean's outburst about the tea, I mean?"

Nana and Laverne traded glances, as they often did.

"There was one thing," Laverne said. "But it wasn't the dean, it was his wife. She snuck off into the kitchen and got out her phone. She was whispering into it. I, uh . . . happened to be near the door and heard her tell someone that he—or she—only had a short time to 'get it done' before it was too late. She saw me and stopped, gave me a dirty look—not exactly dirty, but frigid—so I left her alone."

"The person only had a short time to '*get it done*' before it was too late," Sophie repeated.

"That could mean anything," Nana said.

"Or it could mean she was talking to the dean's killer," Sophie said.

Someone hammered on the door downstairs and Sophie leaped up, almost fell because one foot was asleep, and sprinted down the stairs. It was Cissy at their side door, and she looked red-faced and cross. "Sophie, Grandma is having a fit. She told you all to be over there at ten."

Sophie ducked back in, looked up at the big clock over the stove. "It's just ten now, for heaven's sake."

But Cissy had whirled on her heel and had already stomped back across the lane to Belle Époque.

Sophie returned to her grandmother's kitchen. "It's time. Madame Earnshaw has given us our marching orders, and if we know what's best for us, we'll mush."

Five minutes later they were all sitting around one table in the Belle Époque tearoom. Cissy was eying her nails with a frown; something was wrong, but Sophie didn't have time to pry it out of her. Cissy usually needed someone to coax her to spill her troubles, *a way to get extra attention*, Sophie thought, and then she got mad at herself for being mean. She'd talk to her friend after.

Mrs. Earnshaw was smirking and nodding, as she looked around the table at each one of them: Laverne, Nana, Cissy, Gilda and finally Sophie.

"I got a secret, but I'm going to tell you all before I tell the police. Everyone thinks I'm a nutty old lady, but I'm not. See, I know who killed the dean. It was—"

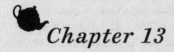 *Chapter 13*

A crash outside made them all jump, and Sophie raced out the door and peered down the lane toward the street. Three police officers stared at two cars that were crunched together. One man climbed out of the front car and circled to look at his bumper as he hollered his displeasure at the other driver, who had rammed into the back of him. A nice-looking fellow in his thirties got out of his dark blue Beamer sports car and approached the irate driver of the front car.

Sophie slunk along, hoping the police wouldn't notice her getting closer. One officer was taking notes and strolled over to the cars as Wally, who was still working the scene of the murder, approached the two men.

"You jerk, what the hell were you doing? Talking on your iPhone, or something? Didn't see a car stopped?" the man in front yelled.

Sophie eyed the two men and realized with a start that she

recognized the one from the Beamer. It was Paul Wechsler, who was the systems engineer at Cruickshank, and who had been lingering about the previous evening, but had accosted the dean as he was leaving. *And* who was one of the other potential grade alterers. *And* the dean's wife's boyfriend!

She definitely needed to talk to him!

"Dude, I'm sorry," he said, hands splayed out in a placating, pleading gesture. "Look, I'm in trouble, too, because this is my girlfriend's car and she's going to freak out. Can we just . . . I mean, there's not much damage, right?"

"Not much damage?" The first man hopped and punched the air. "Look at it . . . just *look* at it! My bumper is dragging. I'm going to—"

"Relax, fellas," Wally said, approaching the two men. "We can settle this. Why were you stopped here anyway?" he asked the first man.

"I heard about this on the news," he said, waving his hand toward Auntie Rose's, "and wanted . . . none of your business anyway!"

"It has become my business with a crash investigation to come. What's your name, sir?"

"*That's* none of your business, either. Why don't you ask *him*?" he said, jabbing his finger toward the other man.

"Your *name*?"

He gave it—Sophie couldn't hear what it was—and Wally wrote it down. "Okay, so you were rubbernecking, stopped in the middle of a public thoroughfare," he said. He turned toward the other guy. "What's *your* name, sir?"

"I don't want any trouble," Wechsler said, backing away. "Look," he said, to the other driver. "Can't we go somewhere and talk about this? I can't report . . . I mean . . ."

Wally's gaze sharpened. "What's your *name*?" he said to the Beamer driver.

"Wechsler," the guy said. "Paul Wechsler. I'm late for work, so maybe we can—"

"No way," the front guy said. "We're going to settle this right here and now. The cops are here, I've got proof, it's your fault. You're the one who ran into me."

This was all very interesting, given her conversation with Julia that morning. Jeanette Asquith had been whispering on the phone to someone last night to get it done or they'd run out of time. Was it Paul Wechsler she was talking to? Even though he was right there, she wouldn't risk being seen talking to him, especially not if they were plotting to kill her husband, but they could both talk on the phone without issue. Was that why he had been speaking with the dean, to maybe make an appointment to speak with him later? And had he come back this morning to visit the scene of the crime as assailants, according to the old saying, apparently did? Was he afraid he'd left some clue behind?

Wally took the guy in front aside and began questioning him, so Sophie sidled up to Paul Wechsler, who was bent over his front bumper, examining it. She would never get another opportunity to get this particular guy alone.

"Hey, are you okay? Do you need a coffee or anything?" she said.

"What?"

"You look like you're shaken up. Can I get you anything?"

"No, it's okay."

"You look familiar," she said, eyeing him. "Oh, I know! You work at the college, right? With computers."

"Yeah," he said, straightening.

He was nice looking but in a serious, bespectacled way, not someone she would have thought of as a cougar's boy toy. "You were here last night, weren't you? I saw you talking to the dean. Did he have you looking into this grading problem I've heard about?"

"What do you know about that?" he asked, his eyes narrowing, dark brows drawn low. He had a nice mouth and a strong jawline, with a bristle of dark hairs along it; a good-looking guy in a very serious way.

"Oh, everyone's heard about it. The whole town is buzzing. Word is that it's a real mess. *Hundreds* of grades changed," she said.

"Not *hundreds*," he demurred.

"But more than the one, right? I mean, it only stands to reason there must have been more than just one."

"Why do you say that?" he said, looking a little alarmed.

Wally was eying her, and she knew she only had a few more moments with Wechsler before Wally came to ask him about the accident. She met the fellow's gaze. "There is no reason why just one grade would be changed. Did you tell the dean that last night, when you spoke to him?"

He compressed his lips. "I wanted the dean to know the bottom line. I was trying to help him, for God's sake! He was set on announcing who did it this morning, but he was taking a real chance because there was no way of knowing the exact person based on the computer information. When I scanned the data I found a pattern of alterations, and they all occurred in two specific areas except for one anomaly that—"

"Mr. Wechsler, if I could speak with you now? I need your license and registration. Now, you say you've borrowed this car?" Wally gave Sophie a stern look.

Drat! The guy was on the verge of telling her important information. Maybe she could accost him later.

When Wechsler moved back to the car to get the registration out of the glove box, Wally muttered to Sophie, "You need to back off." He pointed to the tearoom.

She looked over her shoulder. The others were crowded at the window of Belle Époque. She was torn; Thelma's bombshell reverberated in her head. What did the woman mean? Did she actually know who did it? In that case it was a waste of time to investigate further. But on the other hand, when had Mrs. Earnshaw ever been right about *anything*?

But she couldn't go against what Wally, as an officer of the law, was saying. "Okay, I'll go. But Wally, this guy was at the tea stroll last night, and he spoke to the dean," she muttered. "I wanted you to know that. I have to wonder why he was driving by here this morning."

"I already recognized the name. Paul Wechsler has been summoned in to talk to Detective Morris. We do know what we're doing, you know, and don't *always* depend on citizen involvement to solve murders."

As she slowly walked away, she heard Paul say, as he handed over his information, "I'm borrowing this car while mine is in the shop. It's registered to Mrs. J. Asquith, a . . . a friend."

The others crowded around when she reentered Belle Époque, all except Mrs. Earnshaw, who sat stiffly at the table, her mouth primmed in a straight line, with purse-string wrinkles tightened into deep grooves.

As she led the ladies back to the table, Sophie explained what had happened. "What I don't get, though, is why Paul Wechsler was driving down this street, distracted enough that he didn't notice a car stopped in front of him."

"He would have heard about the dean's death," Nana said.

"And it would spook anyone to know that someone they spoke to the night before was dead," Laverne added.

"He *did* hear about it; the police have already asked him to come in and talk to them." She considered his troubled expression. "Okay, so say he's not guilty . . . he'd especially be upset if he gave the dean information last night that caused the man to speak with someone, and let them know he was going to announce their name this morning as the grade-altering culprit."

"Is Wally okay?" Cissy said, her voice small.

"Why wouldn't he be all right?" Sophie asked her friend.

"We kind of had a big fight yesterday, before he went to work," she murmured.

Sophie felt her heart constrict. As annoying as Cissy could be, she was still a good and loyal friend, and deserved empathy at the very least. "But he came back and slept at your place, didn't he? I mean, he told you about the murder."

Cissy cast a worried expression over her shoulder at her grandmother, and whispered, "Yeah, but he was grumpy and sarcastic and only slept an hour before he left this morning without a word."

Sophie put her arm around her friend's shoulder. "Let's talk after we figure out what we're doing about all of this. Come over and we'll talk up in my apartment."

Cissy brightened. "Okay."

They all returned to Thelma, who needed to be coaxed to repeat her assertion. Cissy did this best. She threaded her arm through her grandmother's and laid her head on her shoulder. "Come on, Grandma, we want to know. Who do you think did it?"

"It's not who I *think* did it, it's who really did it." She patted her granddaughter's hand and sat up straighter, glancing around the circle of expectant faces.

"So who did it?" Nana asked. Her tone was serious, but she winked at Sophie.

Even a broken clock was right twice a day, her Nana had been known to say, so Sophie listened carefully. Maybe Thelma would have some insight, after all.

"Well, this is what I saw with my own eyes. I saw that Asian fellow, you know, the one who works for the college."

Sophie thought for a second. "Vince Nomuro, the registrar?"

"I guess. Anyways, he asked me if I had green tea, and I told him I wouldn't keep something that went green, no matter what folks say about Belle Époque."

Laverne snickered. Sophie thought of correcting her about green tea, but what was the point? "And . . . ?"

"And he went away with that group. But then he came back later."

"Later? How much later?" Sophie asked.

"How about just before I told Gilda to get her butt downstairs and take the garbage out?"

Gilda shrieked and leaped to her feet, her boney fingers thrust through her hair. "You didn't tell me that, Thelma. That you saw someone? Why would you do that, send me out when there was a stranger sniffing around?"

"I figured you'd see him if he was up to no good."

"But you didn't *tell* me!"

"Because then you wouldn't have gone out, stupid!"

Gilda harrumphed and retreated to the kitchen, where she banged around some pots and pans.

"Anyhoo, I saw him, that fella, bending over your hedge. I'll bet he was checking to make sure that fellow that he killed was good and dead."

"How do you know it was him?" Sophie asked.

"He was wearing that stupid hat, a tweed one. Looked like he shoulda been on a golf course, or driving a fancy sports car. I call it an Andy Capp, because of the cartoon, you know."

Sophie was stunned; Mrs. Earnshaw had seen Vince Nomuro that close to Sophie finding the body? It seemed a clear indictment. Sophie went out, spoke to Wally—the two drivers were in a squad car now, presumably giving their stories of the accident to another officer—and had him call in for the detective to come out to question Thelma about her sighting. He told them Detective Morris was on her way.

She hoped it was the answer, and that the crime would be solved swiftly. It all tied in, in a way; the registrar was one of the few people who could have changed Mac's grade, and if the dean was about to expose him as the culprit, then he certainly had motive, though it seemed weak. It would tie up both crimes, then, and let Jason off the hook.

She tried to ignore a niggling doubt in her brain, though. If the dean was about to expose Vince as the culprit in the grade change scandal, then why had he taken the time to warn Jason to update his resume? She couldn't assume Thelma was right about anything, so she'd keep looking into it. Otherwise, Jason was as much in danger as ever.

Cissy trailed her back to her apartment upstairs from the tearoom after they got Mrs. Earnshaw settled talking to Detective Morris in the kitchen of Belle Époque. Nana and Laverne were taking inventory in the tearoom kitchen, since they couldn't open, and then Sophie was going to help Laverne thoroughly clean the carpets in the tearoom. Unless Laverne succeeded in getting her to leave the task to her and get on with investigating, as she kept saying.

Cissy slumped down in one of the powder-blue over-stuffed chairs in Sophie's small living room. She stared at the teapots on the floating wall shelves and yawned. "I didn't sleep at all last night, what with the fight with Wally, and then hearing about the murder, and waiting up for him later."

"What did you guys fight about?" Sophie asked as she brought in a tray with tea and some scones, with a pot of maple cream she wanted to taste. Cissy picked at one nail, frowning down at it and splaying her hand out, examining her ragged manicure. The girl never let anything go, one of her faults. She'd whine about the missed manicure for days.

"He just . . . I don't understand Wally. All I was doing was talking about how Eli is going to propose to Dana, and he got all bent out of shape."

"He seemed fine this morning, just businesslike," Sophie said. Though in truth he did appear on edge for Wally, the most even tempered of fellows. "Do you want me to talk to him if I get a chance?"

"Would you?" Cissy said, dropping her feet to the carpeted floor. "I don't understand him. I was just . . . I know how Eli is going to propose, because he checked in with me to make sure Dana could get the day off. He's going to take her on a cruise on Seneca Lake; he's booked the boat special so they can do a sunset cruise, which they don't usually do this time of year, you know, being autumn. He's going to wait, and as the captain points the boat toward the sunset, he's going to get down on one knee and tell her she's his choice until the sunset of their lives!"

She clasped her hands together and sighed. "I was telling Wally, and saying how romantic it was going to be, how sweet Eli was. How I've never seen Dana so happy. He got all moody and asked me if I was going to talk about Eli and Dana all evening. I asked what his problem was, and then he stomped out."

"Where did he go?"

"To work. I mean, he came back, like I said, but he was grumpy."

"But he did tell you about the murder when you asked, so he's talking to you."

Cissy sighed in exasperation. "Yes, but he was still upset. I could tell. I don't understand why!"

Sophie had a suspicion of why Wally was upset, and

would explore it with him when she had a chance. Her cell phone chimed. "That's Dana," Sophie said, checking her phone. "She said she'd send me a text message when Kimmy was coming in, and that's right now. Can I follow you back to the bookstore? If that's where you're going?"

"I'm going to get that manicure first. I can't stand my nails ragged like this. I feel like everyone's looking at my hands."

"Cissy, no one is looking at your hands. I barely look at my own."

"You ought to. They're a mess."

Sophie looked down at her hands: square, hardworking, dry skin from being in hot water repeatedly, with blunt short nails. "They look all right to me."

Cissy wrinkled her nose, grabbed her purse and said, "I'll talk to you later."

Sophie found her keys and checked in with Nana and Laverne, who were still doing inventory in a leisurely fashion as they worried at a solution to the crime that had assaulted their doorstep. She raced out to the parking lot and jumped in her Jetta, driving down the lane to the street. The cars from the fender bender were gone, but there was still a heavy police presence. She shuddered as she paused; was the body even gone yet? A chill raced over her as she thought about someone killing the dean right outside their house, while her grandmother slept just yards above.

This could not go on. Jason needed to stay well out of all of it, but *she* didn't. She drove out of the lane, turned right and headed toward the town's common, patterned somewhat after Ithaca's center of town, with cafes and restaurants, cute shops, and brick-paved streets for walking. But she turned left before the common, down Cayuga Street, where the bookstore was.

Peterson Books 'n Stuff took up the main floor of the house in which Cissy and her brother Phil had grown up. It was a large redbrick Queen Anne, too big for a modern family, with picture windows along the front protected by the wide porch. Sophie parked on the street and dashed up the steps and into the bookstore, a string of silvery bells tinkling to announce her.

As her eyes adjusted, she could see that there were a few people inside, at least one a student, from the looks of him, with a backpack and glasses, shaggy hair falling forward, concealing his eyes. He sat on the floor in the literature section reading a copy of *The Bell Jar*. Dana made her way to the front through the shelves, paused by the young man and said something sharp to him, after which he lumbered to his feet, put the book back and trudged out, followed by another customer who had just finished paying.

"Kimmy is in the used textbooks section," Dana whispered, sidling up to Sophie. "She's looking for a guide to literary theory while I get her order rung through. It's probably for Mac, something that explains *Light in August* in one-syllable words. Now that his grades are all being reexamined, he needs to get them back up to snuff with a series of exams, or something."

"I'll go talk to Kimmy."

Dana caught her by the arm and glared into her eyes. "She's my friend; don't you upset her. She's distressed enough as it is. The dean was just murdered, for heaven's sake!"

Sophie sighed. "I'm not going to upset her. What kind of a creep do you think I am?"

"You don't want to know," Dana replied, but with a wink and smile. She nudged Sophie. "You can be as single-minded as a terrier with a rat down a hole when you're focused on a problem. Anyway, I'm also working on something else for you, a little gift. But first, go on, talk to her. The sooner this is solved the better."

Sophie still paused for one moment. "Do you think Eli can find out any information for me?"

"Captain America?" Dana said. "No way. He's careful about stepping on anyone else in law enforcement's toes, and this is not his town, even if he was born here."

"Okay. Just thought I'd ask." Sophie rambled through the dim bookstore. Fortunately for her, the cookbook section was right near the used textbook section where Kimmy was perusing a stack of texts. Cookbooks; how could she resist! She actually found a couple of collections of recipes by well-known mystery authors that she thought her grandmother would enjoy.

But she was not there to shop. She cradled the books in her arms, glanced around and backed—purposely—into Kimmy, dropping the books she held. "Oh, I'm so sorry! I . . ." She stopped and stared. "Kimmy Gabrielson, right?"

The girl's dark eyes widened. "Oh . . . uh, Jason Murphy's girlfriend, right?"

"Sophie Taylor," she said, avoiding an affirmation. "I hope you enjoyed the tea stroll." She paused for a beat, then said, "It's so awful about the dean. It happened right outside our place, and I'm the one who found him." The falter of her voice was genuine, and so were the tears that filled her eyes. "I've been trying not to think about it. That's why I'm here; I needed to get away. Cookbooks always soothe me. But it's hard to stop picturing it."

Kimmy's uncertain expression mellowed into warm concern. She picked up Sophie's books and took her by the arm, guiding her to a little alcove off the main area of the store, where there was a soft love seat in a quiet, dim corner. Beauty, the Persian bookstore cat, ambled over to them and leaped up on Sophie's lap, settling himself.

"You poor girl," Kimmy crooned, patting her arm and

setting the cookbooks at Sophie's feet, topped by the book she was reading. "How awful that must have been for you. I think if I found a body I'd never sleep again."

"I didn't," Sophie said. "I mean, I haven't slept yet. My grandmother and godmother seem okay, but then, they didn't see the body. I did!" Sophie felt a little bad overstating her angst as she was. Kimmy was empathetic, and Sophie was playing on her emotions, but it was for a worthy purpose. "Did you notice anything at all last night during the tea stroll?"

"Like what?"

"I don't know, anyone following the dean?"

Kimmy shook her head.

"Have the police spoken to you yet?"

"No, why would they?"

"I imagine they'll be talking to everyone who was at the tea walk last night. Just for witness accounts, you know. Did anyone have an argument with him?"

Kimmy was about to shake her head again but paused. "There was something." She looked down at the carpet, tracing the pattern with the toe of her loafer. "His girlfriend. That woman doesn't know when she is being dumped good and hard."

"You know about Sherri Shaw?"

"Sure, I'm surprised you do. *Everyone* at the college knew. Did Jason tell you?"

"Jason doesn't pay attention to that kind of thing. No, I overheard them at the tea convention, arguing," she said. "I couldn't believe it when I saw her at the tea stroll. What was she thinking?" She cast a sly look up at Kimmy. "My first thought was that he had a new girlfriend lined up and that's why he was dumping her."

"Hmph. Maybe someone less obvious than Cleavage for Brains."

Sophie snorted in unexpected laughter, then felt bad about it. "I shouldn't be laughing. The poor man is dead."

"As bad as I feel about it, I'd say he brought it on himself. The guy was unbelievable, willing to help anyone take a forward dive off a cliff as long as no one saw him shove from behind."

That was a very vivid image, Sophie thought, and indicated a nasty trait of self-involved cruelty. She eyed Kimmy with interest. "Is that what he was doing to Jason? I feel like the dean was targeting him. I've heard that he didn't like Jason's support for Professor Dandridge and Dr. Bolgan's hope to make the humanities department stronger."

Kimmy gazed at her, a startled look on her round face. She plucked at her hair and draped a curl over her forehead with quick, agitated movements. "You sure seem to know a lot about Cruickshank politics!"

"I've been listening to Jason and Julia talk, I guess." She eyed the girl, who now seemed nervous, when she hadn't at first. "Am I right?"

Kimmy nodded, slowly. "If we can assume Jason didn't alter the grade, and that the dean knew that, I'd say Dean Asquith was holding a threat over Jason's head, kind of . . . mmm, emphasizing his control, you know?"

"So he knew it wasn't Jason, and he already had his target set, but he thought he'd throw some shade on Jason to try to bring him in line."

Kimmy nodded and rolled her shoulders. "If I had to guess."

"Would the dean have done anything stupid, like . . . oh, telling the real guilty party that he was going to expose them this morning?"

"I don't know the dean that well, but my *guess*? I'd say

he wouldn't have been able to help himself. He would have relished the idea that the person would sweat all night."

"Sounds like he didn't have a lot of common sense." Sophie thought about all the people the dean could have talked to. Every possible grade alterer that she knew of was nearby, and there were folks who had other motives for murder, too, like Sherri Shaw and Jeanette Asquith. It was a nightmare investigation, but the police would be able to question people and get to their real alibis, while she didn't have that ability.

It was not her problem to investigate, and she should do as she was told and stay out of it. *However,* the police would most definitely be looking square at Jason, since he admitted to having an argument with the dean that very evening. "I wonder, did Mac know his grade had been falsified?" Sophie asked.

The other woman's gaze was becoming less direct. "He says he didn't, but I don't know. Mac is one of those guys who thinks that anything they get, they deserve."

There was a faint impression of bitterness. She longed to ask if Kimmy was fond of Mac beyond the adviser role she played, but that was a delicate subject, and Sophie didn't want to appear to accuse the woman of unethical behavior. It was tricky when she didn't know what the ethics of the situation actually were. "What is Mac like? As his adviser you must work with him closely. I know we talked about his brains, but what is he like, I mean, his personality?" She was a very intelligent woman; would she defend him or not?

"He's not my only student, you know. I don't spend *that* much time with him, but I try to do the best I can for every single one of my students. He can be a sweetheart, but . . ." She shrugged. "He's okay."

"You said he was a sweetheart."

"Comparatively speaking, he is. Some of my students are real pains in the butt."

So that didn't get her anywhere. "Do you think the dean's death is related to this whole grades thing?"

"Your guess is as good as mine, but it doesn't seem likely."

"I heard that there were many more grades falsified."

"The idea should shock me, but it doesn't."

Sophie paused for a moment, trying to find a way to phrase what she wanted to say. She watched the young woman, examining her dark eyes, made up carefully with pale blue shadow, navy eyeliner and thick mascara. "I've been wondering if it was some kind of grades for dollars scheme. If that was true, who would you suspect?"

"Hmph. Brenda Fletcher," she said, her pink glossed lips twisting in a grimace. "I can't stand that . . . that witch."

Well, that was vehement. "I don't know much about her. Why don't you like her?"

"Nobody needs a reason to dislike Brenda."

"Why do you say she'd falsify grades, though?"

Kimmy shrugged. "I don't really know anything, but she's the kind of person who would do it. I have to deal with her on occasion when one of my students has a problem that can't be resolved by the student services office. She's got such a crappy attitude about stuff. When I went in to talk about Mac's problems, she told me if he couldn't cut it, he should go somewhere else, but then said no college would have him. I can't *stand* her!"

But that didn't mean Brenda changed the grade. In fact, it rather argued against it, in Sophie's estimation. If she was worried about being exposed, she'd likely be more diplomatic to someone who could potentially do some digging and point the finger at her. Her dislike of the assistant registrar seemed to say more about Kimmy than Brenda.

"Anyway, who would kill someone over a grade?" Kimmy went on. "I will say, Dean Asquith's wife won't be shedding any tears but the crocodile type over his coffin."

"Why do you say that?"

"She's been wanting to be rid of him for years . . . *hates* the collegiate life. She'd rather live in a condo in Manhattan overlooking Central Park. But their families are too closely entwined for them to have ever divorced. Their fathers were in business together, and other family members still are; the company assets are so closely lashed together that if one of them left, the whole boat would sink. This way, Jeanette is free and can sail off into the sunset with her Geek god."

Chapter 14

Geek god . . . Paul Wechsler, who had crashed Jeanette's car while rubbernecking at the scene of the crime. Maybe making sure he didn't leave any *i* undotted, any *t* uncrossed? Had he killed the dean on his own, or perhaps at Jeanette's command? Her words overheard by Laverne hinted that Mrs. Asquith was involved, and Paul was right there, on the scene. Maybe she called Paul, giving him the go-ahead; they were running out of time, it was now or never. He could have made some excuse to meet the dean later, perhaps, and killed him.

"Kimmy, you seemed a little tense last night, and you pulled Mac aside. Was everything okay? What were you talking about?"

The girl stood and picked up the remedial book she was buying for Mac, a simple guide to literary theory. "What an odd thing to ask," she said, staring down at Sophie. "Anyway,

I have to go. I'm meeting with the MacAlisters. I think I've got them talked into hiring tutors so we can get Mac up to snuff with his grades."

She picked up the other books she had ordered and left Peterson's in a hurry.

It was possible that it was Kimmy who upped Mac's grade, but Sophie didn't think she would kill the dean to hide that fact. Sophie sat for a moment, collecting her thoughts, then was about to emerge from her hidey-hole, when Dana charged back, finger to her lips.

"I did it. I told you I had a gift for you, and I do," she whispered. "There is someone who has just come in who I think you ought to try to talk to."

"Who is it?"

"Brenda Fletcher, the assistant registrar. One snarky student who comes in here all the time calls her the Ass Reg. That's what her desk nameplate says."

Sophie's eyes widened. The assistant registrar; when would she ever have another chance to meet her on such informal, anonymous terms? Who would know more about Vince Nomuro, the best suspect they had, than his assistant? "How did you get her here?"

"I ordered some books for her. They came in last week, but I don't like her much, so I was going to wait until my day off to have her come in while Cissy was here. But I'll tell you this; if anyone knows what's going on at Cruickshank about the grading thing, she will. So, voilà . . . she's here to collect her books."

"What should I say? How can I talk to her?"

Dana thought for a second, then said, "It shouldn't be that hard; the woman is a gossip. Follow my lead." She moved toward the textbook section, waited for a few seconds, then said loudly, "I don't care, Sophie, I will *not* help you figure out who is framing Jason Murphy for the grading scandal!"

Sophie gasped. What the heck was Dana doing? But she had to play along and assume that her friend knew what she was doing. Trailing her, she said, "But Dana, I don't know what else to do. With the dean gone now, I'm afraid the college will railroad Jason, and he doesn't deserve that."

Dana had led her right to Brenda Fletcher, but there was no sign of recognition on the woman's face when she eyed Sophie.

"Maybe he did it," Dana said, turning, with a malicious sparkle in her eye. "Have you ever thought of that? Maybe your golden boy Jason actually did it."

"He did *not*!" Sophie said fiercely, glaring at Dana. How could she say that, even in jest? "If there is one person in this world I'd trust, it's Jason."

Dana glanced over at the assistant registrar. "Oh, hey, Brenda. Do you know Sophie Taylor? She's chef at Auntie Rose's Victorian Tea House, and she's going out with Jason Murphy. I'm trying to tell her there is no way to know who changed Mac MacAlister's grade at Cruickshank, but she won't listen to me. You're the assistant registrar; maybe *you* can convince her."

Sophie switched her attention to the other woman, who looked surprised and a little disgruntled to be accosted in such a way. Sophie thought she'd better tread carefully. It was smart of Dana not to directly address the dean's death, but rather the less-explosive topic of the grade-fixing scandal. If she handled it right, it would allow her to talk about both. "People keep saying that the dean was going to tell everyone this morning that he had caught the grade fixer, and it was Jason. I say there is no way for anyone to know *what* he was going to say. Do you agree?"

Brenda Fletcher huddled into her ancient coat, a dark green bomber-style jacket that was frayed at the cuffs and worn in spots along the sleeve. It must have been an old favorite, spotted with pins and badges: an apple, a Sagittarius zodiac sign and a smattering of little pins with acronyms. She wound her dark woolen scarf more closely around her neck, blinked and examined Sophie for a long moment. She was a plain young woman, with glasses, a habit of squinting, and her curly brown hair scraped back in a bun; the best thing about her looks was creamy, perfect skin, with a mole by her mouth. But her dark eyes betrayed intelligence, and her pause indicated a certain amount of thoughtfulness. Sophie wondered if Brenda had her own suspicions but didn't want to share them.

"I suppose there are notes of what he was going to say," she finally said. "He must have investigated. And he probably told *someone*. Wouldn't you, if you had made a decision and were going to announce it?" She blinked and tilted her head to one side. "He must have at *least* told the president, right?"

"The president?"

"Cruickshank's top dog, President Schroeder."

"I haven't even heard his name come up yet," Sophie said.

Brenda shrugged. "He's a hands-off kind of administrator, hoping to coast through his last three years without much trouble. He leaves a lot to do with the professors, teachers and grad student TAs up to Dean Asquith. I guess he figures the dean of faculty should look after the faculty, right?"

"I guess. So maybe the dean didn't tell him?"

Brenda shrugged.

"Who else might Dean Asquith have told?"

"No one, really. There's the provost, I guess, Dr. Ruta Vilansky, but she's away right now, so not her."

"It all seems so complicated. I went to a technical school for cooking, and the administration was so much simpler."

"You're out of your league," she said with a sly smile. "Never going to a real college has crippled your understanding."

Sophie sighed inwardly, but nodded. "I suppose you have a point."

"I did wonder this morning if someone killed the dean to stop his announcement," Brenda said, frowning and tugging at her scarf, twisting the fringe around her fingers. "But it seems awful extreme. At its worst, what he had to say would have been just an accusation of grade fixing. Despite what folks were saying, whoever did it would likely just be reprimanded."

"I thought he or she would be fired. Or charged. Something!"

"It's unethical, but not a criminal offense," Brenda replied evenly. "I did a little research for my boss looking for precedents, but it's a tricky topic. If the grade fix was limited in scope, then there wouldn't be any action beyond a reprimand. I don't think it was even in the dean's purview to fire Jason or anyone, if they simply faked a grade."

"I can't believe anyone would do that to help an athlete stay on the team."

"I guess you not going to a regular college . . . you wouldn't know how important the athletes are to a school. I was on a team in college, and it was a great moment to stand with my friends on the podium. It's important stuff." She shifted impatiently. "Look, I have to go. Don't worry; Jason will be okay, I'm sure."

"Do you mind talking to me for just a few more moments? I'm kind of freaked out about this all."

"I'm in a hurry," Brenda said. "I came in to pick up some books I ordered."

"It'll take me a minute to get everything together anyway, Brenda," Dana said, glancing their way. "My computer has been acting up this morning," she continued, with a wink to Sophie, "And I have to get it to boot up again before I can process your order, or you'll be charged twice. We don't want that to happen! Have a cup of coffee on the house." She fluttered her hand toward the coffee machine. "I have that caramel mocha blend you like."

Brenda sighed. "There is nothing like a bookstore that serves coffee, am I right?" she said to Sophie, heading toward the back. The coffee machine was right by the alcove Sophie had shared with Kimmy Gabrielson just minutes before.

"Oh, sure," Sophie replied, following the young woman toward the alcove, even though her own idea of heaven was a kitchen and tea.

Brenda fixed up her coffee, chose the biggest brownie from the tray of goodies for sale and curled up on the sofa. The brew did smell good, like a mocha caramel dessert. The woman seemed pretty relaxed for someone whose colleague had been murdered the night before, but Sophie didn't know enough about her relationship with the dean and how his death would affect her. It would affect Vince Nomuro more, since he was probably the one who was more directly involved with the dean.

"I'm going to sound like an idiot, but even though Jason works as an instructor at Cruickshank, I don't understand much about the actual workings of a college. The only time I went to the registrar's office in my school was to pay my tuition and register for classes. But what all does the registrar do?"

Brenda smiled and sipped her coffee, the expression holding more than a whiff of condescension. Fine, let her underestimate Sophie; that was often a good thing. She didn't feel the need to impress anyone with her intelligence.

"We plan and implement registration, a big job even for a college the size of Cruickshank. So many conflicts!" She took a big bite of her brownie, then carefully wrapped it back up and stowed it in her patchwork hobo bag. She swallowed, and took another long drink. "We keep track of the curriculum, not just scheduling conflicts but prerequisites, that sort of thing. We compile enrollment statistics for the dean's office, collect tuition and resolve issues with credit attribution."

"And you maintain academic records."

She sipped. "Well, sure. That's an important part of what we do."

And why they had access to grades, which meant either her or Vince Nomuro could have changed Mac MacAlister's grade. "What kind of training do you need for that?"

"You need a degree, at least a bachelor's, but a master's is better. It can be in accounting, or social work, like mine. Vince was in pharmacy but flunked out, so he switched to accounting. I kid him because he sure did pick two fields that require precision! There are so many facets to the job, it can be approached from many angles, but you have to be good with technology." She wrinkled her brow and stared at Sophie. "What does this have to do with anything? I thought you were worried about Jason."

"I don't understand much about college life at Cruickshank, so I'm trying to get a general feel of Jason's environment. You're helping so much! My cooking school was a lot different," she replied, downplaying her double major and graduation from one of the toughest culinary courses in the country, as well as her private school background, from which

he graduated with excellent grades. With her background
ind grade point average, she could easily have gotten into any
chool she wanted; she chose culinary school out of love for
he subject. "What kind of man was Dean Asquith?"

"What kind of man was Dean Asquith," Brenda repeated,
n a musing tone. "Let's see, an egomaniacal, philandering,
mean-spirited, obtuse, obstreperous megalomaniac? Does
hat cover all the bases?"

So Brenda Fletcher was not a fan of the dean. "I take it
rou're not sorry he's dead."

"I didn't say that! I'm *very* sorry he's dead. I may not
rave liked him much, but I care about Cruickshank. I'm a
PhD candidate in social work as well as being assistant
egistrar. I'll get my doctorate and move on from the job,
rut that won't be for a while. This throws the whole place
nto turmoil, and who knows what kind of a jerk we'll get
rext? Sorry to be blunt, but just because I didn't like the
man, doesn't mean I wanted to see him dead."

The vehemence surprised Sophie, but she could see
where it was coming from. It gave her some idea of the
extent to which the dean's death would rattle the Cruickshank community. A student might not notice a disturbance,
rut the teaching and administrative staff most certainly
would, especially since he was the dean of faculty. And as
Brenda pointed out, who knew what they'd get next in that
rosition? "So Mr. Nomuro is your boss, right?"

She nodded.

"He was along for the walk last night."

"A lot of us were; it was mandatory to attend Dale's little
cheme to link town and gown. Even the president asked us
o go, though I noticed he didn't deign to attend."

"What does that mean, town and gown?" Sophie asked,

distracted, wondering if that command explained Paul
Wechsler's presence.

"Well, town, obviously, all of you here in Gracious Grove.
And gown means the academic gown, nowadays the gradu-
ate's gown, but way back when academics wore clerical garb,
and I suppose that was the gown indicated, you know, a
priest's or monk's robe." She pushed her glasses up on her
nose.

"Oh. Okay." Sophie paused, unsure of how to use the information Julia had given her without giving away her source,
or exactly what was said between Vince and the dean. "What
is your boss like?"

Brenda eyed her as she drained her cup. "Dana, are you
done with my book order yet?" she called out, not letting her
gaze leave Sophie.

"Nope. Just got the computer to boot up," Dana said. The
bells over the door chimed, indicating another customer
coming in. "It's going through some updates right now,
Bren. You know what computers are like." After a beat, she
said, in her best customer service voice. "Hi, can I help you?"

There was an answering murmur from the customer.

"What are you trying to get at?" Brenda asked, setting
her mug aside and leaning toward Sophie. "You're not trying
to pin the blame for the grading scandal on Vince, are you?
Just because your boyfriend is up to his neck?"

"Of course not." So much for the fake grade not being a
big deal. Brenda seemed alarmed, and Sophie felt the need
to tread carefully. "I'm trying to understand everything. One
of the ladies in their group saw the dean and Mr. Nomura
arguing, that's all."

Brenda blinked and squinted. She looked conflicted.
"What did she hear?"

"I don't know, exactly. Did they have anything to argue about?"

Brenda shrugged and looked off into space, chewing her lip and playing with the fringed end of her scarf. "I don't know. It's just . . . I lost track of Vince at one point. We were supposed to stick together, you know, present a united front. But he ditched me, and when I saw him next he was following the dean into a corner at that awful yoga and tea place at the top of the hill."

That accorded with what she had heard from Julia about the conversation, though in that scenario it was the dean who had *dragged* the registrar away to talk at him. However, if Thelma was right and did indeed see the registrar near the scene of the crime at the right time, perhaps she should point the police toward Brenda Fletcher to expose her boss, and Julia would need to recount what she heard, as well. "Didn't you find out what it was about?"

"Right, eavesdrop on a conversation between my boss and a colleague?"

Sophie's phone chimed and she glanced down. A text message from someone she didn't know. Wait . . . Tara . . . Tara Mitchells, the *Clarion* reporter. Her eyes widened. The girl had done her homework; Sophie's cell number was on the Auntie Rose website as the contact for private party bookings. She put the phone away, though, as Brenda stood, straightening her coat, which had bunched up around her hips as she sat.

"I don't have time to wait. Dana, if you're not ready right now, I'll come back. The college is having a meeting today to discuss what to do about the dean's death, and Vince is in a tizzy. I have to be there."

Dana, who had of course been simply stalling, did have the books ready.

Brenda helped pack them into a box. "I took a brownie from the basket," she said and smiled. "My birthday is nex week; I'll consider it my present, and a bonus for making me wait!"

Sophie approached the cash desk. "I suppose the police will want to talk to you at some point. I'm sure they'll be asking everyone about their alibi for last night, you know after the tea stroll."

The assistant registrar gazed steadily at her and said, "I you want to know where I was, just ask me."

Busted. Okay. "So, where did you go after the tea stroll?"

"That's none of your business, is it?" she said. "But it' no big deal. I went home. Nothing earth-shattering abou that. I told my roommate all about my evening. I talked hi ear off, moaned about it for an hour until he was sick an tired of listening, then I went to bed."

Dana checked Brenda out without further delay. Sophie thought for a moment; Brenda said that Vince was in a tizzy Well, if he had killed the dean, he most certainly would be and there were likely police swarming the campus, talking to everyone. She checked the text message from Tara. Dear A killd at yr place? Need comment for campus ppr.

A comment she would proceed to twist into something entirely different, Sophie thought. However, it did suit he agenda to talk to the reporter, who had resources she didn't Meet me at Auntie Rose's, she texted back.

"I have to go," she said, slipping her phone back in he purse and approaching the cash desk. "That *Clarion* reporter who tricked me at the reception is asking for a quote. I have a few unsuitable ones for her."

"Way to go, Sophie!" Dana said, high-fiving her. "Shut her down! I wouldn't go within a hundred yards of her."

"Oh, I'm definitely meeting her, but this time she won't get anything out of me. She was hanging around last night, and since she was skulking, I figure she may have seen something worthwhile. She'll talk, I'll listen this time."

"A year ago I would have predicted you'd get blindsided again," Dana said, as she typed something into her computer. "But you're not the pushover I thought you were. Or, at least, you're only half the pushover I thought you were."

Sophie leaned on the cash desk and eyed Dana, petting Beauty, the cat, as she wondered if she should bring up a topic she was worried about.

"You look *tres serious*," Dana said, glancing over at her then back to the computer. "What's up?"

"Wally and Cissy are having an argument. I think I know why Wally is upset. Would he talk to me about it if I asked?"

"What did Cissy say?" Dana asked, this time fixing her gaze on Sophie and not looking away. "Why is Wally upset?"

Sophie considered; but shook her head. "I can't divulge."

"Ah, so it has to do with . . ." Dana watched her for a moment, then a slow smile tilted her mouth in the corner. "Let me guess; Eli is going to propose to me. He thinks it's a big secret, but I snooped in his coat pocket and saw the ring receipt from Brummel Jewels in Buffalo." She did a little cha-cha behind the cash desk and Beauty glared at her, then leaped down to the windowsill.

"Okay," Sophie said slowly.

"I think he went to Cissy about it, to ask her opinion, or whatever. She *thinks* she's mysterious, but the girl hasn't got a subtle bone in her body. Maybe I've known her too long, but I know everything from her stupid hints. Anyway, I'd bet she's been going on and on about Eli's proposal plan, thinking that's a great way to get Wally to propose to her."

Sophie sighed. "The amazing Dana; how *do* you do it?"

"I'm very intuitive. Also, I'm fairly self-involved, so I think a lot about this stuff. *And* I eavesdrop like crazy."

Sophie smiled at Dana's self-deprecating humor. She seemed like the kind of woman who would be self-involved; she was gorgeous, spent a lot of time and money on clothes, hair and makeup, and worked hard to get exactly what she wanted in life. She had decided Eli was the one from almost the moment she saw him, and had reeled him in effectively. But she was also generous, helpful and committed to the happiness of those she loved. "I think maybe Wally is put off that she's been going on and on about Eli's proposal plans."

Dana nodded, her expression sobering. "We both know Cissy is a bit of a boob. She has no clue how to handle a man."

"Neither do I!"

"Honey, you don't need to 'handle' Jason, you need to finally be straight with him, for God's sake. Grow a pair and tell him how you feel!"

"So, about Wally," Sophie said, refusing to get sidetracked to her and Jason's personal business. "I agree that's what's going on. Should I talk to Wally?"

Dana paused for a moment, then shook her head. "Let me take care of it. Cissy has been my friend for many years, since we were toddlers, practically. I think I know what to do. Those two kids will be perfect together, but Wally is the kind of guy who will drop down on one knee after the Rooty Tooty Fresh 'N Fruity pancakes at the IHOP. You and I both know that he needs to get creative so he can make it a proposal for Cissy to remember, or she may say no. I know Eli is planning something biggish, but to be honest, I don't care about that as long as I get a proposal. Cissy's another story; she's been ODing on all those reality bride shows on TV, and for her proposal she expects fireworks spelling out *Will You Marry Me?* accompanied by baby cupids with sparklers squeezed into their butt cheeks."

Sophie snorted in laughter.

Dana's beautiful face softened with affection. "And she deserves it. I kid a lot, and Cissy has her problems, but she's sweet. She lets me run this place like it's my own, and she trusts me implicitly. I never had that in my family so Cissy is my sister, at heart. I like to boss people around, so let me distract myself until Eli proposes with helping Wally propose to Cissy in a way she'll remember for the rest of her life."

Sophie circled the cash desk and threw her arms around Dana, tears welling in her eyes. "You're so much nicer than you pretend to be."

"Don't go mushy on me, Soph," she said, squeezing and releasing, pushing Sophie away to arm's length. "I *am* nicer than I pretend to be, and you're *smarter* than you pretend to be. I heard you setting Brenda up. I'll bet she's doing a little investigation of Vince Nomuro right this minute!"

"I hope not; I don't want anyone putting themselves in danger, or getting in trouble." Sophie patted Dana's shoulder. "And now I'm going to go and squeeze some information out of a college reporter who *also* thinks she's smarter than me and everyone else, I suspect. How dumb does she have to be to sabotage me, and then try to use me as a source?"

Sophie drove back to Auntie Rose's. Tara was already there. She was across the street with her camera, trying to get a shot of where the police were working, but they had constructed a tent in such a way as to block anyone's view. As she watched, Tara snuck across the street, popped up over the barrier and snapped quickly. But she was not quick enough. Wally, behind the barrier, popped up too, grabbed her camera, and held it away from her while he scanned through and deleted the offending photo.

Sophie snickered. She was surprised by Wally's swiftness and his proactive move, but pleased that Tara didn't get the picture. "Tara, I'm here," she said, motioning to the girl. "You can come back to the kitchen if you want to talk." She then turned and strode along the lane to the kitchen door.

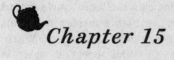

Chapter 15

Tara flung a few choice phrases at Wally, then followed to where Sophie stood waiting with the door open, and stomped in past her. The kitchen was empty, but Sophie could hear murmuring from the general vicinity of the tearoom. Maybe they had moved inventory to the gift nook. It also smelled like Laverne had lavishly sprinkled powdered rug cleaner throughout the tearoom.

"Have a seat," Sophie said to Tara, who plunked down at the table and moodily scanned the photos on her digital camera.

"Jerk cop," Tara muttered, her pale cheeks suffusing with red that spread down her neck. She yanked her windbreaker jacket off and flung it to the floor, her blond hair swinging free as she unwrapped a school colors scarf from her neck and plopped it on top of the jacket.

"The barrier was put up to keep the public out. Why did you think they'd let you take a photo and keep it? Or publish it?"

"Freedom of the press!" she sputtered, smacking the table. "We live in a free country, and they're trying to keep me from exercising my rights."

"Your *rights*? The right to take a photo of the corpse of a murder victim?" Sophie shook her head and examined the girl, the anger she felt from Tara's article about Jason and her exposing him as the supposed cheater bubbling at a low simmer, ready to boil over. "*Your* rights. What about the victim and his family? What about *their* rights? What were you planning to do, splash it on the front page of the *Clarion*? Share it on social media? What kind of lies and misquoted words were you planning to go along with it?"

Tara stilled and glared at Sophie through narrowed eyes. Laverne popped into the kitchen.

"Oh, it's you, honey. We're taking inventory and tidying in the gift nook. It's best to keep busy so we don't think about . . . you know."

Sophie took a deep breath, her godmother's sweet, throaty voice reminding her that this was her happy place, and she would not bring anger into it. It was up to her to handle Tara in a way that calmed the girl and got what she needed out of her. "I'm making some tea, Laverne. Do you and Nana want some?"

"Not right now, honey. We'll get some in a while." She disappeared back into the tearoom.

"Who was that?" the Cruickshank student asked.

"That's Laverne Hodge, my godmother and my grandmother's business partner in Auntie Rose's."

"She looks . . . I don't know, exotic," Tara said. "What's her heritage?"

Sophie paused; the word *exotic* struck her as out of place. Laverne was not "exotic"; her family history was so deep in the Gracious Grove area, there were still places named for the Hodges. But she couldn't think of a reason not to answer, even though it was none of Tara's business. "She always says her family has a bit of every culture in it, but her ancestors are African-American and Seneca Indian, mostly. Why?"

"No reason," Tara said. "My family is so bland. I wish it was more interesting, like yours. I looked up about you. Your dad is, like, mega-rich, right? And your mom is always on the society pages. I saw pictures; she's gorgeous. You're so lucky."

Sophie put on the kettle and sat in a chair opposite the student, regarding her thoughtfully. She would not be deflected from what she had to say. "Tara, you talked about the freedom of the press, but don't you have a responsibility, too? You can say and do whatever you want and label it freedom of the press, but freedom of any kind comes with responsibility. You should be fair. You should be accurate." She paused. "And you should be human."

"As reporters we're not supposed to have feelings about an investigation; we're supposed to stay neutral." Tara blinked, then looked back down at her camera, scanning through her photos again. "It was such a big break, the tip I got about the Mac MacAlister grading alteration. I need more. I need to match that break or—" She shrugged.

"Or you're just a flash in the pan? A one-off?"

Tara nodded.

"Where did you get that information?" Sophie asked suddenly.

"On the grade hike? Someone sent me a note."

"Do you know who it was and just don't want to say? Or was it an anonymous tip?"

"Oh, it was freaking anonymous, all right," Tara said, bitterly. "It was written in all caps, printed off some computer and slipped in an envelope with my name on it. Jeez. If it had been a phone call or a message online, I might have had a chance to trace it. I have a guy who is into computer stuff, and he could have found out where it came from, but no, it had to be old school."

"Which was the point, I guess. Didn't you ever wonder why you were given the tip?" She meant that in two ways, she supposed; she wondered why someone exposed Mac's grade hike, and why in particular to Tara Mitchells.

"No. Should I?"

"I thought reporters were curious about everything." Sophie got up and found the containers of treats she had baked earlier, what seemed so long ago now. How could she say this without being insulting . . . or, in this case, was insulting what she wanted to go for? She turned and gazed at the girl. "I think you were given the tip because someone knew you were the type who would rush to publish the story without a lot of background checking." Sophie had an idea that whomever was actually responsible for the grade scam was also the one who gave the newspaper reporter the tip about Jason. "The important thing is, didn't you think there must be more? Why would just one athlete have his grade elevated? Isn't that the story you want to tell? Expose the fraudster. Get to the bottom of it. *That's* what a good journalist would do."

Tara was silent, staring down at her camera, scanning through photos.

Sophie filled a plate with cookies. "Look, Tara, the problem is, I don't trust you. You lied about what I said, implied awful things about Jason and sabotaged me. You took what I said about Jason's youth and twisted it into something wholly different."

The girl chewed the inside of her cheek. "I won't do it again."

"Aaand we're back to . . . why would I trust you?" There

was iron in Sophie's tone; she had learned, running her own restaurant, that there were times when being nice meant people saw you as soft. So you had to play the bad guy sometimes.

Tara's mouth twitched, and her cheeks stayed red. The kettle whistled, so Sophie got up, found her current favorite blend, a black tea with mandarin peel, spooned some into a diffuser and popped it into the teapot, bobbing the diffuser up and down in the boiling hot water. As she did all that, she kept her eye on Tara. The girl was making a decision, it seemed to Sophie.

Finally, Tara said, her tone snippy, "I think it might be best if you and your grandmother took a more conciliatory approach to me, you know. I'm working as a stringer for a major New York newspaper that is interested in Dean Asquith's murder."

Sophie thought for a moment, considering all the problems with that statement. "Okay, not to be snide, but when you say 'a major New York newspaper,' I wonder; if it was the *Times*, you'd say the *Times*. Likewise the *Daily News*. I have a feeling you are, pardon the pun, trying to fool me with a second-string—at best—newspaper somewhere in New York State, not the city. And why the implied threat? I've already said I don't trust you, and now I think I'll make sure no one I know talks to you. *No* one!" She got her phone out and started writing a text blast for all her friends. "This is what I'll say, and I'll get everyone I know to send it on to all of *their* numbers." She read aloud as she typed: "*If contacted by blond, blue-eyed news reporter Tara Mitchells—or her by any other name—do NOT speak to her; she will twist your words and—*"

"I'm sorry!" Tara looked horrified, eyes wide, body frozen to stillness. "I'm sorry! Look, I shouldn't have done what I did, but I needed a hot quote and you kinda gave it to me, you know?"

"Keep talking," Sophie said, as she rapidly finished the

text and then started adding names from her contact list. Cissy, Dana, Julia, Eli, Wally, Jason and even Thelma.

"How can I get you not to send that? I promise I will report only what you say. I *promise*!"

Sophie shook her head. "Tara, I'm not an idiot . . . or only rarely. I can see all the loopholes in that. Even if you reported accurately what *I* say, you wouldn't feel bound to keep to that with anyone else. No, I think it's best if I warn everyone I know not to talk to you." Her thumb hovered over the send icon as she waited.

"What can I say?" Tara wailed, clutching at her hair. "You won't believe anything I say!"

Sophie nodded. "You're right. That is *exactly* the problem! You might think that nothing you do right now will hurt you, but nowadays the stuff you do as a student can and will follow you. Nothing truly disappears in the digital age." Sophie well knew that; one or two savage online reviews of her restaurant, In Fashion, had followed her. Though it wasn't why her restaurant had ultimately died, it hadn't helped matters any. "You twisted what I said and then lied, writing that I said Jason could easily have hiked Mac's grade. Why?"

"I was . . . trying to open up a dialogue," she said huffily, chin up. "The accusation was out there, so I had to give it a voice, you know, so it could be confirmed or refuted."

"Horse pucky," Laverne said, passing through toward the stairs. She paused and examined the young woman, who stared back uncertainly. "You don't believe that. Stop trying to find an excuse, and admit you did wrong. Tell Sophie *why* you won't do it again, then maybe she'll believe you." Laverne headed upstairs.

Tara was stone faced. She stood and grabbed her jacket and scarf off the floor. "I'll go."

"And I'll send this text," Sophie said, waggling her cell

phone. "Or we could talk, and you could tell me if you noticed anything that night. If you want to report the real story, I'll consider helping, but you have to show me what you're going to write."

Tara paused, eying her, then pulled off her scarf again and removed her jacket, slinging it over the back of her chair, this time. "Look, if we talk, will you not send the text?"

"I'm saving it," Sophie said, hitting save. "If I hear from anyone that you're badgering them, or if I get a whiff that you're lying about what people are saying, it's going out, and it'll expand like a foodie's stomach at a buffet." She laid the phone down on the table. "I saw you hanging around last night. Did you go to each of the tearooms?"

She shrugged moodily. "Kind of. I mean, I followed the group, you know? I took photos."

"So you saw the college registrar and assistant, and the dean and his wife and the coach and his wife."

"And *darling* Kimmy, and Mac, and Mac's parents; I saw them all."

Sophie tried to think about what she needed to know, but she was so exhausted, thinking was becoming difficult. She squinted. Laverne came back downstairs and clapped her hands together.

"Is this young lady staying for lunch?"

Sophie shook her head, but Tara brightened and said, "Sure. What are we having?"

"Sophie made a lovely soup yesterday, a cream of cauliflower harvest vegetable with smoked gouda. I think I'll heat that up and we'll have some of those cheese biscuits you baked in the middle of the night," she said, squeezing Sophie's shoulder.

Minutes later they all sat down together at one of the tables in the tearoom. Nana and Laverne exchanged glances.

"So, Tara, what are you attending Cruickshank for?" Nana asked.

"Communications and journalism," the girl said, then spooned up the soup, rolling her eyes at the flavor. "This is out of this world," she muttered, then buttered a cheese tea biscuit and dipped it in the soup, eating more.

"Everything's so different nowadays," Laverne mused. "With the Internet and cable TV, and mobile devices. Folks get their news from so many sources. My niece Cindy spends half her day online, between schoolwork and socializing. Who knows what to trust online."

"I heard one person at the tea stroll talking about that," Nana said. "She said something about trolls and I thought she was talking about fairy tales, but I guess that's something online?"

"That's people who purposely stir up trouble online. They may even lie or misrepresent things to get folks fighting," Sophie said. Tara was paying attention, she thought, even if she was eating. Time to inject a little pointed reference. "That's the problem; who do you trust? I think that's where news organizations need to step in and become a trusted source."

Laverne snorted. "Hmph . . . too many reporters want to stir things up, not report on the facts. Insert themselves in the story, muckrake, fake quotes, don't do the research."

"Now, Laverne, I'm sure there are good reporters out there," Nana said. "And maybe the new generation will realize that personal ethics are all we have left in this world. Each person has to make a choice as to what they'll do that day, tell the truth or cast slurs and aspersions."

Tara stopped and eyed them all. "I get it. I *get* it! You're all ganging up on me," she said, and threw her spoon down, folding her arms over her chest. "Fine. I'm the bad guy here."

"You were when you lied in print," Laverne said. "Who will hold you to a higher standard if you don't hold yourself to it? You have in your hand the power of the truth. If you don't choose to use that power, if you prefer lies, then what are you?"

"A novelist," Nana said, with a chortle. Laverne chuckled with her friend.

"All right, enough," Sophie said, smiling at her godmother and grandmother. She had an out-of-body moment, brought on by too much drama and not enough sleep, probably. For a moment she saw herself through Tara's eyes, a grown-up, an adult with responsibilities, lecturing a teenager at the dinner table. It was weird. "Tara, I don't want you to feel you're being ganged up on, but they have a point and you know it. One thing is true; you have a choice to make. Are you going to be the kind of reporter people can trust to tell the truth, or are you going to make stuff up to sell papers? I know it's not that simple, but it could be. It *should* be!"

Tara nodded and ate the rest of her soup. She put her spoon down finally, and wiped her mouth. "That was good, thank you. When my mom comes to town to pick me up, I'll bring her here for lunch." She looked at each one of them. "I'm going to be deadly honest for once. Sophie, after I wrote the piece and it was published, I . . . I was sorry. Honestly. I tried *not* to be sorry, but I was.

"It's one thing to type it, but then you see it in print, and hear people talking about it, and I got that the words . . ." She paused and sighed. "The student editor doesn't care; he doesn't take the *Clarion* seriously, not like I do. I want his job next year. I was looking to cause a controversy, get people talking, but I realized too late that the words I wrote changed how some people saw Mr. Murphy. They took every word I wrote as the truth and didn't even question it. I had already decided never to do that again, but I didn't know how to tell you. I'm sorry."

"Don't apologize to me," Sophie said. "Apologize to Jason."

"I will."

Maybe she was being a naive idiot, but she believed Tara. However . . . she'd still be careful what she said to her. "So did you see anything last night?"

"A few things. At some point it seemed like everyone was fighting. Even Professor Dandridge . . . she was upset at something the dean said."

"Why do you say that?"

"She was crying."

Sophie grabbed her phone and texted Julia a note, asking about Tara's assertion. The professor hadn't said anything about that at their meeting that morning. "Anything else?"

"Yeah. I saw the dean's wife sneak off."

"When was this? And where did she go?"

"It was late. Everything was wrapping up for the night. She got in a car and took off."

"A car? What kind of car?"

"How should I know? Something noisy, that's all. It was dark blue and small. She didn't go far, I don't think. I saw that same car parked on a side street not too far from here a little later, as I was waiting for my ride back to Cruickshank."

Jeanette Asquith; Sophie followed a line of thought. Elizabeth Lemmon had said that the dean's wife was a gossip, and had said that a professor was responsible for the grade hike. Could she have been trying to cover up for her boyfriend Paul, who was also a likely candidate for the cheater? And was her phone conversation a confirmation that she told Paul he had better kill her husband that very night because they were *running out of time*; in other words,

Dean Asquith was going to expose him as the culprit the very next day? But why would the dean have had the systems engineer looking into the cheating scandal in the first place? He must have trusted him . . . misplaced trust, perhaps?

It was a puzzle, and she'd have to find some way of establishing Mrs. Asquith's and Paul Wechsler's whereabouts at the time of the crime.

Tara got some quotes from them about how shocked they were at what happened, and how they hoped the police would wrap things up quickly. Sophie agreed to call Tara if she heard anything that she could use for the New York newspaper, which, as Sophie had suspected, was actually a small upstate weekly, not a city newspaper.

Most importantly from the school newspaper's aspect, Tara agreed that she should be looking into whether other athletes' grades were hiked. Sophie had basically gotten that confirmation from Paul Wechsler, who said the alterations occurred in two areas—which if she had to guess meant two different sports, like basketball and football, the biggest marquee sporting events in college—but she wasn't about to feed Tara the info. Let her find out on her own.

After the student reporter left, Sophie retreated to her apartment and curled up on her feather duvet with Pearl, falling into a deep immediate sleep, and didn't awaken until the sun's rays slanted across her bedroom wall in a golden stream. It was late in the day; she had slept for hours. She emerged from her cocoon and descended, yawning.

Cindy, Laverne's niece, was there helping her aunt finish the carpets in the tearoom.

"Laverne, I told you *I'd* help with that," Sophie said, feeling bad for not doing her part.

"Honey, you were up all night and you needed your rest.

Besides, Cindy is happy to help after school and make a little spending money, aren't you, sweet girl?" she said, hugging her niece.

The girl smiled and nodded, her green eyes sparkling. "I'm saving to go to Darien Lake next summer. I'll be almost sixteen by then, and can go with some friends. My mom said as long as I can pay for part, she'd kick in the rest."

Laverne pushed the heavy carpet-cleaning machine away into the corner. "I don't know why this danged thing is clogging up. Just getting old, I guess, like the rest of us. What did you do to it last time it acted up like this?" she asked Sophie.

"There's one filter that's hidden. I'll clean it out for you; leave the machine here," Sophie said.

Laverne returned to the two younger people as there was a tap at the side door. Cindy jumped and hopped over to it, throwing it open.

Josh Sinclair sauntered in, smirking at Cindy, who swiftly disappeared and came back with her jacket thrown over her arm.

"What gives?" Sophie asked, yawning and stretching.

"The natural science exhibit at the college. I'm taking Cindy. Remember?" Josh said, in that tone that implied all the world must know the most important thing in his life.

"I have to go to the bathroom first," Cindy said and disappeared.

"Hey, Sophie, I had a free period this afternoon, so I was out at Cruickshank tutoring a guy on American history," he said, carefully pushing back his reddish-brown hair. He wore a golf shirt over jeans with an oversized Cruickshank College blue-and-silver jacket over it all. He jammed his hands in his jacket pocket. "I got a lift back into town with Miss Fletcher; she's the assistant registrar at Cruickshank."

"I was talking to her this morning about the . . . you

know." Sophie hooked her thumb over her shoulder toward the drama out their front door.

"Yeah, she told me. She said you got her to thinking about a lot of stuff." Josh leaned against the kitchen counter, his eyes thoughtful. "By the way, the cops are mostly gone from out front."

"Josh, I think it's disrespectful to call them cops," Laverne said as she got her own jacket from the coat closet off the kitchen. "They are police officers, or the police."

Sophie rolled her eyes, but Josh nodded. "Yes, Miss Hodge. Anyway, Wally is still outside, so I stopped to talk to him," he said to Sophie. "He asked me to tell you to call police headquarters because Detective Miller would like to speak to you all again."

"Okay. Anyway, how do you know Brenda Fletcher?"

"From registering for summer courses and stuff like that at Cruickshank." Josh was just seventeen, but he had already completed several courses at Cruickshank toward his undergrad degree. He was extremely smart, as evidenced by him tutoring college-level students. "We talk sometimes, about her days in college, you know? She's been cool. I told her a few weeks ago about knowing you and Mrs. Freemont from the tearoom and from the Silver Spouts."

"What did she have to say? You said that I got her thinking?"

"Yeah, right. She gave me a lift," he repeated. "She has got the most rad sports car; *totally* awesome. It's a Porsche Boxster, you know?"

He, like most young fellows, was obsessed lately with cars, now that he had his license. "Yes, all right, *and . . . ?*" Sophie prompted.

He glanced around toward the washroom, shifting from foot to foot. All those teen hormones, Sophie thought, zipping this way and that. He was distracted. "Josh, what did she say?

"Oh, right. She said she's worried. I guess she snooped a bit after talking to you. She asked if I could pass on a message."

"What is it?"

"Well, it's not quite a message, more like a question. She said to ask you, did you think that whoever killed Dean Asquith did it to hide some other kind of crime?"

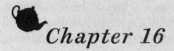

Chapter 16

Sophie wondered what triggered Brenda's question. It merited a face-to-face conversation, though, not a phone call and not a text message. "I don't even know how to answer that."

Josh glanced toward the bathroom, and at Laverne, who was getting her things together. She would be driving the young couple out to the college natural history display, Laverne had explained, because Cindy's parents didn't feel comfortable with Josh driving her yet, even though he now had his license. He sidled closer to Sophie and murmured, "I've been thinking . . . who would she know about other than Mr. Nomuro? And I did a little digging, you know, about the grade-fixing thing? The person with the easiest access to the grades is the registrar."

"Or his assistant," Sophie amended.

"Sure, but he has the final say and takes a final look."

"At least he's *supposed* to; who knows if he actually does?"

"I guess. But he's *supposed* to be ultimate authority, in this case." Josh had a tendency to debate everything. "If he's diligent, he'd check things through."

"That's not enough to convict the man," Sophie said with finality. She was still thinking about Paul Wechsler; as the systems engineer at the school, he would likely know a hundred ways to change a grade even after the registrar had signed off on them, and he was definitely in need of money if he wanted to support Jeanette Asquith in the style to which she was accustomed. Spilling the info to her earlier could have been a quick cover-up on his part, trying his best to act like an innocent in the matter.

And there was still Heck Donovan to consider; he had a distinct reason to want Mac MacAlister, and probably others on his team, to keep playing. She knew virtually nothing about the coach. For all she or anyone else knew, he was a computer genius, or had a hacker son. Too many suspects, all gathered at the tea stroll.

"I was wondering, Soph . . . maybe Miss Fletcher is doing a little digging, you know?" Josh said. "Figuring things out?"

"I hope she's not talking about it to her boss. If he *is* the killer, she could be putting herself in jeopardy," Sophie remarked, remembering what she had heard from Julia about Nomuro and the dean having a heated exchange. "But she didn't strike me as dumb."

Sophie got a text from Jason; he was at police headquarters waiting to talk to the detective again. They wanted to know where he was every minute of the evening, and had told him what he said didn't accord with some of the other accounts of the evening from others about his behavior and actions. A pain shot through her stomach. She texted him a quick note, reminding him of their late texting back and forth, and how, with the police's forensic abilities, they would be able to establish where he was from that. She hoped.

"There *has* to be a way to figure out who was where, maybe eliminate some people from the pool of suspects," she murmured, mostly to herself. To Josh she said, "I'll go out to the college tomorrow morning to speak with Brenda."

Laverne left with Cindy and Josh, and Nana hobbled into the kitchen from the tearoom with a clipboard, which she laid on the kitchen counter. "I'm done in. My feet hurt, my knees hurt . . . *everything* hurts. It's early to bed for me."

Sophie hugged her little grandmother, remembering distinctly what it was like to hug her when she was just a child, and her Nana seemed so tall, her rock in a world where she didn't fit in. "You've been doing too much and worrying too much," she said, not sharing her own concerns about Jason being questioned by the police. "I'm tucking you into bed with a bowl of soup, Pearlie-Girlie and a mystery. Leave thinking about crimes to the fictional world."

Nana set her granddaughter away from her and gazed into her eyes, a serious look on her soft, plump face. "Sweetie, don't think you have to protect me. I know my health scare gave you a rough time. I'm okay, for now, but I am getting up there. God willing I'll be here a few more years, but you must not worry about it." She touched Sophie's cheek. "This is *your* time. We're all given an allotment of years to be young, and I don't want you wasting yours worrying about me."

Sophie paused, compressed her lips, but then saw the determined expression on her grandmother's face. That only meant one thing to Sophie: instant capitulation. "Okay, I've got it. I love you, Nana. I can't promise I'll stop worrying, but I'll remember to have some fun, too."

"Honey, I mean it. You *have* to stop worrying about me. You'll make me very unhappy unless you let go of that, let me live my life the way I see fit. You can't wrap me in cotton any more than I can keep you from suffering the pains and sorrows of being young."

Pains and sorrows, slings and arrows; she stopped, mouth open, about to protest, but then thought for a moment. "I've been doing that, haven't I?" She hadn't even realized that her own worrying about her grandmother was causing Nana sorrow. "Okay, I get it. I don't want you to be unhappy, so I will do my best to stop worrying about you. I guess one way to get my mind off everything else is to call my mother."

Her words were laden with sarcasm, but Nana seemed pleased. "That is a grand idea! Tell Rosalind I'll call her this weekend."

"I have some questions for her. The dean's wife, Jeanette, knows Mom, and I hope she'll be able to tell me what the woman is like, and maybe some things about the Asquith family. But it'll probably go south from there. I want to know the truth about how much Mom had to do with me being hired by Bartleby's, and why she feels the need to keep interfering in my life."

Nana sighed and cupped her granddaughter's shoulder. "Honey, I have no doubt that Rosalind wished she could have had that same conversation with me when I wanted her to come back to Gracious Grove after school, and tried to guilt her into doing it. Go easy on her, honey; you may not appreciate it now, but your mother loves you."

"Okay, I got it. But first I'm going to do something fun. I'm going to take apart the carpet cleaner and see what's clogging it."

* * *

Thelma Mae Earnshaw watched Gilda squirm into the oven to clean it, her butt wiggling like she was a goat trying to get out of a python's grasp. That was the problem with watching all them nature shows; you saw stuff like that, a big snake eating a goat. As Cissy often said, there are some things you wish you could unsee. She shuddered and looked back down at her phone. She had tried sending a text, but all it said was *sending* . . . and it never said *sent*, like Cissy showed her it would. Took darned longer to tap the message in, using that stylist thingie Cissy had given her—stylish, style list, whatever they called it—than it would to call and say what she had to say.

Instead, she got the camera part of it on the screen and held the phone up, taking an unflattering photo of Gilda, though her own arthritic finger also featured prominently in the photo. She'd been doing that a lot lately, using the camera. It sure was fun, but it would be even better if she knew how to send a picture, and had someone to send it to. Folks would get a giggle out of that! She'd been doing that same thing all evening during the tea stroll, taking photos when folks didn't know it, but darned if she could find them now. Sometimes she knew where to look, and at others, they seemed to disappear into some filing system of their own making.

She sighed. She was feeling real fidgety today. They should be open, making money, not sitting there closed, with nothing to do. A couple of groups had had to be turned away already, and it sure didn't do them any good to be tied in with that murder, and all because she had been part of that tea stroll nonsense. How could they capitalize on the publicity it was supposed to bring if they couldn't even open?

"We gotta solve this murder, that's all there is to it!" she said.

Gilda smacked her head on the top of the oven and crawled out with the greasy cleaning rag, staring at Thelma like she'd seen a ghost. "By 'we' you mean 'me' don't you?"

Gilda was still sore that Thelma had sent her outside to take out the garbage the previous night after seeing that fellow from the college skulking around. "No, I mean 'we,' as in me, too. Who knows how long it'll take those doodyheads at the police department to figure this out if we don't take a hand in it? I solved the last two, and I can solve this one."

"You did *not* solve the last two! Sophie Taylor did most of the work, and the police came in and cleaned up the mess."

"You've gotten real mouthy and disrespectful lately, Gilda Bachman! I shoulda never invited you to stay under my roof, but out of the kindness of my heart, I did."

Gilda was about to bellyache back, but at that moment the grand Pooh-Bah himself, Sweet Pea the Siamese cat, strolled down the stairs and into the kitchen, looking around as if trying to find his throne. Gilda immediately went all silly-clingy with the cat, plopping her big butt down on a chair, picking him up, settling him on her lap and crooning over him as if he were a baby, while she stroked his smoky fur and tickled under his chin. He put up with her foolishness, but Thelma knew he was far too dignified to be treated like some dumb normal cat. When they were alone Thelma talked to Sweet Pea, and he had a way of slowly blinking as he looked up at her that let her know he agreed with her entirely.

Gilda had never had kids, and Thelma supposed that was what happened to women who never had children; they went batty over cats. Thelma didn't mind the cat, but he sure did get more than his fair share of attention! All he had to do was meow, and it was as if he was a two-year-old doing algebra; Gilda went nuts about how clever he was.

Though he did seem smart, except that he liked Gilda,

which made her question that intelligence. Or maybe he appreciated having staff.

"I gotta go out," Thelma said, heaving herself to her feet.

"Oh, do you want me to go instead?" Gilda said, with a troubled expression on her plain face.

"No, you stay here and hold down the fort," Thelma replied, as if Gilda was a soldier defending against all comers, like in one of them old gladiator movies. More likely, she'd thaw herself a few or a dozen of Sophie Taylor's cookies and make a big pot of tea and put her feet up, petting Sweet Pea and humming "She'll Be Coming 'Round the Mountain."

But Thelma had things to do, a crime to investigate, so she'd don her invisible deerstalker cap, pick up her magnifying lens and go out hunting. Shirley Holmes, on the trail!

T here was no avoiding it, Sophie decided. After cleaning out the carpet shampooer—what was clogging the hidden filter was an unfortunate amount of cat fur, human hair and shredded feathers, a strange combination if ever there was one—she had to phone her mother.

"Yes, we're fine, Mom," Sophie said, pacing the length of her little apartment on the top floor of the house. After that came a rapid string of questions . . .

"What is going on in Gracious Grove? I mean, really, Sophie, dear . . . three murders in just a few months?"

"I know it's unusual, but we're not in any danger."

"Are you sure? I worry about your grandmother, you know, even though you think I don't."

"We're both fine, and no, we don't need Daddy or you to come here. Daddy's in Shanghai and you're in Tahiti, anyway."

"Not Tahiti, dear . . . I've moved on. It's Bali."

"Oh, Bali. Did I call at a bad time?"

"For you there is no bad time," Rosalind Taylor said, her sleepy voice honeyed with love.

How did you reply to that and still be angry? Sophie wasn't sure what to say. Just the way she had thought of that showed her that she wanted to stay angry at her mother. She was holding on to it, coddling it, stoking her anger like a blast furnace. Why?

She plunked down in a soft chair and amused herself with clicking through the TV channels while her mother described the absolutely gorgeous new resort she had discovered, and how she was trying to get Sophie's father to join her there. When Rosalind Taylor paused for a breath, Sophie decided to take the bull by the horns.

"Mom, when I left Bartleby's the owner said some stuff I'd like you to explain." She told her mother what Adrian Van Sant had told her, that his father had been bribed by Sophie's mother to hire her as sous chef at Bartleby's on Shinnecock in order to get her back to the Hamptons, where there was potential to meet a wealthy mate, rather than be stuck in Gracious Grove near strictly middle-class Jason Murphy. The last bit Sophie had inferred, but felt it was true.

There was silence for a long minute. Then Rosalind said, her voice soft, "Sophie, darling, it's not like that at all. I don't have a thing against Jason, really, but—"

"No, what you have something against is any hope for me to have a happy life." Sophie paused; she didn't like the sound of her own voice. It was hard and sharp, like flint, and ugly.

"You can't possibly be happy there in Gracious Grove, Sophie, not in the long term. Oh, you *think* you will be, but it's not your home."

"Mom, it's not *your* home, but I love it here and you know

that. I'm thirty, Mom, *thirty*! Not sixteen, not ten, not five. I'm staying here, maybe for the rest of my life. You need to make peace with that." That was better; assertive but not nasty.

There was silence for a long minute.

"So did Adrian tell the truth?" she asked. "Did you bribe Mr. Van Sant to hire me?"

"I don't think that matters now, does it?" Rosalind favored avoidance over denial. She chatted about coming home to New York in time to celebrate her anniversary with Sophie's father. "The trick is getting him there at the same time as me," she admitted.

"Mom, changing the topic, I do have another question," Sophie said. It was pointless to hammer away at her mother about the restaurant. "Do you know Jeanette Asquith? She has a home in the Hamptons near ours."

"Well sure, I know Jeanette. We've been on some of the same boards."

"What is she like?"

"A lovely person, even though she's *much* older than me," Rosalind said.

Sophie grinned and shook her head. Rosalind and Jeanette were probably about the same age. *Much older* in her mother's lingo meant a few months, or a whole year, perhaps.

"Last time I saw her, she had let her hair go gray. I hear that's the fashion now, but I will not be following that particular trend." Rosalind Taylor's hair was perpetually a soft, golden, youthful blond.

"Anyway it's her husband, Dale Asquith, who was murdered on our doorstep."

"Oh *dear*! Poor Jeanette! I can't believe that, Dale Asquith? I'll need to send her a note of condolence. What does one say to a widow whose husband has been murdered?"

"I'm sure Emily Post has advice. Who in the family has

the money? I've heard their families were entwined business-wise. Can you find out anything about that?" There was silence on the other end. "Mom, I don't want to make you do anything you're not comfortable with."

"It's not that . . . it's just . . . you've never asked me to do *anything* for you before."

It was Sophie's turn to be silent; she wasn't sure what to say.

"Of course, I'll *do* it! I'm just surprised and . . . and touched. All I want is to help you be happy."

That was what Nana said about Rosalind, but Sophie had never seen it that way. "So who *does* have the money in the family?"

"You've come to the right person. There isn't much I don't know about who has what money among the financially viable of this country." Her tone was unexpectedly wry and full of self-knowledge. "When Jeanette and Dale married, it wasn't so much a marriage as a merger, the joke among our set went. It was an agreement put together by their fathers, and it seems to have worked remarkably well for many years. Neither wanted children, or at least that's what Jeanette always said. That seemed so sad to me; I don't know what I'd do without you or your brothers."

Sophie rolled her eyes, but then stopped. She was being disrespectful, if only in thought, and that was not honoring her grandmother's request that she try to be kinder to her mother. Rosalind Taylor may not be a conventionally huggy-kissy mom, but there had been moments in her life that Sophie remembered; a cool hand on her brow when she was sick, a night spent crying on her mother's shoulder over a dead pet, and how hurt her mother had seemed when every school holiday, Sophie chose to spend it in Gracious Grove rather than whatever big trip her mother planned. She took a deep breath. "So you don't think they ever loved each other?"

"I didn't say that, but everyone knew that they each had . . . outside interests."

"That's still true. He had a mistress and she has a boy toy, a younger guy who is crazy about her. Mom, do you think she'd have any reason to kill him?"

Rosalind thought for a long minute. "I cannot imagine. You've only seen her once or twice, I gather, but Jeanette is exquisitely cultured. She's calm, not passionate. I can't see her killing Dale. Why would she?"

"Not even to leave her life as a college dean's wife? I understand she hates it."

"I don't know who you've been listening to, but there was nothing keeping her there. I think she rather enjoyed the collegial life, and she always has the house in the Hamptons and the pied-à-terre in Paris if she wearied of it."

It was Kimmy who had suggested Jeanette Asquith hated the college life. Did she have a reason? Was it in an attempt to throw suspicion onto the dean's wife? Or an opinion shared as fact? "How are their finances? Did they have money? I mean, money in the sense that Daddy has money? And what happens now that the dean has been killed?"

"Both sides have old money, and quite a bit of it. Dale was ambitious because he thought being a dean gave him a certain image that he appreciated. His older brother was the star of the family, you know; he took over the business reins from their father. I think Dale went out of his way to differentiate himself from that business life, even though he has a business degree from some prestigious business school in Canada. But if I understand their case correctly—and I believe I do—if one of them died, the other inherited everything from their marriage agreement."

"Sounds like a dangerous agreement to have."

"But why, darling? The agreement was very specific as to

what was included and what was not. I know for a fact Dale always used his marriage as a way to keep his girlfriends in their place. He would *never* divorce, and every single one of them knew that. It was probably the same for Jeanette. A very chilly woman, if you ask me, but one who has always known exactly what she wanted and how to get it. And speaking of cold . . . it must be getting positively frigid in Gracious Grove. Winter is coming. Will you come and visit me if I go to Aruba or Sint Maarten over Christmas?"

Sophie paused, but could think of no nice way to say what she felt, that she was looking forward to spending Christmas in Gracious Grove, and to helping out in the tearoom, experimenting with holiday treats. And spending time with Jason, Dana, Cissy and the others, as well as Laverne and Nana. "We'll talk more often, Mom, I promise. But no more tricks to get me back to 'society,' okay?"

"From now on, no more tricks. I'll see if I can find out anything more about Dale and Jeanette, but I don't think there's much more to tell. Their marriage worked for them both, if you ask me. Every marriage is different, darling. Like your father's and mine; we don't spend a lot of time together, but . . . but we love each other. We really do."

When they hung up, Sophie felt slightly uneasy, but she wasn't sure why.

On a lonely back road, Thelma gunned the motor of her old car and tooled along as twilight darkened the sky. She pulled up at the gates of Cruickshank College, turned into the drive and followed it back to the dormitories. Many, many years ago she had snuck out here to visit a boy, back when no one in her set of friends thought of sex before marriage—only bad girls did that sort of thing—and "making out" meant a little kissing under the bleachers.

She sat and looked up at the dormitory building, a turn-of-the-century ivy-covered three-story redbrick with white stone caps and corbels. If what she'd heard was right, then all this hooey and the dean being murdered came down to one spoiled brat athlete named Mac MacAlister, who didn't have two brains to rub together and needed a piece of someone's mind. Maybe some of Thelma's. And if someone had faked up his grade, he would sure as heck know who did it. He'd play dumb—and *be* dumb, sounded like—but maybe, just maybe, a surprise attack would have him admitting who puffed his grade for him.

Enough thinking. Doing was more her style.

She eased herself out of the car and wrapped her heavy sweater around her. She had come prepared, and grabbed a bag full of cookies from the passenger seat, then hobbled up the steps to the dorm, easing through the door as a skinny, pale student came out with an armload of books, holding the door open for her while eyeing her with some surprise.

She grunted her thanks, but then turned before letting the door close behind her. "I'm looking for my grandson, tall feller, reddish hair, basketball player. Do you know where I might find Mac?"

The kid's eyes widened. "Mac MacAlister?"

"Who else, Mac Aroni?"

The guy smiled. "His room is third floor, to the left." He rolled his eyes and shifted his books. "You can't miss it; he's always got some of the other b-ball players hanging around, or some girl who is mooning over him. It smells like beer belches and stale perfume."

Third floor. Why did it have to be the third floor? She

eased into the dorm, letting the door swing shut, and stared; three flights of polished wood stairs wound up. And up. And up!

There was a clatter from above and a girl stomped down the stairs, yelling a string of curse words over her shoulder. As she turned back she spotted Thelma and paused, hand on the polished wood railing, turning beet-pickle red. "Sorry," she muttered, as she continued past Thelma toward the door.

"Hey, you, is there an elevator here?"

The girl paused. "An elevator upstairs?"

"No, I want the one that only goes down," Thelma growled. Seeing the confusion on the girl's face, she said, "Of *course*, an elevator up!"

She shook her head, then paused and said, "Well, there *is* a freight elevator for taking furniture up, you know. But it's locked."

"I guess I'll have to climb," Thelma said. "And you . . . stop swearing. No boy likes a girl with a mouth like a sailor."

"Yeah, well Mac can kiss my—"

"Mac MacAlister?"

"Sure." The girl eyed her. "Do you know him?"

Thelma considered her cover story, but decided not to use it again unless she had to. "You his girlfriend?"

"Mac doesn't have a girlfriend, singular," she said with an angry sniff. "He's got several girls on the string, including his adviser—some desperate chick named Kimmy. Honest, I never saw such a bunch of desperate women in my life!" She made a rude gesture upward, tears glistening in her eyes. "And then he gives *me* the cold shoulder when all I want to do is help him out with his geography term paper. Says he doesn't need my help, he can buy whatever he wants. Well, he can kiss my . . . atlas. He tells me I'm his girl, and then as soon as he gets chugging beer with his buddies he forgets about me. Well I'm *done*. He's dumb as a stump anyway, and not even hot. He may be the best Cruickshank can produce, but that's not saying much."

"You're better off without him, honey, let me tell you that. Anyone who has to bribe his way into a degree probably peaked in high school."

As the girl stomped out of the dorm, Thelma began the long and arduous climb up. This better be worth it.

As she drove home an hour later, she thought it had. Not in the way she expected, but in a totally different way.

Chapter 17

S ophie awoke the next day with determination
in her heart. Jason had called her late the night before
and they talked at length; though the police were still completely polite to him, they had made it clear that he was a
suspect. Someone, they didn't say who, had given an account
of the evening that differed enough from his that they were
trying to substantiate his version.

He had given them his phone and they had one of their
guys go through it; he hoped it helped establish where he
was at the time of the crime. Given their suspicion of him,
he needed to stay out of their informal investigation; how
would it look if he was badgering some of his colleagues at
Cruikshank? Somehow, some way, Sophie needed to figure
out who killed Dean Asquith on their doorstep, and clear
Jason.

She realized that the one person who was unaccounted
for in all of this was Sherri Shaw. What if the dean's murder

had absolutely nothing to do with the grade alteration? That was as likely as anything. She called Dana, who in an aside told Sophie that she would be speaking to Wally about Cissy that day at some point, and asked her one question.

Half an hour later Dana got back to her with an answer; Sherri Shaw worked at a downtown dress shop that catered to the well-heeled in Gracious Grove. Dana offered to visit the shop, since she could do so with the view to look at their wedding dress collection, and find out where Sherri went that night after the tea stroll.

As she made tea and put together a tray with soft-boiled eggs and toast, Sophie pondered what she knew, and what she didn't. The dean had a wound on his neck, but his death had been caused by being stabbed in the chest. But there was also that drool, the bluish skin and the contorted hands, which suggested poisoning. Why multiple wounds? Why poison? And why, then, a final stabbing? Had the intent been to kill him another way and he wouldn't die? Like Rasputin, she thought, remembering from a long-ago history lesson on the Russian that he was both poisoned and shot.

And why was Dean Asquith murdered on *their* doorstep in particular? It could be happenstance, she supposed, but wasn't it more likely that the killer wanted it to happen there, as opposed to in front of SereniTea or Belle Époque, because of the salted tea incident, and her own connection to Jason? If that was true, it indicated a killer who was present at the tea stroll and saw what went down, and who also understood Sophie's connection to Jason, supposedly the prime suspect in the grade scandal.

But was the killing related to the grading scandal, or incidental to it? There were two sets of suspects, those who were involved with the college and the grading scandal, and those who may have had personal reasons for wanting Dale

Asquith dead. This morning, she would handle the college side of things, while Dana helped her with the personal side.

There was still a police presence on their street. Nana was that very morning going with Laverne to police headquarters to speak with the detective, as was Sophie, at some point. Her grandmother desperately wanted to reopen Auntie Rose's, but the front was still cordoned off, though the white tarp enclosure was gone, and the only folks strolling the street were what Laverne called "looky loos." Sophie circled to the back parking lot and hopped in her car, revving the engine and backing out of the parking spot.

Sophie stopped the Jetta while still in the laneway and scanned the houses across the street, knowing that the police would have canvassed every neighbor by then, to find out if they'd seen or noticed anything. Those poor long-suffering folks were likely not pleased with Auntie Rose's at this point. Maybe they could do a neighborhood tea party to try to regain some good neighborly feelings. People on their street were very patient with the increased traffic that came from having several tearooms.

She noticed a neighbor, one of their defenders, standing across the street and waving to get her attention. Sophie got out of her car and crossed. "Good morning, Mr. Bellows," she said.

"Morning, Sophie," he said, his voice as creaky as a door in a horror film. "How is your grandmother holding up after all this?"

Sophie smiled down at the elderly gentleman, a tiny gnome of a fellow stooped over a tripod cane, with a few wisps of hair over a bald head. "She's doing all right. I worry, of course, because of the health scare we had."

He nodded. "You tell her to take it easy and let folks help. She's an independent woman, is Rose Freemont. When my

Mary was alive, Rose was sweet as could be about taking her shopping when I was laid up with the surgery."

Garfield Bellows had been a good friend to Sophie's grandmother over the years. He was one of the few residents still living on the street from before it became a tea drinkers mecca, and had been supportive of Auntie Rose's, though he sometimes got cranky about tour buses blocking his drive. He was also still sharp as a dagger and despite thick glasses, noticed more than most a quarter his age.

"Mr. Bellows, did the police speak to you about that night?"

"The night of the murder? Sure did. Wally first, then that woman detective." He looked up at Sophie, twisting his whole body to do so. He had hurt his back badly in an industrial accident many years before and had some fused disks in his spine, meaning he couldn't turn easily. "I was sitting by my front window, that evening, watching all the hoopla. Best entertainment I've had in years, or it would have been if someone hadn't died at the end of it. I'm sorry about that, for his wife and kids, if he had any."

"He was married, but didn't have children, that I know of, anyway." Sophie was trying to think of a way to ask him if he'd seen anything.

He cast her another sly, body-twisting look. "You might want to know what I saw. What are the police going to do, throw me in jail?" He gave a rusty laugh, and talked, giving her a complete rundown of everything he saw from his side of the street up to and including the late-night skulker that Mrs. Earnshaw claimed was Vince Nomuro.

"Did you get a good look at him?"

"Not really. Can't imagine how Thelma was able to identify him from her window. She was upstairs when she saw him, right? Leastways, that's what Gilda told me. Thelma

Mae Earnshaw may have the sight of a bald eagle, or she may have the imagination of Isaac Asimov, but she don't have both. I'm leaning toward the imagination."

It didn't surprise Sophie that Gilda Bachman had already been over spilling everything about her employer's perfidy in sending her outside to do the garbage when she had seen someone slinking around the property. She had been complaining about Thelma since the day she started working for her, and it didn't look like that would ever change. "So you didn't notice if the person was wearing a hat?"

"Kinda looked like it, but I couldn't swear to it."

"Mr. Bellows, I heard a noise a while before I found the body, and when I looked out, I thought I saw two people embracing. Did you see anything like that?"

He squinted and screwed up his mouth, then said, "Yuh, I think I know what you mean. I was coming back from the bathroom 'bout then. I heard a noisy little car, and I kinda saw it, but I couldn't get a make and model. I think I saw two people talking or hugging, but they disappeared into the shadows. Hey, you see all manner of things if you watch long enough. I told the police all about it." He craned his neck and stared up at her. "You think I saw murder done?"

"It's possible we both saw murder done." A chill raced down her back. She knew the approximate time she had seen what she thought was someone hugging or dancing; if it was true, she had something to go on, and could maybe eliminate some of the suspects on her radar. She should be letting the police handle it all, but she still fully intended to snoop. "What was your impression of the people?"

"Well, now, one looked like a fella, tall, like that dean was, you know. The other . . . I had the impression it was a gal, but I wonder now, was that because I thought they were a couple, hugging? Not that two fellas—or two gals—can't hug, but you know . . . it felt like that." He shrugged and tapped his cane on the pavement. "I don't know what I'm saying. Don't know if you should listen to me or not."

"I'm not sure of what I saw myself, Mr. Bellows. I wish I did. I had the impression one of the two was shorter than the other, but that unfortunately describes almost everyone, given that the dean was quite tall. I'd better get going."

"Give my love to your grandmother, and tell her and Laverne to come visit me sometime. And bring some scones."

Wally was sitting in his cruiser watching her speak to Mr. Bellows. She was undecided for a moment, and thought of going over to talk to him, but instead she smiled, waved, got in her car and took off. She was too anxious to go to police headquarters right away, so she drove out of town. She didn't have a plan, yet, but maybe being there would inspire something.

Cruickshank College campus in autumn was lovely. The old brick and stone buildings were set amid oak, maple and birch trees going golden and red as autumn advanced. She parked in front of the administrative building, a redbrick structure with a bell tower in the center. Jason told her that it was the oldest college building, once housing all the classes as well as administration. The autumn sun made the windows glisten gold.

The parking lot was off to one side, not full, but with probably twenty cars, three of which were Gracious Grove police cars. Detective Morris would not be pleased if she thought Sophie was snooping where she oughtn't and had come out to the college before stopping at the police station, so Sophie kept her wits about her as she dashed up the steps and into the cool, dim entry of the college administration building.

From the directory board in the entrance she learned that President Schroeder and Provost Vilansky's offices were on the second floor, along with boardrooms, while the various deans had offices on the main floor, along with the registrar, administration and various student services.

She passed from the entrance into the inner hallway along with a flow of students hefting backpacks, purses and laptop cases. Cruickshank's stately atmosphere was somewhat diminished by the sight of students squabbling in the halls, examining the cluttered bulletin board on the wall by the office door, and standing in the main office at a chest-high counter complaining to harried staff. It appeared to be a hub for student services, scheduling, finances and other aspects of collegiate life, so kids were whining about class timetables, late grants, extra fees and even dorm conditions. Sophie poked her head in the office, but ducked back out to the hall and glanced around, doing her best to be inconspicuous while getting her bearings.

The halls were wide, with polished hardwood floors and bright lighting that glared off the glass cases holding academic and sport trophies, more of the former than the latter. Along the wall toward the deans' offices (indicated by small signs that jutted out from over each door) was a line of paintings and photos of Cruickshank College presidents, provosts and deans through the years, almost entirely male, older and white. Diversity did not seem to have penetrated Cruickshank administration in the slightest, though the student body appeared diverse enough. She passed the dean of students' closed door, and peeked into the dean of faculty's office; two police officers were thumbing through files and searching his desk.

She definitely wanted to stay away from there, then, but luckily, Dean Asquith's office was separate from everything

lse, befitting his position. She took a deep breath and
ooked around with more purpose as she got her bearings.
Why was she here?

It had occurred to her that despite what Brenda Fletcher
had told her—that the dean likely would not have been able
to do anything to whomever fixed Mac MacAlister's grade—
there might be more to the case. Grade fixing was only the
end result; there were possibly other indictable offenses.
What if whoever did it had hacked into the college computer
system? *That* was surely against the law. So was taking
money to alter grades, she had to imagine.

She had an excuse of sorts to talk to Brenda Fletcher; after
all, the assistant registrar *had* sent that message to Sophie via
Josh Sinclair. She'd follow up on that, and try to bring the
topic around to Vince Nomuro, to see if the assistant thought
the registrar would have changed the grade. If he did, would
he be afraid enough of the consequences to do harm to the
dean? But she hesitated; was Brenda Fletcher purposely
directing her toward her boss? Maybe Sophie should tackle
Vince Nomuro first. What excuse could she use?

As she thought, she examined the bulletin board, staring
at announcements of sporting events—football and basketball
games, archery tournaments, track and field meets—as well
as seminars, year abroad programs and other items of interest
to students. A never-ending flow of students entered and
exited various offices, clusters gathering in the hall like leaves
in a stream caught in one place, then breaking up to drift away
with the flow. She heard Dean Asquith's name whispered
among those who gathered, shifted and left, and among new
arrivals, too, who waited for the office to clear out before
entering to address their own concerns. His death had affected
the student body more than she had expected, if just as a
shocking tragedy.

Enough pondering. She needed to *do* something, and talking to Vince Nomuro would be a start. From there she would track down Brenda Fletcher, and maybe take a little side trip to see if she could dig anything up on Heck Donovan, who she had not forgotten had a huge stake in keeping Mac MacAlister able to play.

She was gathering her resolve when someone behind her said, "Sophie, I'm so glad you came!"

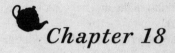

Chapter 18

S he whirled. "Julia!"

The professor stood in the middle of the hall clutching an armload of papers, holding a briefcase with three fingers of her left hand, her purse slung over her shoulder. She looked frazzled, and dark circles bagged under her eyes.

Sophie's surprise turned to concern. She sped down the hall and took the professor's briefcase off her hands, put one hand under her elbow and asked, "Are you okay? You look so tired."

Julia glanced around at the students who eyed them curiously and straightened, sucking in a long breath, letting it out slowly. "I'm all right. This has taken a toll on me, I think. Are you here to meet Jason? He's still with his class, and then I think he has a meeting with Dr. Bolgan. After that he has student meetings for an hour in his office in the arts building."

"I'm not here to see Jason."

Julia leaned in and whispered, "Are you investigating?"

"Do you have a minute to talk?"

She nodded.

Sophie guided her aside to a quieter spot. "You've been a good friend to Jason. I'm afraid for him; the police questioned him again last night, and he won't tell anyone, but I know he's scared."

"Further to our conversation, I've been asking around, trying to see if anyone knows anything. Every single person I've talked to here at Cruickshank wonders the same thing; does the grading thing have anything to do with the murder?"

"Does anyone have an answer?"

"So far, no," Julia said, shifting the stack of papers. "Because of all this nonsense, the department is making me check over all of Jason's work, including his students' lit essays." She rolled her eyes. "Just what I need. I've got morning sickness, raging hormones, heartburn, constipation and extra work. I need to get off my feet for a minute; follow me." Julia led her to a room at the end of the hall, a quiet retreat that she had needed a key to open. There were two couches facing each other across a low coffee table, a soft chair, a shelf with some magazines and a few potted palms.

"What is this?" Sophie asked, looking around.

"This is the reflection room. It's for teaching staff who have reached their limit. This qualifies as a day I've reached my limit. I'm only surprised there isn't a line to get in." She paused and grimaced, scanning the restricted space. "It used to be a storage closet. I swear I still smell the ammonia fumes."

Sophie smiled, but didn't get what Julia wanted. "So what are we going to do to get to the bottom of this? Have you got any more ideas since we talked yesterday morning?"

She nodded sharply. "I most certainly do, but look who

I'm talking to! You're the sleuth, Sophie . . . Gracious Grove's very own Junior Marple! Now that you're here I'm sure you'll know exactly what to ask, and of whom. I'll be your facilitator, right? Wait here. I'm going to get Vince Nomuro."

"But Julia, what . . ." Sophie half rose from her chair in alarm. What was she supposed to say? How could she question a man she didn't even know? But protest came too late; the professor had thrown her papers down on a chair and disappeared out the door.

The stack of papers slid sideways, so Sophie tidied them. They appeared to be grading reports for various students, so she averted her eyes. None of her business. Unless . . . Julia said she had to check all of Jason's printed-out student papers. She rapidly sifted through them and found one with Mac MacAlister's name at the top and the class, which was, as Tara had mentioned, Literary Migrations. His piece was entitled "The Environment in American Literature." She scanned it quickly; there was nothing interesting in it. His grasp of English grammar and spelling was shaky at best. Jason had given him a D, and there was a check mark beside the grade and Julia's initials.

But what else she found in the stack gave her pause. There was a note. She scanned it quickly, a skill perfected from years of reading orders in her restaurant kitchen. It said, in part,

> *JM didn't do anything, but I know who did. Ms.*
> *Dandridge, you should be very very carefull of*
> *all the cheets at this skool.*

JM . . . Jason Murphy? And was that a threat toward Julia? Had she some accountability in the grade change, and did someone know? She heard a noise in the hall and tucked the note back into the stack with a corner hanging out.

The door opened and Julia shepherded in Vince Nomuro, who frowned as he glanced around and then focused on Sophie. "What is this about, professor?" he asked of Julia.

"This is Jason's friend, Sophie Taylor. Remember her from the tea stroll? Dean Asquith was killed on her grandmother's doorstep and she's trying to sort out what happened. I thought maybe we could put our heads together and come up with something, Vince."

Sophie fumed. She had planned to tackle him in his office one-on-one, and hadn't even figured out what she was going to ask yet. It was harder with a third party present. Julia watched her eagerly, her gaze shifting from Sophie to the registrar and back. It was like she expected Sophie to pull a rabbit out of her hat. Or ponytail.

"Mr. Nomuro, I know how upset everyone is about the dean's murder. Can we talk about it for a minute?"

He narrowed his eyes. "Julia, what is this? It feels like an ambush."

"Mr. Nomuro, it's not, really," Sophie said. "I'm just a concerned citizen, mostly because it happened right outside my grandmother's tearoom, *and* because Jason is a friend. His name is being thrown around in this mess. I know he didn't do anything wrong, and I'm sure you know that, too."

"I still don't understand why you've come to me."

Sophie gave Julia a look and she appeared to get the hint, finally. "I, uh, need to see the main desk about some interdepartmental mail. If you'll excuse me, I'll be back in a few . . . in a while." She closed the door behind her.

"Can you sit for a moment?" Sophie asked, trying to make her tone appealing and a little lost.

He sank into one of the overstuffed chairs and crossed one leg over his knee. He was neatly dressed in navy dress slacks and a navy blazer over a white shirt, with a diamond-patterned tie in blue and silver, fastened with a silver arrow-shaped tie pin. He adjusted his tie. "You have my attention, Miss Taylor," he said, his diction precise and formal.

Sophie tried to remember what Brenda had told her about the man. She had implied that he was a college administrator almost by default. His first career course halted when he failed as a pharmacy student, so he turned to accounting. He was on her short list of people who could have changed Mac MacAlister's grade. But more importantly, he was named as someone seen close by the tearoom late the night of the murder. What could she ask him that would conceal her true aim, to find out if he could have killed Dean Asquith?

"I'm sorry Julia hauled you down here, Mr. Nomuro," she said, with all sincerity. "I don't know her very well, but she's been a good friend to Jason and stood by him through all the worry over the grading scandal. Until the truth comes out, he's going to be suspected."

"I believe in letting investigations take their course, Miss Taylor."

"Please call me Sophie. That's fine, but I do think investigations can go off the rail at any time for so many reasons. Anything we can do to streamline the process will help, don't you think? Now that Dean Asquith is dead, what will happen to Jason? Do we even know what the dean was going to say? Was he going to name Jason as the grade changer, or did he have someone else in mind?"

"Why do you think I would know?"

"Your department collects all the data, such as grades."

"True, but as we have discovered, there are holes in our

system we will have to plug." He regarded her steadily for a moment. "Are you implying the dean was killed to stop him from naming the guilty party? That is patently absurd," the registrar said, shifting in his chair, appearing agitated. "At most, Jason, or whomever, would be censured and their grading would be overseen for a while. As is happening in the interim, until it is sorted out. No one would kill over that."

That was reaffirmation of what she had already heard. "But what if whoever did it, did more than just change one grade?"

"Multiple grade changes, you mean? Why do you say that? Have you heard anything? What are you implying?"

His alarm was palpable, and interesting. His complexion had become blotchy, his dark eyes dilated. He was the likeliest candidate for a grade changer, since his office would have last stab at it. However . . . Julia said it happened before she saw the grade, so, between Jason and Julia, it had been altered. The registrar would likely know how to do that, but why would he, rather than wait until he received the grades from the department head, Julia? There would be less potential for being caught after she had signed off on the mark.

"I'm trying to figure things out." She tapped her foot on the carpeted floor, watching the registrar. "You were with Dean Asquith's group the night of the murder. Did you notice anything? See any suspicious interaction?" She was thinking specifically of his argument with the dean at SereniTea, but didn't know how to bring him around to discussing it, directly.

"I did see something, now that you mention it." He glanced at her, then fixed his gaze on the fake silk flowers in a vase in the corner of the room. "It was at SereniTea. I had taken Dean Asquith aside to speak with him about a professional matter that I felt a need to discuss before his announcement."

"Oh? What was that?" she interjected.

"That is incidental to my story."

She clamped her mouth shut, not wanting to agitate or upset him, but if he was innocent of the grade scandal charges, he was probably taking that opportunity to plead his case with the dean.

He sat forward and interlaced his fingers together between his knees. "After Dale and I spoke, he walked away, while I stayed back to speak to that woman . . . whomever it is that Julia has running the place."

"Kirsten Frawling."

"That young lady has no idea how to run a tearoom. The place is a jumble of Eastern influences, or rather Western misunderstanding of Eastern influences. I wanted to correct her on several things. Though SereniTea's use of fusuma—that is sliding panels—tatami mats and shoji screens to create washitsu—that is a Japanese-style room—suggests a traditional tearoom, everything else is a mess."

Sophie stayed quiet.

Vince Nomuro retreated into himself for a moment, looking down at his navy slacks, pleating the crease by pinching it between his fingers, then said, "When I emerged from speaking with the young lady, who seems a scattered kind of person, not a good manager, I saw Dale speaking to, or rather arguing with, a young man, someone I recognized."

Sophie drew her breath in to speak, but then made herself stay quiet. Vince Nomuro was the kind of person who was organized and methodical in his speech, and an interjection would throw him off.

"The dispute appeared heated, and even physical. He was arguing with Paul Wechsler, our systems engineer. He looks after all of our computer needs, designs programs and maintains our intranet. It's a very important job. He should have more help, but so far we haven't been able to attract anybody to the other positions, so he fills in. He's not paid half what he's worth."

This was getting interesting. Julia had said she saw Paul and the dean speaking outside of SereniTea and this was the confirmation! Sophie had seen Paul draw the dean aside later, near Auntie Rose's, and understood the conversation to be about the grading, but the heated disagreement earlier? The registrar had stopped, and Sophie felt it was safe to ask, "What were they arguing about?"

"I only heard a few words. When Dale saw me he drew Paul away into the shadows and I was accosted by my assistant about something." He glanced up at Sophie. "I know all the gossip, Miss Taylor. Sophie. I know that people say Paul is involved with Mrs. Asquith."

"I've heard that from a number of reliable people," Sophie asserted.

"What he and Dale argued about had nothing to do with Mrs. Asquith, I would attest to that. Paul said to him something like, 'if you tell people that tomorrow, you're going to look like an idiot'. Dale said, 'you're the one who told me' . . . but that was when Dale moved Paul away and I couldn't hear any more. I'm planning to ask Paul about that today."

The reference to the dean's Monday announcement must have been about the grading scandal, but did it mean that Paul had told the dean that Jason was the one responsible, or someone else? And did it come from Paul in his position as systems engineer? She had no doubt the college had been delving into the problem from a technical aspect since all grades were entered on a computer.

Though she wasn't quite sure how. "Mr. Nomuro, how are grades entered by instructors and professors?"

"We have a content management system, of course. Our staff log on, give unique identification and hopefully log off when they are done."

Sophie could see many problems with that, including what he implied himself, that if a staff member failed to log off, anyone using his or her computer might be able to change things without anyone being the wiser. "But the grade alteration would have a timestamp, or electronic fingerprint, right?"

"Sure. But any system is only as good as the humans utilizing it."

Lots of cracks and possible problems, then. And no one would know that better than those in charge of using it constantly, like Vince and Brenda, and the one charged with maintaining it, Paul Wechsler. If she eliminated Jason and Julia from contention, then the most likely grade alterer was among those three.

But she couldn't forget that this information was coming from Vince. She had Julia's account that the dean had questioned Vince himself about his spending habits. Sophie inferred from that, that the dean still hadn't fully made up his mind yet on the guilty party, even just hours before he was to make the announcement. He clearly still felt it was possible that Vince had taken bribes to change Mac's grade.

Maybe when Paul pulled the dean aside near Auntie Rose's, he was telling him that if he named Jason he'd look like a fool, because Vince was really the guilty party. Or . . . maybe he pulled the dean aside to tell him that he would look like a fool if he named the registrar, because it was someone *else* who was the guilty party. She sighed, feeling no closer to the truth. "So you haven't tried to speak with Paul yet?"

"He hasn't come into work today," Nomuro said. "And he didn't call, either, the office told me."

* * *

Rose and Laverne exited the police headquarters into the brilliant, hard October sunshine. It was a crisp day, one meant for hot tea and scones, and for hosting groups at Auntie Rose's. Without the daily rhythm of the tearoom, Rose felt bereft. "I'm worried, Laverne. Why do you think Sophie hasn't been in to see the police yet?"

"That girl is off chasing a murderer, if I know her."

"Detective Morris warned me to make sure she stays out of trouble."

Laverne snorted as she unlocked the car and held the door open for Rose, who climbed into the low old vehicle with some difficulty. She circled and climbed in behind the wheel, started the engine and cranked up the heat. "As if either of us could make Sophie do or not do something she had on her mind. That girl is as obstinate as her grandmother."

Rose smiled wearily and put her head back. "Laverne, who did this awful thing? And why outside our tearoom?"

"I know Sophie is doing her best to figure it out, but I think it's time the Silver Spouts leaped into action."

"What do you mean?"

"There is nothing a group of snoopy older folk can't ask," Laverne said with a chuckle.

"You're right," Rose said, sitting up straighter. "And I think we ought to start with our old frenemy, as Sophie calls her, Thelma Mae Earnshaw. She's the one who claims to have seen the college registrar, but what did she really see?"

They headed home, and as they pulled in noticed Gilda outside with a bucket cleaning the siding by the front step of Belle Époque. It was such a surprising sight they stopped and Rose rolled down her window. "Gilda, what are you up to?"

She looked around stealthily, then scooted over to the car window, leaning over and poking her frizzy head in. "I'm staying out of the way. Madame has her knickers in a twist," she said sourly.

"Why this time?" Rose asked.

Gilda looked furtive. "It was a phone call this morning that set her off."

"Just tell us," Laverne said, leaning across Rose. "What phone call? Who was on the line?"

"It was from the college. The dean of students wanted to chew her out for going to the dorm last night and upsetting Mac MacAlister."

Rose and Laverne exchanged looks. "We *have* to hear about this," Rose said.

Ten minutes later they had coaxed Thelma and Gilda over to Auntie Rose's and had them ensconced in the tearoom at one of the smaller round tables with a cup of Auntie Rose's Tea-riffic Tea Blend and a lemon scone with Devon cream and fresh berry coulis, something Sophie had made the day before.

"So, what happened, Thelma, and why was the college upset?"

In a halting and sniffly manner, Thelma related what had happened, finally, after many interjections and exclamations, arriving at the part where she had labored up the stairs and found the room in which Mac MacAlister held court. "You'd think he was Rudolph Valentino as the Sheik, with all those giggly girls lying around, cooing over him. One was even combing his bushy hair, for cripes' sake!" Thelma said, her pudgy face red with indignation. "It would be a cold day in the blistering underworld before I'd do that. Girls are so stupid. Cissy's over the worst of that, but she's waiting around for a proposal from that wet noodle, Wally, when she should be proposing to him herself, if that's what she wants."

Rose and Laverne exchanged a look. Once Thelma got up on one of her high horses, it was hard to make her dismount. The only way was to force the issue.

"So Mac MacAlister was in his room with a bunch of college girls giggling over him," Laverne said.

"What did you say when you barged in there?" Rose added.

Thelma clattered the teacup against its saucer and moved the teapot, a figural representing a graduation cap resting on a stack of books, around. "I said, 'Who do you have to bribe around here to change your grade?' and he kinda looked offended. That's when he called dorm security."

"That was it?" Rose sighed. She'd thought the woman actually found something out.

Thelma gave her a cagey look. "Who said that was it? I skedaddled out of his room and down the hall, and this blond girl took me aside, pulled me into a room. I recognized her; she's a reporter for the college paper, the one who's been hanging around so much, and was at your tearoom talking to Sophie yesterday."

"Tara Mitchells," Laverne said.

Thelma nodded. "Anyways, she asked me a bunch of questions. I didn't know the answer to any of 'em. Then she said something strange. She said that she had seen two people together who didn't fit, and it made her wonder if they were all barking up the wrong tree."

"Did she name names?" Rose asked.

Thelma grimaced. "Can't remember. One was something that made me think about appliances."

"What could make you think about appliances?" Laverne asked.

Thelma shook her head.

"Blender?" Rose mused. "Oven? Mixer? Vacuum? Beater? Are there any names in the case that sound like any of those?"

Laverne was biting her lip to keep from laughing, but she got control of herself and asked Thelma, "So you can't remember the name, but what else did she say?"

"She said this fella, the appliance one, was in a car with someone she never thought she'd see him with."

And that was it, that was all Thelma could tell them. Tara had shut up after that and snuck Thelma out of the dorm as Mac complained loudly to security.

"Now, what about this other thing, you saying you saw the registrar skulking late that night," Rose said. "When you sent Gilda to take out the garbage?"

Gilda sniffed and crossed her arms over her chest. Pearl ambled into the kitchen just then, though, and with a glad cry Gilda sank to the floor and enticed the cat into her lap. The delicate Birman hesitated, glanced up at Rose, then climbed into the generous velour-clad lap. From then on Gilda's mood was significantly better, as she fed the cat scones with dabs of cream.

"I did see him," Thelma said. "Or at least . . . I saw his hat."

"You already told us that, the duffer cap," Rose said. "So what was it made from?"

Thelma shrugged, her floral printed caftan rippling with the action. "It was a funny kind of tweed material, you know?"

"That's not enough to accuse the man," Rose said.

With that, Thelma got huffy again. "Well, he was the only one wearing one of those that night," she said, and dragged Gilda back to Belle Époque.

"We need to tell Sophie to get a hold of Tara Mitchells and ask her what she told Thelma," Rose said. "I hope that girl doesn't do anything rash."

"Tara?"

"No, Sophie!"

Chapter 19

Vince Nomuro retreated to his office and Sophie sat for a moment, gathering her thoughts. When Julia came back with a hopeful look on her face, Sophie said, "Can you sit for a moment? We need to talk. What does this mean?" She pulled free the note in the pile of papers, read it over more completely, then handed it to Julia. In full, it read,

> *Mac's grade is just the tip of the iceburg. JM
> didn't do anything, but I know who did. Ms.
> Dandridge, you should be very very carefull
> of all the cheets at this skool.*

The professor read it, and pink flooded her cheeks. She settled herself for a moment, then looked up at Sophie. "I don't know what this means. You're not going to believe me, but I don't."

Sophie regarded her for a moment. All this time, despite doubts pinging at the back of her mind and knowing that the professor could use some extra money, she had chosen to believe Julia when she said she had nothing to do with the grade changing. Mostly, she acknowledged, because Jason trusted her. "The JM mentioned is Jason, don't you think?"

Julia nodded, carefully avoiding Sophie's eyes.

"Why was this note written to you? And why does it tell you to be careful?"

"It was stuck into my departmental mail slot this morning, and I piled it in with this stack of papers. I hadn't even read it until this moment." She frowned and shook her head. "I don't know what it means, why it tells me to be careful. Is it . . . do you think it's a threat?" She put her hand over her stomach.

"It doesn't sound like it," Sophie said. An anonymous note. *Another* anonymous note, like the one that had tipped Tara off to the grade alteration in the first place. Who was the whistleblower? And why was Mac the one pinpointed?

"Julia, you never did answer my text. I sent you a note; I was told that you were crying the night of the tea stroll, that the dean said something to you, and you were upset."

"Oh, Sophie, it wasn't important. He told me our food was awful." She rolled her eyes. "Yes, I burst into tears. I do that about three times a day right now. It wasn't important; that's why I didn't mention it."

Sophie watched the professor, and decided to try out one of her theories. If she was right about any of this, there was little chance that Julia was guilty of the grade change, and certainly not the murder. "I do wonder about what it means, that Mac's grade is the tip of the iceberg. It could mean other of Mac's grades were altered, or—more likely—that there are other departments involved, more students' grades changed. Vince Nomuro explained how the content management system here works. When you use your work computer, do you ever leave the office with the computer on? Have you ever come back to find someone else in your office, or just leaving it?" She should be asking Jason the same question, and she would.

"I don't remember a specific instance, but . . ." Julia shook her head. "I'm horribly confused," she confessed. "I feel like my brain is going into hibernation, asleep a great deal of the time."

Sophie regarded her. "I had a waitress who said that the only real problem she had while she was pregnant was that she was thinking of a thousand things at once and worrying, so she didn't get enough sleep and was forgetful."

Julia nodded. "That sounds like me. I never should have gotten into the tearoom business. What was I thinking? Now, with the baby coming, I can't afford to keep going with it if it's ultimately going to fail."

"Do you want my true opinion? The ruthlessly honest truth from someone who has failed in a restaurant?"

Julia nodded.

"I think you need to decide what you want from the business. If you've discovered that it's not your thing, there's no shame in that. Sell the business and the building. You'll lose a little money, but you'll be out of it. However, if you can be happy with it breaking even for a couple of years, you can use that time to find your niche. It's not necessarily a bad idea, but either you find someone else to manage your place, or Kirsten needs to take a management course. And you definitely have to hire a better cook. She can't do everything, and right now she's not doing anything well."

"But she's a friend, and a great yoga instructor! I can't fire her, and I don't know how I'd tell her to shape up!" She shrugged helplessly, tears in her eyes. "Maybe I should sell SereniTea."

"Maybe," Sophie said. "Or maybe not." She felt for her. "After this is over, let's talk."

"Okay."

Sophie pondered the note and what it could mean; the spelling was comically atrocious, but was that purposeful? Why warn Julia? Had anyone else received notes, or just her? Sophie decided she needed to put it on the back burner for now. Maybe her subconscious would have a better idea than she did. "Julia, I appreciate the idea you had, of sticking me here and bringing people to me to figure this out, but I don't think that's the best plan. I'd prefer to see people in their natural habitat, if you know what I mean."

Julia nodded. "I guess I was overzealous. I want this to be over for all of our sakes. Is there anything I *can* do, though?"

"Sure. I know we said you or Jason should handle Coach Donovan, but we both know it's best if you guys stay out of it. I'd like to talk to him. Where would I find him?"

"Heck has an office here in administrative, but he's not usually in it. If you'll help me get this stuff to my office," she said about the stack of paperwork, "I'll help you track him down."

Ten minutes later Sophie was standing in the lobby of the gymnasium where she had attended the basketball game. Heck Donovan had his main office in the auditorium complex, but his schedule had indicated he was coaching a basketball practice at that moment. Julia had offered to come along and introduce her, but Sophie wanted to do this on her own. She wasn't sure how she was going to proceed, but from her hopeful expression it appeared that Julia had a much better opinion of Sophie's investigative abilities than she had of herself.

Her cell phone chimed and she noticed that she had several

ext messages and a missed call. She found a secluded alcove
and checked out the text from Josh. It was actually a string
of texts, as he was in class and couldn't call. He had done
ome research and found a few toxins that could have pro-
duced the convulsions and drooling that the dean apparently
uffered. He mentioned everything from ricin, fairly easily
distilled from the castor bean plant, to exotic Amazonian cane
oad poisons, like the ones he and Cindy had seen at the
xhibit at the college. There was a more likely one, though,
ae said; monkshood was a locally available plant, and deadly.

She appreciated the information, but did it help? If she was
even right about the dean being poisoned, how was it introduced into his system? Was it in something he ate? And he
didn't die of poisoning, he was stabbed to death. Also, there
was the wound on his neck; was it an attempt at a first stab,
or something entirely different? Without access to the police
nformation, she might never know.

She sighed deeply, staring off into space. What she wouldn't
give for a gabby police informant right that minute. How con-
venient for amateur sleuths in novels when someone on the
police force happily spilled all the information the amateur
happened to need right when they needed it. She was lucky
ndeed that Wally had told Cissy what little he had, that there
was poison in the dean's system.

The missed call was from Nana. Heart pounding with
alarm, she stepped outside of the auditorium into the cold
clear air and called the tearoom line. Nana answered and
reassured her everything was fine. *She* was fine. It was just
hat they had a talk with Thelma Mae and she had informa-
ion she thought Sophie might want before talking to folks
at the college. Sophie listened with amazement to the tale
of Thelma Mae's misadventures in the dorm, and her chat
with Tara Mitchells. She could hear Laverne chuckling in

the background, the warm throaty sound that had taken he
through numerous teen crises, usually accompanied by he
godmother's pat on the back and a *this too shall pass*.

"I need to find Tara Mitchells to have a talk with her abou
what she meant by having seen two people together who didn'
fit. I also need to track down the systems engineer, Pau
Wechsler. He's not been in to work today, which could mean
anything, I guess. I don't even know if anyone has seen hin
since yesterday, when he had that accident outside Auntie
Rose's. I think I'll pay the registrar another visit, though
when I'm done here."

They chatted a moment longer and she ended the call, then
reentered the auditorium. Practice was still going on; she
could hear the squeak of shoes on hardwood, and the coach':
whistle, with some swearing and loud admonitions. She made
her way into the gym and watched from the shadows for a
while. Coach Donovan was red-faced and yelling much o
the time. Mac MacAlister seemed off his game and missec
most of the shots he attempted. Sophie knew little about bas
ketball, but it appeared his timing was off. Maybe his mine
was somewhere else, or maybe because he was suspendec
and couldn't play in games, he didn't care. The whole team
appeared lackluster.

Finally the coach dismissed the players. Sophie wondered
if she'd have a chance to talk to Mac about his grade hike
but he stormed from the court with his teammates and she
was not about to follow him into the locker room. The coach
however, was another thing entirely. He stormed past her
and she followed until they reached his office.

He unlocked the room, stomped in, got a can of root beer
from his desk drawer, popped the top and took a long swig

"Coach Donovan?" she said.

He whirled and glared at her. "Who are you?"

"We've met," she said, striding across the room and holding out her hand. "I'm Sophie Taylor. Jason Murphy's friend? We met the night of the basketball game at the reception for the alumni donors."

He looked at her thrust-out hand and back up to her face, but didn't shake. She pocketed her hand. "What do you want?" he asked and took another long slurp of his drink.

He was a no-bullcrap kind of guy, she assumed. Okay, straightforward, then. "Your star player has been accused of having one of his grades raised to keep him eligible for the team." Even if he didn't officially have access to the CMS, he might know a little about how it worked, probably enough to take advantage of a computer left logged on to alter a grade. He might be smarter than he looked. "I don't know whether he asked someone to do that for him or not, I only know Jason didn't do it. Do you have any idea who did?"

The perpetual scowl on his face deepened, the grooves bracketing his mouth shadowed and bristly with beard hairs missed during his morning shave. He was as unprepossessing a fellow as she had ever seen, but it was mostly his glower that made him so. "If I did, why would I tell you?"

Her father had told her, during one of their rare talks, that when faced with a combative individual in the business world, his best strategy had always been to disarm him with honesty, and then keep him off balance with rapid questions. Sophie wasn't sure if she knew how to do that, but it didn't hurt to try, since she couldn't think of a single reason why he'd tell her anything otherwise. "Because I can tell it's getting to you. You need to talk to someone, and I don't matter; why not tell me? All I want is for Jason to not get in trouble." She paused, but he stared at her, wordless. Well, at least he hadn't tossed her out yet. "Coach, did anyone approach you about Mac's grades?"

"We all knew he needed to get his grades up, but I never asked anyone to cut him any favors. All I said was he needed some remedial help, and could they get him a tutor."

"Who did you say that to?"

"His adviser, Kimmy. She's a great gal; really went to bat for Mac."

Sophie was back to square one, in a sense, because Kimmy could still have been the one who altered the grade. "And no one else?"

"His parents; we discussed it at length. Dean of students, Lilith Klein. She was the one coming down hardest. All I asked *her* was to cut Mac some slack." He grimaced and took a swig of root beer, hand on his stomach. "Ha, fat chance. She hates athletics. Hated that Asquith was trying to get them featured more prominently at Cruickshank. She'd like to have mathletes, not athletes." Even a joke came out growled from Heck Donovan.

From the sounds of it, the coach was the last person who would have wanted to harm Dean Asquith, and she thought it was probably safe to rule him out as the killer. "Was she pressuring Dean Asquith to find out who among the faculty or staff had boosted Mac's grade?"

He nodded. "Hell, yeah. She was putting on the pressure. She's all about STEM," he said, using the acronym for science, technology, engineering and math. "Makes her sick that more money comes to colleges from athletics than from math or science. No one ever bought team color jerseys for mathletic events, did they? I told her to suck it up, buttercup, and she got all red-faced. Mad as hell that I make more than her, probably."

Sophie took a deep breath, and felt a moment of compassion for Dr. Klein. She also spared a thought wondering how

Heck and his wife, Penny, got along. She seemed a firebrand kind of woman, mousy *looking* but not mousy acting. She was strong-minded and resented Cruickshank. How did they deal?

Sophie was a pragmatist; if the college's biggest problem was that athletics brought money in, they were doing all right. She was probably vastly oversimplifying the problem and she was sure Jason would have an argument against it, but it wasn't much of a problem, in her mind. Now that she knew a little more about the coach, she proceeded, altering her methods slightly. She sank down on a hard plastic chair by the door, jamming her hands in her jacket pockets.

"It's so awful that this is all going on. I don't know what to make of it. But Jason didn't do the grade altering; I've known him for years, and I'd bet on that! And now with Dean Asquith being murdered right outside my grandmother's tearoom . . . I don't know what to think." She looked up at him as he swigged his root beer. "Coach, who would do such a terrible thing? You were with the group that evening; who do you think did it?"

"I was there, but me and Penny took off early. Not my scene. I only went because Dale made such a big deal out of it and he was good to the athletics department. But I headed home as soon as I could scoot. Needed a beer to wipe out the taste of tea."

Okay, if that was true he was in the clear. "Who do you really think did the grade altering?" she asked, persisting. Another thing her father had said was, if you didn't get an answer, keep asking the question in different forms. "Some people are saying the dean was going to make an announcement yesterday morning. Who would he have said?"

He looked conflicted and slumped down in his chair

behind his desk. "I shouldn't even be saying. Whoever did it didn't do me any favors. I thought that maybe Lilith Klein had a hand in it."

Sophie squinted, wrinkling her nose. "The dean of students? You just said she didn't care about athletes. She surely wouldn't want to help Mac by upping his grade."

He leaned forward and shoved some papers aside, agitated. "Don't you get it? She could alter his grade, then expose it, get Mac put off the team and make it a major scandal for the athletics department. Like we're all cheaters or something." He glanced toward the door and whispered, "I think Dale Asquith was onto her, and that's why she had him killed."

It was so far out of left field she truly didn't know what to say. "But you don't have any proof of that, right?"

"I know what I think," he said. He shrugged. "Nah. Not really. Truth to tell, I'd bet Jeanette had him killed. That bitch is as cold as ice."

And that was it for the coach's information, such as it was. Every path led to a deceiving and manipulative woman, with no information to back it up but his own supposition. It was a miracle he was married, given his gloomy view of womankind.

Confused and baffled, she left the athletic arena and walked across the campus, hands buried in her pockets, enjoying the breeze and the flutter of golden leaves that drifted along the walkways. Students crisscrossed around her, using the paths or the grass, as they wanted. Most stared down at phones, or were lost in the music streaming through earbuds in their ears, but a few pairs and trios conversed as they walked, heads together, texts in backpacks or bookbags.

From a distance she saw a girl with a shiny sheet of blond hair, wearing a plaid short kilt and knee socks on plump legs. She called out Tara's name and the girl looked up from her phone. She spotted Sophie and seemed conflicted. Sophie loped across the grass up a hill, reaching the girl near the dorm block.

"Hey, Tara," Sophie said, by way of greeting. She gasped, catching her breath. "I heard you had a senior run-in last evening." When the girl looked blank, she said, "Mrs. Earnshaw; you met her when she invaded MacAlister's dorm room?"

Tara broke into giggles. "She was a hoot! I wish my great-grandmother was half as interesting instead of moaning at me all the time about how all I do is text and that I should do something with my hair, and that no man will ever want me if I don't lose ten pounds and wipe the smirk off my face."

"Sounds like my mother," Sophie said sympathetically. "Mrs. Earnshaw said you mentioned something about seeing two people together who didn't fit. What did you mean?"

"Oh, that. Right. Nothing important," she said, her gaze slipping away off to the distance.

She'd come back to that, Sophie thought. "I've been trying to find out what's going on with the investigation into the grade-altering scandal. Have you heard anything?"

She looked troubled. "I don't know. People are assuming it was Professor Murphy now. I'm so *ticked* about that. I took the easy way out when I mentioned him, and now I can't convince people he didn't do it. It's like the whole thing has taken on a life of its own."

"That's the problem with gossip and innuendo; it does tend to get stuck in people's head. I get peeved when people say stuff like *'no smoke without fire.'* Sometimes that's all it is, smoke puffed into your eyes by someone else with something to hide. Anyway, Tara, you can make it right by helping find out who actually did it."

"I've been trying. But what more can I do? Who do you think I should go after?"

Sophie eyed her. Could the girl be trusted? "Do you plan on nailing someone else to the wall without checking your sources, or retailing gossip and innuendo in the paper?"

"Look, I already apologized. My stupid editor is cranky mad, right. Normally he doesn't care about anything, but before he died, the dean threatened to shut the paper down if anything like that happened again. I have to come up with something solid, and he's going to be vetting every article I write for a while."

So it seemed that Dean Asquith wasn't behind the story, and perhaps then was not trying to railroad Jason. Sophie shared what the coach had said about Dean Klein, and asked what Tara knew about her.

Tara rolled her eyes. "What an idiot. Dean Klein never did anything, and if he's implying she killed Dean Asquith, he's barking up the wrong tree for sure."

"Why do you say that?"

"There's no way she could have done anything. Dean Klein is in a wheelchair."

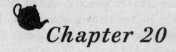

Chapter 20

"**O**h, okay." It seemed the coach only brought up Dean Klein's name as a distraction. "Tara, why don't you tell me who it was you saw together who didn't fit?"

"Because it doesn't matter; I don't think it's related."

"Let me be the judge of that; just *tell* me!"

But her blue eyes were clouded with doubt and she shook her head. "I don't want to get the wrong person in trouble this time."

Great time to grow some caution. "Tara, you can trust me not to blab. Finding a murderer is serious business!"

"I know. *You've* done that twice," the girl said.

Her reputation came back to haunt her. "Just tell me who it was."

"Later," she said, whirling on her heel and striding away. "I've got to get to class right now; I'm late."

Sophie sighed. "Just don't get in any trouble!"

"I won't," she called over her shoulder. "Don't worry about it; it's nothing!"

Sophie sat down on a bench and texted Jason, telling him she was on campus, and that she had a question. Had he ever walked away from his office and left the door unlocked and was still logged in to the program he used to enter student grades? It was the kind of thing anyone might do, and it could be the easy answer as to who had altered the grade; anyone *could* have who walked past his office.

However . . . even as she still explored that possibility, she had a sense that this went beyond someone simply sneaking into an office and changing one grade. If she was right, there was a systematic raising of grades among key athletes. Paul Wechsler said that there was a pattern (to the raised grades, it was implied) except for an anomaly. She wondered if that anomaly would tell them anything.

She headed back to the administrative building and entered. The place had quieted down some, and she wandered the halls, which smelled of floor wax and oddly, tuna-fish sandwiches, thinking about her next move. She found the registrar's office. The main door accessed an outer room with a desk, chairs lined up against the wall, and a coatrack. A couple of jackets hung on it, including one that she recognized as Vince Nomuro's from Sunday evening. But no tweed duffer cap. Not that that told her anything; hats were the kind of thing you changed for different purposes. The desk had Brenda Fletcher's name on it, with the ASS. REG. designation that amused Dana so. But Brenda was absent. Sophie tapped on the inner oak door with the gold plate that said REGISTRAR—VINCE NOMURO—MACC. She heard a peremptory "Come in," and eased it open.

Vince looked up from a stack of paperwork, adjusting his glasses. "Oh, it's you again."

It was said in a neutral tone, which seemed to be his only tone. He was very low key, especially given this was her second time interrupting his day. She sat down across the desk from him in a comfortable black-and-chrome chair that had the scent of real leather. His office was spacious, with floor-to-ceiling windows filled with lush tropical plants, and a view beyond of the parking lot. Shelves of pottery lined the wall behind his desk. Above the shelves was an impressive collection of samurai swords, lethal-looking knives with elaborate hilts, and some reproduction art of Japanese swordsmen and archers.

He was a collector. Her attention was especially attracted to a lovely Japanese Satsuma tea set, golden glazed porcelain, with dragons writhing around the teapot and depicted on the tea bowls surrounding it. He also appeared to collect urns and jars; some were Japanese vases and ginger jars, with ornate enameled designs of dragons and tea ceremonies. One looked like an old Grecian urn, with archers in a chariot chasing a stag on it, but there were a few that looked Egyptian, with processions of stiff figures carrying goodies to a dog-headed god seated on a throne.

It never failed to amaze her the stuff people collected, she thought, as she tried to frame what she was going to say. He watched her, waiting, glancing over at his computer screen from time to time and moving his mouse. "That's a lovely tea set," she said to break the ice. "I have a friend who comes from a Japanese family; she gave a talk to my grandmother's teapot collector group on the tea ceremony of her family's people. It was fascinating!"

"That is what Julia should be doing at SereniTea," he said, tapping a pen and turning his computer monitor away from her line of vision. "I think people would enjoy it."

"You must tell Julia that! My friend SuLinn could help her with it."

"SuLinn Miller?" he said. "I know her. Her husband is an architect and did some design work for my home. I'm trying to return it to its midcentury-modern floor plan." He appeared friendlier at the connection.

Interesting. The dean had referenced his renovations, but surely a man of the registrar's pay level could afford that?

"Is Cruickshank College a good place to work?"

"What an odd question," he said, frowning across the desk at her.

"I'm trying to get a feel for the place. If Jason is going to be working here awhile, I'll be at more functions, you know."

He gave her a slight smile. "It's a bit like a dysfunctional family, with some infighting and cliques. We're a normal workplace, I suppose, with all that implies. We have a picnic every summer with our families, and we even do Secret Santa at Christmas, though it's never much of a secret. I've had the same person get my name two years in a row, and she always gets me something *she'd* like, instead of something I'd like."

Sophie smiled. "My mother does that. She gets me French perfume and jewelry when I'd rather have the latest kitchen gadget." Okay, so they'd made friends and shared stories; it was time to be blunt. "Mr. Nomuro, what would you say if someone said they had seen you late the night the dean was killed, right outside our establishment where he was murdered?"

Without hesitation he replied, "I'd say I was not there, so someone is trying to frame me."

"And why would anyone do that?"

He steepled his long, boney fingers in front of his mouth. After a lengthy pause, he said, "I wouldn't like to hazard a guess."

"But you have suspicions?"

He shook his head, staying silent. Everyone was stone-walling her, it seemed. She'd try another approach. "Did you and the dean get along?"

"For the most part," he said, flattening his hands on the desk surface. "Miss Taylor, why are you asking me all these particular questions?"

"So if someone said you were arguing with him that night, they'd be lying?" she persisted.

He hesitated a moment, but then said, his tone firm, "I would not occasion a guess as to what people may or may not assume from my demeanor."

That was a deflection, not an answer. Sophie recalled the conversation she had overheard between him and his assistant the night of the basketball game. He was tense, keeping his eye on Dean Asquith. What had he said, that he didn't trust the dean? That Asquith was desperate for the scandal to go away before it hurt fund-raising or his job. That he was intent on keeping his eye on Asquith implied that he was afraid the dean would try to pawn blame off on someone handy, someone dispensable, maybe even the registrar. But did Vince have a reason to be afraid of what a thorough investigation would uncover?

She eyed a photo among the pottery pieces on the shelf behind. The registrar had a wife and two teenagers. "I didn't get a chance to meet your wife the night of the tea stroll. Was she there?"

"No, she travels a lot on business." His tone betrayed a growing impatience. "She's in Hong Kong right now."

And teenage kids wouldn't be likely to keep tabs on when dear old dad came home. He could easily have been the assailant. Just then the door swung open and Brenda Fletcher leaned into the room. "I'm back, Vince, and I've . . . oh, you've got company. Sorry."

Sophie turned in her chair, and the assistant registered her recognition.

"You!" Brenda said. "What are *you* doing here?"

"Brenda, don't be rude. However, it's a timely interruption; I'm sorry, Miss Taylor, but I do have a lot of work to do," he said, waving his hand at the stack of paperwork and computer. "I'd appreciate it if you showed yourself out. I hope you'll excuse me."

She sat for a moment, wondering if she could get any more questions in, but it would look too pointed if she did, certainly, and he was already tired of her. She scanned his wall of certificates, including his MAcc, and various plaques from local nature conservancy groups. He was Man of the Year two years before for his work in preserving natural plant species.

Plant species. She glanced back toward him; he watched her with his dark brows knit, then he shoved some graying straight thick hair off his forehead and glanced pointedly at his computer monitor. "I'm keeping you," she said. "I'll go."

She followed Brenda to the outer office and closed Vince's door behind her, but paused while the assistant registrar took off her bomber jacket and hung it up on the coatrack, fussing with one of the pins that caught on the lining. Distracted by an idea she had no clue how to pursue, Sophie lingered, as Brenda sat down at the desk. "You told Josh Sinclair to ask me, did I think that whoever killed the dean did it to hide another crime. What made you ask him that?"

"I don't know. I was just trying to figure it out."

"But what in particular did you mean?" Sophie pressed.

"I was just wondering out loud, I guess." She shrugged. "I didn't have any tangible clue; I'm no investigator."

Sophie was disappointed; it would have been nice to have someone else's input. "Could you tell me where Paul Wechsler's office is?"

"Paul Wechsler? Why do you want to see him?"

"I'm trying to figure things out, you know? I'm still worried about what this is all doing to Jason's reputation." Or at least that was her cover story for asking questions.

"You mean the grading scandal?" She pushed her glasses up on her nose. "All I know is, the dean had Paul going through the whole system, trying to figure out when the grade was changed. I think he asked him if he could tell what computer was used."

That confirmed Sophie's suspicion about the computer that was used being recognizable to the system, even though they were all likely on a mainframe. "Isn't that a little irregular?" When Brenda looked puzzled, she went on, "I mean, isn't it irregular to have someone doing that kind of forensic examination of the computers when he's one of the possible suspects?"

The woman frowned down at her hands on the desk and scrunched up her mouth as she thought. "I guess I never considered Paul a suspect. You mean just the grade change, right? Not Dean Asquith's murder?"

"If he was the one who changed the grade, couldn't he also be the murderer, if Dean Asquith discovered he was behind the grade tampering and accused him of it?"

Brenda moved in her chair, looking agitated. She glanced toward the registrar's closed office door. "Look, I'm worried about some stuff. Maybe . . . can we get out of here for a minute? I'll glance into Paul's office for you on our way out and see if he's here."

Sophie nodded, wondering what was up. Brenda grabbed her jacket and they left the office. She slunk down the hall, then scooted into the main administrative office. Sophie followed. Vienna Hodge was at the desk, dealing with a student whose schedule was apparently messed up by some change in the curriculum. The fellow trudged out of the office as Brenda ducked past the desk and trotted through, weaving between desks as clerks glanced up from their computers.

"Where is *she* going?" Vienna asked Sophie.

"She's checking to see if Paul Wechsler is in today."

Her dark eyes sparkling with mischief, she said, "He is not, *and* he hasn't called in sick, either. We were all wondering if he and Mrs. Asquith took off together." She sobered, and the mischief dissipated like mist. "But she actually came in a while ago to talk to the police, who are going through files in the dean's office."

Why come *here* to talk to the police? Sophie wondered. Why not go to police headquarters? Though maybe she had already done that. "What's your take on all of this?" Sophie asked, folding her arms on the counter and watching Vienna sift through a stack of papers. "There must be gossip. Usually support staff know a lot more about what's going on than their bosses think they do."

Vienna glanced over her shoulder, but the older woman who was usually at the desk behind the administrative counter was absent, and the other clerks were too far away to hear. "It may sound mean, but there is kind of a betting pool on who changed the grade, and also on who killed the dean!"

Sophie concealed her distaste. "And how are bets running?"

"Don't you dare tell Auntie Laverne about the betting thing," Vienna said, shaking her head slightly, her heavy earrings jangling. "But *my* money is on Mrs. Asquith. She's as cold as ice, and . . . Mrs. Asquith!" Her gaze had shifted to over Sophie's shoulder and her tone had changed. "How nice to see you again!" she said, her eyes wide as she gave Sophie a look.

Sophie turned. The dean's wife, appearing as neat and calm as ever, strode into the office. She glanced at Sophie without appearing to recognize her, then strode past the counter, her high heels making clipped tapping noises on the terrazzo floor. "I need to take a look at something," she said, but didn't explain further.

Sophie leaned across the counter and murmured to Vienna, "What offices are back there? Not Dean Asquith's."

"No, back there is secretarial, engineering and the mainframe."

"Engineering . . . you mean, like, systems engineering? Paul Wechsler's office?"

Just then they heard a screech and two voices engaged in an argument. The voices rose in volume as the two women emerged from the back room, with the exquisitely controlled (usually) Jeanette Asquith following Brenda Fletcher.

"What were you doing in his desk? I want to know," Mrs. Asquith asked.

Brenda, red-faced, turned to her. "Mrs. Asquith, I'm sorry, but you don't work here, and you don't have any right to . . . and anyway, that's my own business."

"Do you know where Paul is?" Jeanette shrieked, following. "Do you? Does anyone?" She looked around the office and Vienna shrugged. "He's not answering my calls," she continued, her gaze landing once again on Brenda, who appeared alarmed. "He's not in his apartment," the dean's widow said, on a sob. "Please, do any of you know where he is?"

"I certainly don't, Mrs. Asquith," Brenda said, walking past the counter. "If I knew, I'd tell you." As she strode past Sophie, she grabbed her arm and muttered, "Come on, I need to talk to you."

Sophie let herself be pulled outside to the bracing autumn air. Both of them stood on the front steps of the administrative building for a moment, adjusting to the brilliant hard sunshine of October. Then Brenda started down the few steps, with Sophie tagging along. "Brenda, what's going on? Were you going through Paul Wechsler's desk?"

"Yeah, and Mrs. Asquith caught me at it. I was trying to find his daily planner; we all have one issued by Cruickshank, and we're supposed to keep both our computer planner and our hard copy updated with where we are at all times. His is gone. *He's* gone."

"What does that mean?" Sophie said, trotting to keep up.

"I wish I knew," she said, slowing as she pondered the question. "I'm trying to figure out why Mrs. Asquith is so upset, and what she was doing there. It changes everything. Or . . . maybe not." She stopped and turned to Sophie halfway to the parking lot. "Do you have any clue who killed Dean Asquith? It's driving me crazy, and now the theory I had was just blown out of the water."

"What theory was that?"

"You first," she said.

But Sophie was not about to break first. "No way. You work with all of these people; you must have an idea."

She looked undecided, but started across the parking lot and settled on a bench under a tree that had shed a blanket of golden leaves. Sophie followed and sat down next to her.

"I've been torn apart," Brenda said. "I mean, on the one hand . . . I don't know. But now I want to know, where *is* Paul?"

"Brenda, you're going to have to be clearer than that. What are you talking about?"

"Okay, all right, but I don't want the police involved yet. I want to ask him myself."

"Him who? What are you *talking* about?" Sophie turned on the bench and put her knee up, staring at Brenda and waiting.

"Did you notice, when you were talking to Vince, his collections?"

"The pottery? Sure."

"He has expensive tastes. I think . . . I'm pretty sure he's the one who altered the grades."

Sophie thought back to what Brenda had said to Josh about the murder being committed to cover up another crime. Maybe she knew or surmised more than she had initially been willing to admit. "Why do you say that?"

There were tears in her eyes as she shook her head. "I don't want it to be true. I've always gotten along with Vince. But he keeps buying expensive stuff, and taking trips, and doing renovations. I mean, one of those things, sure, but *all* of them? And with a family, kids near college age? I began to wonder where he was getting the money. I think . . ." She paused and shook her head. Her voice clogged in her throat as she said, "I think he's been taking money to change grades for some time."

"Are you saying that you think he killed the dean?"

"No, no of course not! In fact, he couldn't have. He just *couldn't* have!"

"But?"

"What?"

"I thought I heard a 'but' at the end of your denial."

Brenda squeezed her eyes shut. "Okay, yeah. *But* . . . Paul Wechsler, who was looking into the grading thing and may have figured out from keystrokes or passwords or whatever who did it, is missing. And the last time I saw him was yesterday, in Vince's car."

Chapter 21

It all fell into place; Tara had told Thelma that she had seen two people together who didn't belong. And Nana said that Thelma swore one sounded like an appliance. Wechsler; could that sound, in Thelma's mind, like *waxer*? She explained to Brenda what she had heard, though not who she had heard it from. "Is that what my informant meant, then, about seeing two people together who didn't fit? Were they friends? Did they hang out together usually?"

"Well, no, never. I mean, Vince and Paul were about as different as you can get, and I don't think they spoke to each other unless it was work related." The woman looked stunned. "I don't want it to be Vince. I don't. He's been decent to me, and always given me time when I needed it to study for my dissertation defense. He's even fed my cat when I had to go out of town suddenly! He's a decent egg." She shook her head suddenly. "Look, there is no proof—*none*—that it's Vince."

"Well, I wouldn't say there is *no* proof," Sophie demurred. "I can think of a bunch." Her eyes widened as she thought of one more, one that tied together a bunch of little threads, but she wasn't about to share that idea right then until she'd had time to process it.

"I won't believe it."

"Brenda, let's be clear . . . you're worried that Paul's disappearance has to do with the dean's murder. Does that mean you're worried that Paul said something to Vince that tipped him off, and that Vince has done something to him?"

Brenda's expression cleared. "No, hearing it out loud like that . . . it's ridiculous. You've met Vince; he's the cool, calm, collected type. There must be an explanation. I have one surefire way of figuring this out, and then I can tell you everything."

"What do you mean? What way?"

But Brenda shook her head. "Look, I don't know anything, and I'm certainly not going to throw Vince under the bus until I know for sure. There has to be another explanation."

Sophie nodded. That's exactly what she would say and do in Brenda's shoes.

"So what if Paul and Vince were together; they're colleagues, for heaven's sake, right?" Brenda said. "They don't have to be best of friends to be in a car together. They could have been just talking or . . ." Her eyes widened. "Maybe *Paul* is the culprit and has taken off now for good."

Sophie considered; it was possible. "Paul crashed the car he was driving yesterday, so maybe he needed a lift somewhere. I could go back and ask Vince."

Brenda shook her head. "Look, if I'm wrong and Vince *did* kill Dean Asquith . . ." She paused and shook her head. "I can't believe I'm even entertaining that notion, but okay . . . if that's the case and you confront Vince, that'll show your hand. It could ruin things. Right? If there is a case against him?"

Sophie nodded. "You're right. But do you think Paul's in any danger?"

Brenda shook her head. "No way. I don't really think Vince is the guilty one. I've worked with the guy for two years, and he's not the type. But all I'm saying is, Vince will be here all day—he never leaves early—so we know where he is."

"You aren't going to do anything foolish, are you?" Sophie asked, watching the other woman's eyes, the calculating expression, the intense stare. "Please say you won't take any risks."

"No, no way. I like living too much." She shivered and fingered her lapel pin, the Sagittarius, maybe a lucky talisman. "Just promise *me* you won't tell anyone what I'm thinking about Vince, and you won't turn him in. If he didn't do anything . . . look, I don't want him to go through . . ." She shook her head. "He's a good guy. Unless I'm completely wrong. But . . . no, I'll tell you later. Can I call you?"

They exchanged cell phone numbers, and Brenda made her promise not to do anything until she got back to her later. She then strode off across the grass, back to the administrative building.

So that was that, for now. Sophie's cell phone chimed; it was a text from Jason, who was waiting for a student in his office. He said, Never leave my door unlocked and computer logged on; one of the things I told Dean A and Paul W. Gotta go; talk later?

So that answered that. She tapped in See u later, and just then the phone rang. She answered.

It was Dana. "So, I have a million things to tell you. I talked to Wally."

"Nothing about the investigation? I thought you were going to—"

"Humor me, Sophie. Let me tell things my way."

Sophie sighed and sat back on the bench. There was nothing to do when Dana had something in her mind. She'd do it her way, or no way at all.

"I talked to Wally, and told him what's up with Cissy. The dufus is so freaking relieved! He was afraid Cissy had feelings for my man. Can you believe that?"

"What's he going to do?"

"What I told him to. If you can hurry up and wrap up this case, he can get some time off and take Cissy for a weekend in the Poconos. I have a friend—an old boyfriend—who has a cabin he'll lend me, and I'm sending those two kids on a weekend alone so he can propose properly without Thelma calling her every half hour."

"If I can hurry up and wrap up this investigation?"

"That's what I said. And by the way? He was so relieved, I got Wally to spill some details. There *was* poison in the dean's system, but not enough to kill him, just to make him woozy. Something called aconite? I guess it can come from a local plant, the monkshood?"

Sophie immediately thought of Vince Nomuro's Man of the Year plaque for preserving local plant species. She *really* hoped Brenda didn't do anything that tipped him off to their suspicions.

"By the way, 'woozy' is not the official word; that's mine," Dana added. "Anyway, the cause of death ultimately was a stab wound to a major artery feeding the heart. He bled out quickly and died, possibly within a few minutes of being hit. A lucky strike, Wally called it."

"No weapon?"

"The killer must have taken the weapon with him. Or her. If whatever he was stabbed with had stayed in, he may have had a better chance, from what I understand. It looks like, according the doctor, he was ripped up inside as the weapon was pulled out. Wally says the doctor was kind of puzzled and wouldn't commit himself as to what kind of weapon it was, but maybe a barbed knife. I looked it up online; there's this knife called a zombie killer, a throwing knife, and it is wicked!"

"That's awful."

"I'll send you a pic of one I found."

Sophie received the message and examined the knife. It was odd looking, like three arrow points on a shaft.

"Yikes, that looks lethal!" Something like that sure would do damage as it was pulled out of a wound.

"I know. I went to the dress shop to talk to Sherri Shaw. Nice place, by the way. You should go there, get some decent clothes. I found the cutest sundress for next year, half off! I'll wear it when Eli and I go on our honeymoon to Madrid."

Sophie shook her head, trying to get rid of the cotton between her ears. Dana was occasionally scattered and her thoughts were rapid fire, like a machine gun, rat-a-tat-tat, a barrage of words and half thoughts. "So did you find out anything from Sherri at the dress shop?"

"She's mad and sad, all at once," Dana said, her tone more sober. "That'll be forty-three fifty-seven; cash, credit or debit?"

"What? Oh, you're at work."

"Yes, I am. Thank you. Have a nice day!"

Sophie was about to ask what again, when Dana said, "Now, where was I? Sherri . . . poor girl. This has hit her hard. She said the dean told her she was the love of his life, that he'd do anything for her, and that they were going to run away to New York together."

"And she bought it?'

"She's one of *those* women," Dana said. "I don't mean that the way it sounds. Just that she buys it. She believes it. He says things, she takes them in, embellishes them and spins them into a fairy dream castle with her as the pretty pink Barbie at the center. Can I help you?"

"What? Oh . . . Dana, I've got another call coming in and you've got a customer. Can I call you back? Or, you call me when the store is deserted."

"'Kay. We have a sale on textbooks for this season. What are you looking for?"

The other call was Josh. He had sneaked out during a study period. "Sophie, I wondered about something. We were trying to figure out how the poison got into the dean's system, if there was any."

"There was; I just got the confirmation. Aconite, maybe from a local plant called monkshood."

He told her his idea, and it meshed exactly with what she had been thinking. It all worked together, eyewitness accounts, her own observations, even the physical evidence. Every little bit of information she had jibed. However, one thing worried her deeply; where was Paul Wechsler? Jeanette Asquith said she had been to his home, and he wasn't there. Brenda was clearly worried about him, too. Sophie looked up at the college administration building. Jeanette had not emerged. Maybe she was still there and Sophie could catch her.

"I have to go, Josh. Thanks for the chat."

"What are you going to do?"

"I'm not sure. I guess I'll give everything I have to the police and let them sort it out."

"Good. I was worried you were thinking of tackling the killer yourself."

"No. I have no plan to do that."

Dana called moments after she finished with Josh, but she didn't have much information, though it all confirmed what she already thought. Sherri knew that Jeanette and Paul were together, and she had even spoken to him. Both paramours were hopeful that their dalliance would turn into a permanent relationship. Sherri had left the tea stroll after Dale Asquith promised her he would come to her that night, to *talk things over*, but he never showed up.

He was concerned mostly about how he came out of the scandal, and not so much who actually did it, according to Sherri. Trouble was, his intent to go into full damage control by announcing he'd reveal who made the grade change, or changes, may have given his killer a reason to not wait another minute and kill him that very night. At the very least, in Sophie's estimation, it tied his murder to the grading scandal.

"It's odd that Paul Wechsler is not to be found today," Sophie mused, but another customer came in that moment and Dana had to go.

Jeanette Asquith emerged from the administration building and headed down the walk to the parking lot. Sophie skipped across the green and caught up with her.

"Mrs. Asquith, I'm so sorry about everything you're going through."

The woman, her eyes red rimmed and bloodshot, her face lined with worry, stared at her. "I beg your pardon? Who are you?"

"I'm Sophie Taylor, you remember? Rosalind Taylor's daughter? We've spoken a couple of times, the last was at the tea stroll. I work for my grandmother at Auntie Rose's Victorian Tea House?"

"Yes, of course. You must forgive me. My brain is . . .

with everything that's happened I just . . ." She reached a champagne-colored Mercedes sedan and stood, her whole body wavering. She clutched the door handle but looked like she was holding on to keep from falling rather than about to get in the car.

"Mrs. Asquith, why don't you come and sit down for a moment. You look like you're about to faint." Sophie felt terrible for her, but was also hopeful she could learn more and get the woman's story. She led her across the grass to sit on a bench that was along the walk up to the building.

They sat in silence for a moment.

"How is your mother?" the woman asked, straightening her spine, her exquisite manners taking over even in the midst of her breakdown.

"She's well, in Tahiti right now. Or Bora-Bora. I can't remember. I talked to her yesterday." Sophie hesitated a moment, glancing over at the late dean's wife, who sat stiffly, rigidly upright. "I told her about your husband and she sent her condolences."

"Oh, yes, I've been getting lots of those . . . condolences. What does that even mean? Condolences; from the root word 'condole'; to express sympathy for a person who is suffering grief, or loss." She glanced at Sophie. "I'm a fallen woman, according to my late unlamented mother-in-law. She knew I had my . . . outside interests, and she knew Dale did, too. But she blamed *me* for both of them. Said if I was any kind of woman, I'd be able to keep him faithful. How about that? I not only strayed, but I was also to blame for my husband straying."

She snorted an ungenteel laugh that ended on a sob. "No one could keep Dale faithful because his whole ego was tied up in being that kind of man, the one all women wanted. I know because for a long while I actually tried. But especially lately. He was worried about losing his appeal as he aged, so he had accelerated his pace of late. Poor Sherri, she thought she could change him."

"Why didn't you leave?" Sophie asked, genuinely curious.

"I knew what I signed up for. We weren't in love; we were well matched. I didn't think I'd get to care, you know?" She sighed. "I did care. I didn't love him, not in that way, but we spent a lot of years together and we made a compatible couple for much of it."

Sophie sat sideways on the bench and watched her, seeing the frosty exterior as a cloak now, a cover to keep from caring, or at least to keep people from knowing she cared. "I'm so sorry. I truly am. No one can know how you feel but you." She waited a moment. "I know you are . . . uh, friends with Paul Wechsler. Nobody seems to know where he is today. Where could he be?"

Tears welled in her gray eyes and she shook her head. She pushed back her shoulder-length silvery hair, tucking it behind her ears. Reaching in her purse, she drew out a tissue and blotted her eyes carefully, trying not to dab away her pale blue eyeliner. "After he crashed the car yesterday, we had a bit of a fight and I didn't see him last night. I told him I had things to do. And now he's not answering his phone, he's not at home, he's . . . I don't know where."

Sophie had a gnawing sensation in the pit of her stomach. Her suspicion of the registrar was growing, and with it, her fear for Paul. She'd have to tell someone; she just had to. But not Jeanette Asquith, not until she knew more. "Have you called his friends, or family?"

She shook her head. "What would I say? They don't know about us."

"Mrs. Asquith . . . may I call you Jeanette?"

She nodded.

"Did he share anything about this grade-change scandal with you? I happen to know Paul was looking into it for your husband, and I overheard him saying some stuff to him that night, the night your husband was murdered."

She swallowed back her sobs and nodded, blew her nose, tucked the tissue back in her handbag and cleared her throat. "Dale asked to speak with him late last week. He had Paul go through every mark given and trace the computer trail. I don't pretend to understand. At the time I thought it was Dale's way of being nasty, because I told him Paul and I were going away over Christmas and he could go to his family gathering, which I loathe, alone."

"But?"

"But Paul told me Dale actually said he trusted him. He didn't want to bring in an outsider, and he wanted to be able to reassure the Board of Governors and President Schroeder that he had it all under control."

"I've heard some stuff that makes me wonder if Paul originally told him one person was the guilty party, and then later changed his mind."

"No, not at all. Paul told him one of two people were most likely to have changed the grade, but because of some security issue he had discovered, he wasn't sure, and that Dale would have to wait. But stupid Dale . . . so sure of himself. So self-important. He thought he could pressure Paul into bringing him the name by Monday morning, so he made that stupid announcement."

"It was like asking to be killed before Monday morning, if it was that serious an issue," Sophie said. "I spoke with Paul briefly and he indicated that he had discovered a pattern of grade changes except for one anomaly. What was that? Do you know?"

She nodded. "Cruickshank apparently has an Olympic hopeful in its ranks of athletes."

When she told Sophie the sport, it was not a surprise. Some things were beginning to make sense in a way she had not expected, though there were still a few loose ends, things she didn't understand. "Has he spoken to the police about any of this yet?"

"No, he was supposed to be going there yesterday at some point, but I don't think he made it. He was upset when we last spoke."

"Mrs. Asquith, I have to ask something. I hope you don't get offended, but someone overheard you saying something that night, something . . . well, I didn't know what to make of it. You were on your cell phone and said something about getting something done before you ran out of time. What was that about?"

The woman looked mystified for a moment, before a ghostly smile lifted one corner of her mouth. "Ah, yes, I know what you mean. I was speaking to my antiques dealer. He's having a Louis Quatorze sideboard refinished for me, and I needed him to get it done before Thanksgiving." She shook her head. "It seemed so important at the time. I always have people at the house for Thanksgiving, and I wanted it done to showcase the Sevres."

It figured that something so ominous sounding would turn out to be innocent. Sophie made a quick decision that went against her promise to Brenda, but she felt justified. A man's life may be at stake and that mattered more than anything. She told Jeanette what she had heard, that a witness reported last seeing Paul Wechsler in Vince Nomuro's car. She recommended that Jeanette go to the police and file a missing person's report on her boyfriend. They might not be able to do anything, but since they had information that e was involved in the evidence collecting for the grading candal, they just might. Paul had information, and the olice needed to speak with him; that would prompt them > search for the systems engineer.

Jeanette sped off in her sedan. Her sports car was likely > be in the shop indefinitely, given how complicated repairs n foreign cars could be.

Her sports car, which Paul had been borrowing. Sophie emembered the night of the murder, and the sound of a porty car revving around the time of the murder. Something osh said came back to her. If what she suspected was true, aen she now knew who the killer was.

The more she thought about it, the more certain she was f her theory. But what to do? Just turn the info over to the olice? She knew how good the police were at doing their obs. She had nothing against them, but she also felt that ometimes her ability to circumvent the rules allowed her > uncover the truth much more quickly.

How much better would it be if she could enlist her riends to set the killer up to exposure? She nodded. Sereni- ea, in this instance, would be the perfect place. She left a message on Jason's phone, and decided to head back to Aun- ie Rose's.

Thelma was playing with her phone again, but it was hopeless. The only thing she had figured out with any urety was the danged camera function, but the stupid thing ad a camera on both sides, because along with some photos f Gilda's big bottom were a few fuzzy- and wrinkly-looking nes of what Thelma had at long last concluded were of her: jowl with a few hairs sprouting, a double chin, and a bleary ye set in wrinkled folds of skin.

She had also finally figured out how to scan through tl photos. Aha! There were the ones she remembered takin after the tea stroll from her bedroom window on the fro of the house down to the street, which had been kinda dar She was just able to make out a little car in one, and tv figures together in another.

"Gilda!" she hollered.

"What do you want?" Gilda asked, tottering into tl room on new two-inch heels.

Thelma stared. "What are you all gussied up for? Nev mind." She picked up the phone and stared at a pictur "Look, this is you the night of the tea thingie, when yo were taking out the garbage. Remember? Well, I took son photos before that, while you did it, and later, trying to g the hang of this. Do you see the car?"

Gilda got close and brought up her cheaters, which da gled around her neck on a fancy string of beads like son useful version of a necklace. "Yeah. I see it."

"And the next picture, do you see those two people?"

Gilda stared again. "Yeah. I still can't believe you se me out knowing someone was lurking! I could have bee jumped and murdered, or worse!"

"Stop whining. Nothing happened, did it?"

Gilda tottered to the back door where there was a mirr on the wall and pulled an orange-colored lip balm out her purse. She stroked some on her lips.

"Where are you going anyway?"

She stuck up her nose, snooty as could be, and said, "O With friends." She tottered out the door.

Thelma stared closer at the pictures, but couldn't be su of what she was seeing. Her vision was not what it used be. There was only one thing *to* do. She grabbed the re phone, the reliable one that didn't take a college degree in computers to work, and called Cissy.

R ose was working on the accounting and sighed at the end of a long line of numbers. She sure hoped they could open again, and soon. Not because they were losing money—though they were—but because she didn't know what to do with her time. They had cleaned the place from top to bottom, and taken inventory. And now she was lost. Laverne had gone home to give her father something to eat, after which she, Gilda, and Laverne's father, Malcolm, would be going to the Tuesday night church social.

Wherever Sophie was, Rose hoped she was safe. Her granddaughter had inherited her uncle Jack's adventurous spirit, the resolve that had sent him, after they lost her other son, Harold Junior, to the Vietnam War, to the West Coast to join the antiwar protests. He got lost along the way, his deals tainted by drugs and a broken heart. His brother was everything to Jack, and losing him changed him forever. Sometimes it felt like sorrow would close around Rose's heart and smother it, but then she stiffened her spine and remembered Rosalind and her wonderful grandchildren, especially her own darling Sophie.

The phone rang. "Auntie Rose's Victorian Tea House. How may I help you?" It came automatic after so many years.

"Is Sophie there?" It was a young woman's voice.

"No, I'm sorry, she's not. May I ask who's calling?"

There was a moment of hesitation. "Do you know when he'll be back?"

"No. May I take a message?"

"Can you tell her Kimmy called? Kimmy Gabrielson.

I've got some information, and I'm not sure what to do abou
it. I need someone to trust, someone who isn't connecte
with the college." Her voice held a note of desperation. "Sh
seemed determined to get to the bottom of things."

"Oh, honey, maybe you should tell me so I can tell her?

"No, I can't do that."

"No hints?"

"I saw something weird, and I need to talk to her. I trie
her cell, but she's not answering. I didn't leave a messag
because I didn't know what to say. When you see her, te
her to call me right away. She has my number."

"Honey, are you okay? Kimmy? I'm worried about you
Are you all right?"

"I don't know. I'm going to see someone right now to tr
to straighten things out. Just give Sophie that message." Th
line went dead.

Chapter 22

The day had wasted away. It was late afternoon and Sophie felt exhausted. She had been asked to stop at the police station, but if she went there it would take hours to tell them everything she was thinking, had conjectured and was wondering about. It would have to wait. She was determined to get down to the truth, now that she had an idea what it was. She entered through the back door to be met by Nana, who was pacing, with Pearl at her feet.

"Oh, Sophie, I was so worried. I tried calling your cell phone. Why didn't you answer?"

Sophie grasped Nana's forearms and made her sit down, concerned about how pale her grandmother looked. "I was in the car. I never answer while driving, you know that."

Nana nodded. "Of course. Kimmy Gabrielson called. She wouldn't tell me what was wrong, but asked if you could call her. She said something that worried me a bit; she said she was going to see someone right then to try to straighten things out."

"That doesn't sound too worrisome."

"You didn't hear her tone. She was . . . puzzled. And upset."

Sophie eyed her grandmother and nodded. Nana had excellent people skills and was empathetic, which meant she must have sensed something over the phone line to be so worried about it. "What specifically are you worried about?"

Nana picked Pearl up and cradled the cat in her arms. "That she was upset by whatever she saw, and yet was going ahead to talk to whomever it was that was involved."

Sophie pulled her phone out of her purse and checked it; Kimmy had tried to call multiple times, but whenever she was in the car driving Sophie ignored the phone. She hit the call button, but this time it was Kimmy who wasn't answering. She left a message to call her, saying, "Hey, Kimmy, it's Sophie. My grandmother was concerned about your call. Is everything okay? Call me back as soon as you can."

There was a tap at the kitchen door, and Sophie hopped over to answer it. Cissy Peterson, a cell phone in one hand and her other arm supporting Thelma, said, "Can we come in? Grandma needs to show you something."

Sophie pulled Cissy into the warm kitchen; the poor girl was shivering. She was always shivering if so much as a mild breeze was blowing. Thelma toddled in after her, and Sophie guided both women over to the small table and made them sit down. Thelma was oddly withdrawn, and Cissy abnormally buoyant.

"What's up?" Sophie asked.

"You're not going to believe this," Cissy said. She played with the cell phone for a moment, bringing up images. "Grandma can't figure out how to use this as a phone, but she sure has figured out how to take photos, even when she doesn't know she's taking photos. She took these from her second-floor window the night of the tea stroll, after everyone had

gone, before she sent Gilda out to do the garbage. What do
you think?"

Sophie held it so Nana could see the screen. "It's hard to
tell what any of that is," she said. "Wait, I think I can zoom
in on this picture. Or even better . . ." She raced upstairs to
her desk and linked the phone and her printer, then printed
off the photos. By the time she came back down, Nana had
hot cups of Auntie Rose's Tea-riffic tea blend sitting in front
of Cissy and Thelma. Sophie plunked the photos down on
the table. "These are grainy, but . . . oh, good lord!" she said,
staring more closely at the pictures, two in particular.

"What is it?" Cissy and Nana said simultaneously as
Thelma grunted.

Sophie got a pen and circled something in the passenger
side seat of the sports car she had heard that very night, and
which was parked at the far curb. "Look at that, sticking up;
that is the weapon, or at least a part of the weapon." She
circled a section of another photo of two people in an embrace
of sorts. Sophie shivered and pointed her pen to the circle.
"And that is a killer and murder victim. Dean Asquith never
saw it coming."

The other women stared at it, and Nana got it after a
moment. "I think we know who that is," she said, and named
the killer.

Sophie nodded. "You're right, Nana. Mrs. Earnshaw,
you're a genius, and you may have given us proof that the
police can't ignore." She took the older woman's hand.
"Thank you for this."

Mrs. Earnshaw nodded. "I'm glad it helps. Couldn't make
hide nor hair of who it was myself, but you seem to know them
all better than me. I'm glad because . . . well, because I know
I caused you mischief with the salt in the sugar packets."

"Why on earth did you do it?" Nana asked.

Mrs. Earnshaw shook her head. "I don't know. Sometimes I swear, I see the world like it's turned upside down."

Sophie kept her mouth shut. After years of managing employees, she felt like she'd attained some insight into human behavior; for some it was virtually impossible to release a grudge, no matter how old. She had her theories as to why Thelma did what she did—it involved old unresolved jealousy of Nana—but it wouldn't do any good to rehash that distant past once again. Everyone thought that by talking things out they could dismiss old problems, but for some folks that didn't work. That was true of Thelma Mae Earnshaw, still holding on to the sixty-year-old grievance that Rose stole her supposed beau.

The photos were too grainy and too far away for anyone but those who knew what they were looking at to decipher. Cissy went back to Belle Époque, taking the photos and her grandmother with her. She was going to call Wally, who was at home right then, and tell him Sophie's plan at just the right time. Sophie would let her know when.

Nana was worried; Sophie could tell. But she would never stop her granddaughter from doing what she thought right. When Sophie graduated from high school Nana was the one constant, unwavering source of support for all her plans and dreams of culinary school and opening a restaurant.

Her mother had always said that Sophie inherited her father's business drive. She had certainly listened to him anytime he talked; those moments were precious to her, the longing to have his approval was constant in her teen years. Something he once told her had stuck; he said that in every case when he thought he was right, he preferred to beg for forgiveness *after* doing something, than ask for permission *before* doing it.

She was putting that into action. Sophie left a message

n Josh's cell phone to call her as soon as he was able, then
honed Julia and explained what she now knew and what
he planned, if Julia was willing to help.

"Oh, my goodness . . . are you sure? I mean, can that be
rue? I never would have expected this."

"I'm pretty positive, but what alarms me most is that Paul
Wechsler is missing and I'm concerned about the message
rom Kimmy Gabrielson, who is *not* answering my calls. I
hink we need to act on this right away so nobody else gets
urt. I know the police should be involved, but I'm afraid if
hey take control, they'll have to wait for warrants and sub-
poenas, and I'm scared to death when we have a human life,
nd maybe two, hanging in the balance." She paused, thought
 through, then said, "But can you do your part if we do this
ny way? Can you play it off?"

"If what you're telling me is true, then I will do it, and I'll
o it well. In my misspent youth I was actually in, among
ther works, a rather awful off-off-Broadway play about a
irl who manipulated people into giving her exactly what she
eeded. I was very Method; my parents still remember it as
heir six months of hell, because I lived in that bitchy girl's
kin. I did a lot of research, and tried out some of the tech-
iques on people. I can do this."

"But do you *want* to?" Sophie persisted. She was begin-
ing to get cold feet. She could back out now, give all the
nformation to Detective Morris and . . . and what? Wait
vhile the detective and the DA decided if they had enough
o nail the killer? Worry about Paul Wechsler, who no one
ad seen or heard from in twenty-four hours? Try to find
Kimmy Gabrielson, who had gone off to who knows where?
Her resolve hardened, but still . . . "I wouldn't put you in
arm's way, Julia; not for the world. I'd never forgive—"

"Sophie, this is *my* choice. The police could investigate

this and likely make the arrest, or at least, *try* to make the arrest, but if we can provide them with a stronger case without it seeming like entrapment, I'm willing to do my part. What if you're right and Paul Wechsler is in danger?"

They set it up, and Julia made the calls that she needed to make, then reported back to Sophie that it was done. The meeting was set.

"Really?" Sophia asked. "It was that easy?"

"It was. But I think I'm being set up, if you wanted to know the truth. I said I wanted to get in on the bribery action. Our culprit is canny and insisted on knowing how I figured it all out. I said I wouldn't talk until we met face-to-face."

Sophie had an uneasy feeling in her gut, a heck of a time for that to start acting up. "It's not too late to back out, you know. In fact . . . Julia, we need to shut this down," she said, her voice trembling. "I'm going to call the police and—"

"No!" Julia said. "If you do that, I'll set up the meeting for right now and do this on my own. We are going ahead."

Alarm growing, Sophie tried to talk her out of it, but ultimately she knew that the professor would be safer if they went ahead as Sophie had planned, because she had backup built into the plot. Over the next few hours she prepared and finally heard back from both Josh, whose technical ability was vital to the plan, and Jason, who was going to be Sophie's escort.

He listened as she explained the plan, and then burst out. "Sophie, that is *insane*! How could you put Julia in danger like this?"

"I've had second thoughts about it. Jase, I *tried* to call it off, but Julia won't let me. She threatened to go ahead alone. The only thing we can do now is be the safety net and get it right."

"No, there's another way. *I* can be the pigeon. I'll meet the lunatic and say I'm looking to get in on the action."

"That won't work, and you know it," Sophie said, pacing in her apartment, and then ducking to glance out the window in her front-facing bedroom. "You were set up to be the fall guy from the beginning; there's no way you'd turn around and want in on the action." She glanced at her alarm clock. "Time is too tight now to change it up. Josh is all set. You need to meet me there in half an hour so we can set everything up, make sure it's right." There was silence for a long minute, and Sophie felt everything hanging in the balance, including her future relationship with Jason. "Please, Jase! I know you don't like this, but now that we've committed to it, it's important to keep Julia protected."

"If Julia can't be dissuaded, then we'll work together to make sure she's safe."

"I hope you know I never intended to put Julia in harm's way. I should *never* have gone to her like I did; I should have waited until I could run it past you. But now she won't back down. I'm sorry. I really am."

"I know. We'll have to make sure nothing goes wrong."

Sophie supervised the setup at SereniTea, but she hadn't been able to eat dinner when they came back to Auntie Rose's. Jason had wolfed down a few sandwiches. He had some course work on his laptop that he was checking over. He explained that in his course he left it optional to his students to submit their work on paper or electronically, but that he was going to change in future to all electronic. That way he could demand that his students run their work through a plagiarism-checking software. He had been too trusting for too long, and had recently become aware that some of his students were even paying others to do their

essays for them. He had been naive, thinking he was bein
watchful enough, but no more.

Sophie half listened, anxiously watching the clock. Nan
luckily, seemed distracted and spent the time on the phor
and fussing around up in her own apartment. Sophie pace
ran upstairs to change her clothes into dark yoga pants an
a sweatshirt, raced back downstairs and resumed pacin
But finally, it was time to move.

When they emerged from Auntie Rose's in the twiligh
they were witness to an awesome sight. Their street wa
often populated by folks walking dogs or out strolling; th
was not so unusual. But tonight it was who was there th
was strange. Two elderly gentlemen (Malcolm Hodge ar
Horace Brubaker) helped Mr. Bellows, who leaned on
rollator walker as they strolled slowly up the street, in th
direction of SereniTea. Nana was outside of Belle Époqu
having a heated argument with Thelma Mae Earnshaw, wh
had a large purse over her arm. Laverne pulled up to th
tearoom with Gilda Bachman in her passenger seat.

Sophie stopped dead. "Oh, my heavens! We have th
Silver Spouts Investigative Team in full battle readiness."

Jason stifled a laugh as he took Sophie's hand. "Indee
we do."

"I wish they weren't doing this, but you cannot keep thos
folks down."

They walked up the hill, slipped into SereniTea, ar
concealed themselves in the private tearoom that shared
wall with the office. Josh had wired in a simple recordir
setup, and borrowed from his school's audio video clu
some pairs of wireless headphones for Sophie, Jason, ar
himself, of course, because he would *not* be left out. Soph
had the cold shuddering horrors as she realized what sh
had done, dragging a pregnant woman, a teenage boy, h

kinda-sorta boyfriend and even—inadvertently—a collection of oldsters into her mad scheme to out the villain.

"Next time I get a brilliant idea I'm going to run it past you first," she whispered fervently to Jason. "You're the level head to my impulsivity."

"Next time," he murmured back, squeezing her hand. "We're in it now, so keep your head in the game."

They sank down together in the shadows by the wall, right near the door into the office, and Sophie prayed as she crouched in silence. There was some noise in the office. Sophie could hear Julia clear her throat and shuffle some papers, and she said softly, "Testing." Sophie rapped on the floor in their prearranged signal.

There was silence for a while, just the sound of Julia sighing, rattling through papers, muttering under her breath and her chair squeaking. But finally there was a tapping at the back door, which led directly from the office out to the parking area behind the shop. Sophie almost held her breath, listening.

"You came," Julia said. "I wasn't sure you would."

There was a murmur. Sophie's prayer switched to an earnest one that the confession-slash-revelation they hoped to get was audible on tape. Had Josh done everything right? Was the recording device on? Would the killer reveal everything they needed for a conviction? Had the police showed up outside, which was Cissy's part in this all?

"Have a seat and let's get down to business."

Sophie almost didn't recognize Julia's voice, and she exchanged a glance with Jason. But he nodded; like most people, she probably had a voice she used normally, in conversation, and one she saved for talking to difficult people when the need to be stern overrode any desire to placate. Jason would have heard that businesslike tone before.

"Let's. I'm not quite sure what you meant by what you said on the phone, but if you think I have something to do with this whole grading mess, then I'm ready to listen."

Sophie took in a deep breath. So that was how Brenda Fletcher was going to play it, as the mystified innocent; okay, then Julia would have to be canny. She let her breath out quietly, hoping the professor could handle what was on her shoulders.

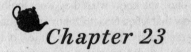

Chapter 23

"**C**ome on, Brenda, I *know* you're behind it all. Do you think I haven't been working on figuring this out since Asquith first talked about the fake grade? And do you think I ever for a *moment* assumed it would be just one student's grade? Quite frankly, Jason's not smart enough to take money for changing a grade."

Sophie squeezed Jason's hand in the dark. There had been no response from Brenda.

"But *I* am," Julia said.

Sophie felt a spurt of fear; right now, on tape, that would play like a confession of grade changing from Julia. They needed Brenda to come through with her own confession.

"Why don't you tell me what happened?" Brenda asked, sitting down and shifting position, from the sounds coming through the headphones.

There was silence for a long minute. Then Julia said, "I'll

tell you what I know. After a little digging I know that you were on the archery team while an undergrad." That was amazingly simple to find out, since Brenda had done her undergrad degree at Cruickshank. It was all there, in the recent athletic history of the school. Sophie had discovered it in minutes once she knew what they were looking for.

"And I know that when Coach Donovan approached you about upping the grades of some of his critical players, like Mac MacAlister, he also promised the cooperation of the football coach," Julia continued. "You got the idea to also help out a particular grad student who is poised to go to the Olympics if she can keep training with the Cruickshank archery coach. For that she needs to keep her archery scholarship, which requires a B or better."

Sophie nodded. She was sticking to script.

Brenda was silent, and so was Julia. But finally the assistant registrar said, "That's quite the fairy tale you've spun." There was suspicion in her voice.

This was the moment; Sophie felt it. When you were trying to get someone to do something, there was always a moment when it hung suspended, on the precipice. Anything Julia said now would either tip Brenda over the edge into trust, or make her back away from the edge in hardened suspicion.

"Brenda, I need you to let me in on this," Julia said, urgency threading through her tone. "Now that Dale is dead, I can find a way to hush this up," she continued. "I don't know what Dale was going to tell the media, and I don't care. It's lucky he died before being able to speak. I'll bet Paul killed Dale, he was so anxious to get Jeanette to himself. Or maybe Jeanette killed her husband; I never did like her."

There was a protracted silence. Sophie waited. She and Julia had decided against having her admit to Brenda that he knew the assistant registrar was the dean's killer. Brenda was unlikely to believe that Julia would shield a murderer out of greed so she could get in on the scam.

Sophie crossed her fingers as she glanced at her lit watch dial. Eight o'clock. Josh would have provided the police with a headset now, and they'd be listening in. She hoped they didn't interrupt, as they may feel they should.

"Okay, say I believe that you can hush up the grade scandal thingie," Brenda said. "Though I don't admit anything. Why would you, a hoity-toity professor on the tenure track, be willing to risk it all to alter grades?"

"Because I can," Julia said, her tone smug, with a hint of laughter. "That's exactly why; no one will suspect me."

"I don't believe you."

"I *need* this, Brenda, badly," Julia said, her voice breaking.

Sophie's eyes widened. Good touch!

"I'm keeping things together, but just barely. I'm almost broke, I'm . . . I'm pregnant, and my husband is going to leave me if I drive us into bankruptcy with this stupid, god-awful teahouse," she said, her voice harsh and grating. "I hate it! You saw what it was like the night of the stroll; bad food, bad management. What was I *thinking*? And now I'm going to bring a baby into this . . . this *mess*. I'm going to have to sell this place, but if I don't get some money soon, I'll lose everything. I'm desperate."

"So you *need* me," Brenda said, her tone gloating.

Bingo. Sophie squeezed Jason's hand. They had her.

"I didn't say that," Julia replied. "I could go ahead and set his up on my own, and I think I'm probably smarter than you, so *I* won't get caught."

Sophie's eyes widened. That wasn't part of the script! *No, no! Julia don't blow it*, she thought.

"You think you're smarter than me?" Brenda bellowed.

Or maybe taunting an egoist like Brenda was just the right move. *Brava, Julia*, as Jason would say.

"I *know* I'm smarter than you. After all, I figured out your scheme, right?"

"Every professor and teacher at Cruickshank thinks they're so damned smart," Brenda griped. "Bunch of frickin' losers. If you were so smart, you wouldn't be teaching at a third-rate college with the rest of these boneheads. I'm *so* much smarter than all of you, because I figured out a way to double my measly salary. I did it *all*, my own plan. You're dead wrong, you know. Heck Donovan didn't approach me; I approached *him*, even though he didn't know it was me! He *thought* he was dealing with Vince, can you believe it?"

Sophie almost gasped in surprise. That was kind of brilliant, to do all of that and yet hide behind a third party.

"Asquith didn't know it was me, either," she said.

"Well, no; he thought it was Vince, right?"

Brenda chuckled. "Yeah, I had everyone confused. Vince thought it was Paul, and Paul thought it was Vince. The dean thought it was Vince, too, and wanted Paul to prove it."

"That couldn't have gone on forever," Julia said. "Was it just luck that Dale was murdered that night?"

Sophie tensed; how were they going to get Brenda to admit she killed the dean? Surely she wouldn't just say she did it. The confession they needed felt like a long shot now; maybe they hadn't planned it quite well enough. So far all they had was the grade fixing.

Brenda sighed. "You know what, I'm sorry it's come to this. But I can't let you join my little scheme, and I certainly can't have you approaching student athletes on your own. I think . . . yeah, you're going to have to be a sad victim of circumstances."

"I don't understand."

"Paul may have suspected that you were the grade fixer all along; I can find a way to support that. So you killed him, then out of remorse came back here and took your own life. It's messy, and not what was supposed to go down, but it has as good a chance as any of working. Big risk, big reward."

Sophie stared into the shadows, listening to the madness.

"Brenda, what are you talking about?" Julia asked, a note of real fear quavering through her voice.

Sophie felt for Jason's hand and squeezed one more time. It was time to end this farce. She slowly, quietly rose from her squatted position, but her feet were numb and she stumbled slightly.

"What are you looking for?" Julia said sharply, her words covering up, hopefully, the faint noise Sophie had made.

"That's a nice letter opener, kind of Oriental, and pointy." There was a clatter. "You know, Dale never saw it coming. I'm sure he felt the arrow I shot from across the street in the dark, even though it just nicked his neck. Enough to get a little aconite in his bloodstream, anyway, and make him shaky and weak. I'm a pretty good shot; I should have gone to the Olympics myself, but I have other plans." She paused, then said, in a conversational tone, "Trouble was, Dale was going to name the wrong person, true, but a little digging by anyone, even that stupid news brat, and folks would have figured out it was me who altered the grades using Vince's computer and password."

"But the worst that would have happened was you'd get fired, right?"

"Maybe. But then I wouldn't be able to get another job as registrar, right? So many schools, so many student athletes, all longing for good grades. Cruickshank was just the beginning for me. I'll do it again, and do it better. I needed a distraction, a fall guy. I wasn't entirely sure what I was going to do to cover my tracks, but getting rid of Dale seemed like a good first step. He met me there like the schmuck he was—he always did underestimate women— and never saw it coming until the moment I got real close and plunged my arrow in his chest, twisting it before pulling it out. The snob had it coming to him." The sound of a chair pushing away from the desk rattled in their headphones.

Julia, her voice quivering with honest fear this time, said, "Brenda, you *killed* Dale? I didn't think . . . I mean—"

"Of *course* you didn't think."

There was a noise outside, a car door slamming.

"What was that?" Brenda said.

"The police, coming to get you!" Julia shrieked. "Jason, Sophie!"

That was their cue; together they surged toward the office door, but it flung open and knocked them backward onto the floor. Brenda, swearing, clattered through the dim rooms to the tearoom entrance; the front door banged open, a motion detector alarm going off. "Jason, make sure Julia is okay," Sophie said, springing back onto her feet. "I have to follow Brenda!"

Jason grabbed her and kissed her and said, "Go get 'em, tiger! But don't do anything stupid."

Sophie dashed through the dark tearoom after Brenda and out of the front. A police car was on the other side of the street, and the detective was getting out, her service revolver in her hands. Brenda dashed down the street toward her pricey little Porsche Boxster.

"Stop! Police!" Detective Morris shouted, pointing the gun at Brenda's back, but the woman started zigzagging.

Sophie raced after her and saw the beautiful moment when Brenda Fletcher went flying, tumbling down the sloped street tripped by a rolling walker shoved in her way by Mr. Bellows and his two companions. Thelma Mae Earnshaw hobbled over to the downed young woman and began whaling away at her with a heavy ancient pocketbook constructed out of the finest alligator skin, shouting unintelligible swear words. She had to be hauled off the murderess by Officer Wally Bowman, who contained her as Detective Morris shoved Brenda Fletcher's face down into the dirt and grass and made the arrest, with all the appropriate warnings.

Three hours later, as Sophie and the rest waited in Auntie Rose's tearoom, they got the news. Paul Wechsler and Kimmy Gabrielson had been found unharmed in Brenda Fletcher's basement. Paul admitted that he had gone to see Brenda to try to blackmail her, since he had figured out she was behind the grade scam. She agreed to pay him off and convinced him she had a safe full of money in her basement. He underestimated her. She led him there and knocked him out, tying him up while he was unconscious. Her intentions toward him were unclear, but Sophie wondered if she was going to stage something that would make it look like Paul was behind it all, and had killed the dean, too, before committing suicide out of remorse.

That plot was messed up when Kimmy Gabrielson came hammering on her door demanding answers. Kimmy, gullible as could be, followed the assistant registrar downstairs, where Brenda said she had all the information that Kimmy would need to expose the real guilty party. Kimmy, too, was neatly knocked out and confined with Paul Wechsler as Brenda went to meet Julia, trying to decide what the professor knew, if anything.

Brenda Fletcher was digging herself deeper and deeper
into a hole, despite her posturing bravado toward Julia. Her
plot was becoming tortured and overcomplicated, and she
would have been found out at some point soon, since the
police were closing in on her and Vince Nomuro as the
logical suspects. Brenda had already brought attention to
herself by being the one who questioned Jason's timeline
with the police. It seemed she was not above throwing shade
wherever she could. But thanks to Sophie, Julia and the
others, Paul and Kimmy were unharmed, and the police had
what appeared to be an airtight case against the assistant
registrar.

"What gave you the idea that it was Brenda behind
the grade altering and not Vince?" Julia asked
the next day, as they all sat in the now-open Auntie Rose's
tearoom.

Sophie poured her a cup of mint tea and smiled, deeply
grateful that the professor seemed none the worse for a
frightening confrontation with a killer. "There were a few
things. It snowballed, I guess. Random facts. I noticed all
the pins on Brenda Fletcher's jacket when I met her in the
bookstore the day after the murder, but what I didn't realize
was the pin I thought was for her birth sign, Sagittarius,
couldn't be, because her birthday is the end of October and
Sagittarius doesn't start until late November. She's a Scor-
pio, a scorpion.

"Why would she wear a Sagittarius pin, then? Well, she
wouldn't, but I realized if it wasn't a zodiac sign, then the
pin was simply an archer. When I found out what the postu-
lated weapon in killing the dean was, that it had to be barbed

to do the damage it did internally, I thought of an arrow, and more specifically a poison arrow, which could have caused the nick on the dean's neck and his other symptoms. Furthermore, when I cleaned out our carpet cleaner, there were feathers clogging it. I couldn't figure out where they came from until I learned Brenda was into archery, and I remembered a friend in prep school who made all her own arrows. Brenda was one of the few people who actually was in the tearoom, so I wondered if they came out of her coat pocket. I'll never know for sure, I guess. We know the rest from her own words; she actually did use poison on the arrow, aconite, which incapacitated the dean somewhat. Then she came right up to him and stabbed him with another arrow, pulled it out, and carried it away with her."

"I can't believe she did that," Jason said. "Quiet, meek little Brenda. I never looked at her twice!"

"She sure didn't seem meek to me," Julia said, shivering.

"She was wearing a different jacket the night of the tea stroll, a nice one, but she never wore it again. I was surprised she didn't wear something nicer to work other than that ratty old jacket with all the archery pins. But now I realize, the *nice* jacket must have been splattered with the dean's blood and couldn't be worn until cleaned. Those other pins, an apple and some scatter pins with initials, were all archery related, too. An apple is a common archery pin; I guess it probably came from the old William Tell story, of the apple on his son's head. But the others . . . after I started getting suspicious of her I looked up the initials on them—at least the few I remembered—and found out they were from school teams she'd been on. And by the way, that ratty old jacket was worn more on one sleeve than the other because it's the one she used to wear when she practices archery.

Archers wear a protective guard along their bow arm, and I think it rubbed on the fabric, wearing it out unevenly."

"Clever girl! So, what about the sightings of Vince Nomuro in his tweed cap late that night?" Nana asked.

"He *was* wearing the duffer cap, but at some point Brenda stole the cap, probably from his car before he left, and wore it to do the murder so her face would be concealed by the brim. They're about the same height." She paused and frowned. "You know, I realized suddenly that her alibi was predicated on having a roommate that she stayed up with and told everything to about the evening. But she told me, among other things, that Vince was nice enough to feed her cat for her when she went out of town. If she had a roommate, why did she need someone to come in and feed her cat? I was pretty sure that there *was* no roommate, and of course now we know that, because she felt completely safe in locking Paul and Kimmy in her basement. No roommate, no alibi.

"By the way," Sophie continued, "she was his Secret Santa last Christmas and gave him the arrow tie clip he wears. I figured that, though I wasn't sure. Tara called me this morning with some info; a few folks in the office told her that Brenda Fletcher was behind his recent ten years of service gift, a reproduction urn with the images of archers on it. Like a lot of people, she planned gifts according to what she likes, rather than considering what the person would like to receive. When I began to suspect it was an arrow used to kill the dean, those items, the arrow tie pin and the urn with the archers on it, threw me off for a while; I thought maybe Vince was the grade scammer *and* killer."

"And the sports car in Grandma's photo?" Cissy asked.

"Yeah, the sports car. I was thrown off by that as well, because everyone seemed to drive one, even Vince. But so did Brenda, and if I'd paid attention to something Josh said earlier, I would have wondered how an assistant registrar who was paying for her doctorate could afford a newish Porsche Boxster. Dead giveaway. You could kind of see, in that picture, the outline of the bow sticking up in the passenger seat."

Chapter 24

The scandal rippled through the college ranks. Dozens of student athletes had their grades adjusted. Heck Donovan was fired and arrested for his part in the affair, as financial records proved the bribery was funneled through him, and that he actually took a cut off the top before putting the rest of the money in a safe deposit box in the bank. Penny left him and moved back to New York, taking her job back at the nonprofit.

An interim dean of faculty was named. Computer security was made a priority, but they had to hire an outside firm to take care of it. Paul Wechsler moved to New York with Jeanette Asquith, leaving his job for his own start-up, funded by his wealthy girlfriend, who by all accounts loved him in ways she had never loved her husband.

And Mac MacAlister was expelled, not for the grade alteration, but for skimming through school on bought papers paid for by his ambitious parents. Tara exposed it all with the help of Kimmy Gabrielson, who had been trying to get Mac to eschew the easy way out and actually study. That was what she had been telling him the night of the tea stroll when she pulled him aside, that if he didn't start writing his own papers, she'd turn him in. In fact, Kimmy confessed that she had been trying to stir things up without getting into the mess herself, and that was why she had slipped the badly spelled note into Julia's mail slot; she was hoping Julia would investigate further.

The unlikely pair Tara Mitchells saw was Paul Wechsler with Vince, who gave him a lift the day he crashed Jeanette's car. She got her byline on a piece in the Rochester newspaper on cheating by college athletes, and every word of it was the truth.

Almost two weeks later, Dana Saunders was a happily engaged young woman, and had gotten her friend to let Wally and Cissy book the cottage on the lake for a romantic weekend away, just the two of them. It was a Saturday, and Belle Époque was full, with Thelma seated at a table in the middle of things, regaling the tea sippers with her story of how she beat the killer into submission so the police could haul her away.

Auntie Rose's was busy, too, but Cindy, supervised by Laverne, was happily working away, making scads of money in tips. For the moment there was a lull, as everyone had their tea and goodies. Sophie washed some dishes as Nana sat at the register in front. The Auntie Rose phone rang.

It was Wally. "Sophie, you, Laverne and Mrs. Freemont better get over to Belle Époque right away! Something major is up," he said, and then the phone went dead.

"What now?" Sophie hurriedly explained to her godmother

and grandmother what Wally said, and hustled them across the alley. Gilda let them in the side door and led them through the kitchen to the tearoom, a silly smirk on her face. As they entered from the back, they saw Dana, Eli and Jason at a table with Cissy. Wally, uniformed, stormed in the front door and rushed to the table.

And dropped to one knee by Cissy. "Cissy Peterson, when I first saw you, you were a little girl in a flowered dress a little too big and knee socks that sagged down around your ankles. You were six and I was seven, and I fell in love with you." His voice broke, and he paused, clearing his throat.

Cissy, eyes wide and again wearing a pretty floral dress, had her hands clasped in front of her. Thelma, grinning, had turned from her group and sat, her hands propped on her knees, watching.

Sophie hopped up and down, grabbing Nana's arm and hauled her closer. "He's going to do it right here and now," she muttered to her grandmother.

Laverne whispered, "My good lord, he is!"

He pulled a ring box out of his blue police shirt pocket. "Cissy Peterson, I would be the happiest and proudest man on the planet if you would allow me to serve and protect you for the rest of our lives."

Cissy burst into tears, and the tea drinkers broke out into applause, but among the blubbering, clapping and cheering, Sophie could understand one word: *yes.*

Only it sounded more like "Yesyesyesyes."

A while later, as Cissy and Wally sat at a table in the corner canoodling, as Thelma called it, Sophie and Nana sat with Jason, Eli and Dana. Dana explained that Wally told her he was not going to leave Mrs. Earnshaw out of the most important moment in her granddaughter's life, not when it was so important to her that Cissy was happy. He was sincere.

but it didn't hurt that it would earn him major brownie points, either.

"So, we're all taking the plunge," Dana said, waving her left hand with her own nice-size sparkler, as Eli gazed at her adoringly. "When are you two kids going to get down to brass tacks?" She eyed Sophie and Jason with one raised eyebrow.

Everyone laughed, but Sophie wondered, what did Jason really think?

A little while later, Jason said, "Can I walk you home, Soph?"

"All the way across the alley? Why certainly, sir."

The others exchanged glances, but no one said a word. She followed him out the front door.

"Let's go for a drive instead," he said.

"It's pretty cold," Sophie said, eyeing the sports car Jason had once again borrowed from Julia. "You have got to stop borrowing that car."

"I didn't borrow it, it's mine. With the baby coming she needed to get rid of it, so I bought it."

"Really? Cool!" She hopped in, and he put the top up. He drove her to the lake, where as teenagers they hung out all summer every summer when she wasn't at Auntie Rose's and he wasn't working in his father's hardware store. Hand in hand they walked down to the dock and sat on a bench. All the boats were gone, and the lake looked deserted. She could see all the way across the beautiful blue stretch to the long low hill on the other side of Seneca Lake, clothed in a solid forest of gold, red and brown trees. It made a gorgeous tableau that reflected in the still water.

He turned to her. "Sophie, I've been thinking about this for a while. When we were teenagers you got under my skin pretty good. I was heartbroken when you left, but I get now why your mom didn't want us to get too serious. We were kids."

"Uh-huh." She stared into his light brown eyes, swept his longish hair behind his ear and caressed his stubbly chin.

"But we're not kids anymore. Soph, I'm still nuts about you. I think about you all the time. Even with all the crazy stunts you pull, I think I might be more than a little in love with you."

"Jason, I—"

"No, let me talk, he said, grabbing her hand and clasping it between his, warming it against his chest. "I don't know where your heart is, but I hope it's right here," he said, flattening it over his heart. "Will you make it semiofficial? Can we tell people we're together?"

"Finally! I was afraid you were going to break up with me. Yes! I'll be happy—ecstatic—to do whatever it is we're doing, only with each other." She leaned into him, still feeling his heart beat against her hand, and touched his lips with her own, sinking into a proper kiss, one that promised many more to come.

Blueberry Pecan Yogurt Tea Cake

From Auntie Rose's Kitchen

Serves: 12–16

Note: This may seem like it has a lot of instructions, but it's really a very simple—and simply delicious—dessert, moist, fruity and luscious.

TOPPING:

   1 cup white sugar
   1 tsp cinnamon
   ¼ cup all purpose flour
   ½ tsp salt

BATTER:

   2 cups all purpose flour
   1 tsp baking soda
   ½ tsp salt
   ½ cup butter, room temperature
   1 cup light brown sugar
   ½ cup white sugar
   1 egg
   1 tsp vanilla extract

1 cup fat-free Greek yogurt
2 cups fresh blueberries
1 cup coarsely chopped pecans

1. Preheat oven to 350° F. Lightly butter a 9 X 13 pan.
2. In a small bowl mix the topping ingredients until well blended. Set aside.
3. In another small or medium bowl, whisk together the flour, baking soda and salt. Set aside.
4. In a large bowl, cream together the butter and the sugars. Using a handheld mixer, mix on medium-high to high for approximately 8–10 minutes. Set aside.
5. Whisk together the egg, vanilla and yogurt in a separate bowl. Add to the butter mixture in two parts, mixing with your handheld mixer on medium and making sure that the first part is fully incorporated before adding the rest. Increase speed to medium-high and mix for 1 more minute.
6. Add the flour mixture to the wet, and mix on medium for 1 minute.
7. Spread half the batter into the prepared pan. This layer will be thin! Don't worry about that; it's important to have enough left for the second layer.
8. Sprinkle half the blueberries over the layer of batter, then half the pecans. Over all this, sprinkle half or a little more than half of the topping mixture.
9. Now spread the remaining batter; this may get a little tricky, but dropping the batter in small spoonfuls all over the top will make it easier to spread the batter out.
10. Top with the rest of the blueberries, the rest of the pecans, and sprinkle the remainder of the topping mixture over the whole.

12. Bake for approximately 45 minutes, or until the cake seems set when lightly pressed. It will be soft, you just don't want liquid in the center.

Let it cool slightly, but this is best served warm with a big dollop of whipped cream or scoop of ice cream. You *can* heat it up the next day for more yumminess. Stored in a plastic tub, it'll stay moist for days.

Steeped to Perfection

A Brief Description of Tea Strainers and Infusers

By Karen Owen aka Karen Mom of Three
http://acupofteaandacozymystery.blogspot.ca/

Tea strainers are as functional and collectable as teapots and teacups and saucers. Known for both their function and practicality, with a tea strainer, you can spend a little or a lot to infuse your favorite blends of tea in your pot or cup. Strainers were historically made from silver, but today they are commonly made from materials such as stainless steel, plastic, silicone, sterling silver and porcelain.

Traditionally, tea leaves were added to the teapot. A strainer was then used when the tea was poured into the cup. Tea strainers like these work well for the first few cups, but as the leaves sit in the pot, they cause the taste of the tea to become bitter. Here is a brief description of the different types of tea strainers and infusers available to today's discerning tea drinker:

Tea Strainers: I was surprised the first time I had a pot c
tea made the traditional way in a British tearoom. My first tw
cups were wonderful, but as the tea sat in the pot containin,
the leaves, it became bitter. While I didn't enjoy the tea, I di
adore the lovely silver tea strainer that balanced delicatel
on my bone china teacup, then in its matching bowl whe
not in use. It was ornately engraved and beautifully made.
came home and looked on eBay to add one to my persona
collection. I quickly learned that these tea strainers were i
high demand to collectors; the more ornate they were, th
higher the cost. You can purchase a plain metal strainer fo
your teacup with a bowl for under ten dollars, but a vintag
silver tea strainer will set you back a few hundred or even
few thousand dollars.

Tea Balls: Tea balls are the most practical choice fo
infusing tea leaves in a teapot, and they offer the user th
ability to easily remove the tea leaves before they ca
become bitter and tannic. Tea balls can be found online o
in stores for a fraction of the cost of the silver tea strainer
used in high-end tearooms. Tea balls are most often a stain
less steel or metal mesh ball that fits inside your teapot an
can be removed easily by the short attached chain.

When selecting, pick a large tea ball for a teapot and ,
smaller one if you are a mug person. The larger the tea ball
the more space the leaves have to expand in your infuser
allowing them to disperse their full flavor. If you're someon
who likes the occasional mug of tea, a smaller tea ball is th
best choice.

Tea Brewing Baskets or Infusing Baskets: Tea brewin,
baskets are popular for today's busy tea lover. Often sol
along with oversized tea mugs, these baskets allow for eas
infusing and discarding of loose-leaf tea leaves. An infuse
will often fit in the top opening of your teapot, so the freshl

boiled water surrounds the leaves, allowing them to expand and release their intoxicating flavors. It can then be removed to prevent oversteeping. They can be metal or ceramic. The London Pottery Company creates truly wonderful teapots with built-in stainless steel strainers that are designed to fit inside the teapot with the teapot's ceramic lid. The lid will fit perfectly over the strainer. If you can get your hands on one of these teapots, you will be very pleased.

Tea Socks: Yes, you read that right: *tea socks*. When I heard about this I was a little put off, but there are places in the world where an everyday sock is used to brew the most exotic of teas. Commercially you can purchase what is known as a "tea sock," made of cotton and metal. This tea strainer resembles a butterfly net and is quite functional for brewing your tea leaves. Then again, you can always try a clean sock . . .

Silicone Tea Strainers: Silicone tea strainers make excellent gifts and party favors. You can find them in so many fun shapes and designs, from hearts with arrows piercing through them, to fruit-shaped strainers, flower-shaped strainers, sea life such as manatee-shaped or shark-shaped silicone strainers, submarine-shaped, Eiffel Tower–shaped and my personal favorite, tea-bag-shaped silicone strainers. Look for them in gift shops and on eBay, priced from around one to twenty dollars.

Novelty Metal Strainers: Novelty metal strainers are also popular, more for their shapes than their functionality, though. They do work; however, they are often harder to clean and more for show. From robot- and spaceship-shaped strainers to monkey-shaped and even umbrella-shaped fun strainers, these metal tea strainers can be found online on eBay and in specialty shops year-round but are most popular around gift-giving holidays. Usually priced from five to thirty dollars, these strainers are highly collectable and fun.

Plastic or Metal Teaspoon Strainers: Plastic or metal tea-spoon strainers have a long neck like a spoon, with a shaped basket on the end. The strainer basket can be a simple orb, or may be heart shaped. It opens so you can put your leaves inside, and snaps closed to be used in your teapot or mug. There are also more novelty teaspoons made of plastic in the shape of swans or musical notes. A popular "scoop-style" plastic strainer that I enjoy using and giving as gifts looks like a coffee scoop, but with a bent plastic mesh basket that sits on the side of a tea mug and holds only the amount of loose-leaf tea required for a mug of tea. These are great for the office or the home and for a quick spot of tea. These strainers can be found on eBay, priced from just under one to ten dollars.

Tea strainers are a tea enthusiast's delight. There are so many wonderful options in every price range. Each of these strainers offers their owner a vessel for the voyage toward the perfect cup of loose-leaf tea.